E 10/17

LARA ADRIAN

"Action-packed, sexy and enticing…Lara Adrian's wild imagination and creativity is amazing."
–Reading Divas

"With an Adrian novel, readers are assured of plenty of dangerous thrills and passionate chills."
–RT Book Reviews

"Ms. Adrian has a gift for drawing her readers deeper and deeper into the amazing world she creates."
–Fresh Fiction

TINA FOLSOM

"Folsom's stories and characters are as unforgettable as they are beautiful, sexy and passionate…"
–Aobibliosphere

"Intensely affectionate and blazingly hot."
– Joyfully Reviewed

"Tina Folsom's super sexy romances will be your favorite guilty pleasure!"
–Stephanie Bond, New York Times bestselling author

9030 00004 5607 8

Other Books by Lara Adrian

Midnight Breed Series
A Touch of Midnight (prequel novella)
Kiss of Midnight
Kiss of Crimson
Midnight Awakening
Midnight Rising
Veil of Midnight
Ashes of Midnight
Shades of Midnight
Taken by Midnight
Deeper Than Midnight
A Taste of Midnight (ebook novella)
Darker After Midnight
The Midnight Breed Series Companion
Edge of Dawn
Marked by Midnight (novella)
Crave the Night
Tempted by Midnight (novella)
Bound to Darkness (August 2015)
Stroke of Midnight (novella, October 2015)

Masters of Seduction Series
Merciless: House of Gravori (novella)
Priceless: House of Ebarron (novella)

Historical Romances
Dragon Chalice Series
Warrior Trilogy
Lord of Vengeance

Other Books by Tina Folsom

Scanguards Vampires Series

Samson's Lovely Mortal
Amaury's Hellion
Gabriel's Mate
Yvette's Haven
Zane's Redemption
Quinn's Undying Rose
Oliver's Hunger
Thomas's Choice
Silent Bite (novella)
Cain's Identity
Luther's Return

Out of Olympus Series

A Touch of Greek
A Scent of Greek
A Taste of Greek

Eternal Bachelors Club

Lawful Escort
Lawful Lover
Lawful Wife
One Foolish Night
One Long Embrace

Lover Uncloaked (Stealth Guardians, Book 1)

Venice Vampyr (Novellas 1 – 4)

PHOENIX CODE
Novels

Cut and Run

Hide and Seek

HIDE AND SEEK

PHOENIX CODE SERIES
Books 3 & 4

NEW YORK TIMES BESTSELLING AUTHORS

LARA ADRIAN
TINA FOLSOM

ISBN: 1941761054
ISBN-13: 978-1941761052

PHOENIX CODE SERIES
© 2015 by In Media Res Publishing, LLC
Cover design © 2014 by CrocoDesigns

HIDE (Phoenix Code Series: Book 3)
© 2015 by Lara Adrian, LLC

SEEK (Phoenix Code Series: Book 4)
© 2015 by Tina Folsom

All rights reserved. No part of this work may be used or reproduced in any manner whatsoever without permission, except in the case of brief quotations embodied in critical articles and reviews.

This book is a work of fiction. Names, characters, places and incidents are either products of the author's imagination or used fictitiously. Any resemblance to actual events, locales, or persons, living or dead, is entirely coincidental. No part of this publication can be reproduced or transmitted in any form or by any means, electronic or mechanical, without permission in writing from the Author.

www.PhoenixCodeSeries.com

Available in ebook and print. Unabridged
audiobook edition forthcoming.

CONTENTS

HIDE

Lara Adrian

1

Heavy summer rain pounded the roof of the cabin like a barrage of gunfire. John Duarte cursed as another thin stream of water began to drip from between the log rafters of his small, hundred-year-old mountain home.

The deluge had been going on all day. Driving, relentless. It showed no sign of slowing down, even as the clock on the stove in the single-room living space rolled past midnight.

Taking a swig of his freshly opened Coors, he glared up at the steady stream of rainwater that was splashing onto his living room rug. *Fuck*. He'd patched two ceiling leaks already tonight and was just about to take off his boots and settle in for a late meal and a cold beer.

No such damned luck. At this rate, the odds of him eating or getting any shut-eye tonight were slim to none.

Not that he made a point of doing either on a regular basis. Blame it on too many years deployed to one hellhole or another as a combat Marine, followed by too many years working covert missions for a different, less public and highly specialized program after his official tours of duty in the sandbox had ended.

Add to that, the past three years he'd been living up on this remote North Carolina mountain, hiding away from the very people—the very duty—he'd once pledged his life to as a Phoenix program operative.

Three years that he'd been waiting for the program's enemies to catch up to him. Three years preparing for a battle he would unleash on whoever was responsible for the death of Phoenix's founder and the subsequent threat against everyone else associated with the covert agency.

Duarte took another long drink of his beer as the sum of all those years washed over him. Now, he lived totally off the grid by choice. Alone by necessity. Just him and God and the elements—two of which seemed determined to drown him off the mountain tonight.

Scrubbing a hand over his dark beard, Duarte set the bottle down on the scuffed countertop. His meal would have to wait. He put a lid on the pot of bubbling venison stew he'd warmed up, then turned to take a closer look at the leak he needed to patch.

He didn't get halfway across the old wood plank floor before a high-pitched beep sounded from the console of monitors on the other side of the room. Hard to hear it over the steady drum of the rain, but Duarte would know that sensor alarm anywhere.

Since he'd gone underground, he'd conditioned himself to register the faint warning even in his sleep.

And he knew what the alarm meant.

Someone was on the mountain with him.

He glanced at the blinking red light to see which sensor had been tripped. The one down by the road—if the narrow, twisting dirt path that led off the mountain pass and up to his cabin could be mistaken for a road.

Which it wouldn't be, not by anyone who didn't have any business coming up here.

And not by anyone fool enough to brave traveling

this far and this high in the middle of the night. In the pouring rain.

Couldn't be wildlife either. A few months after he'd installed the sensors around the perimeter of his property, Duarte had made adjustments so the deer, black bears, and other woodland animals didn't trip the alarms. He'd painstakingly fine-tuned them to react only to the body temperature and two-legged gait of human intruders.

Like the one currently heading right for him in the dark outside.

Another alarm beeped, this one a motion detector situated in the woods off the main path, some hundred yards out from the cabin. Either there was more than one person coming for him, or whoever approached had now veered into the thicket to make a more circuitous route forward.

"Shit."

He'd been anticipating the moment his hiding place would finally be discovered, but did it have to be on the darkest, soggiest damn night of the year?

Duarte strode over to his workstation and woke up his laptop. The remote feeds from his half-dozen surveillance cameras mounted in the woods filled the screen. He clicked to infrared mode and glanced between the array of night-vision green images of the woods and rocky terrain that lay beyond the cabin.

His bogey wasn't hard to find.

Only one, but the son of a bitch was closing in fast.

The hooded, huddled shape moved hastily in the southwest quadrant of his surveillance field. Maybe he had the bad weather to thank for the way his intruder humped so carelessly through the thicket. Either that or

Phoenix's enemies had sent up one of the least professional assassins in their stable to try to take him out.

Duarte knew better than to discount the incoming threat based on initial appearances. Overseas, he'd seen more than one battalion nearly blown to smithereens by decrepit old men dropping IEDs in the middle of a village, or smiling goatherds shuffling along the road wearing forty pounds of explosives wired to them under their tunics.

Hell, in his thirty-two years of living, he'd seen enough bar brawls and domestic disputes to understand that anyone with an inclination or motivation toward violence was to be taken seriously. And dealt with appropriately.

Permanently, when the situation called for it.

As for the creeper who'd infiltrated Duarte's domain tonight, the bastard was about to get an unfriendly welcome courtesy of Mr. Smith & Mr. Wesson.

Duarte opened the desk drawer and pulled out one of several firearms he kept at the ready around the cabin. Tucking the pistol into the back of his jeans, he got up and killed the flame under his pot of stew.

Taking one more long swig of weak beer for the road, he quietly exited the cabin's back door and headed out into the rain to greet his unwanted visitor.

2

How much farther could it be?

Lisa Becker reached into her jacket's hood to smear a wet hank of hair away from her eyes as she peered through the gloom to the path ahead of her. At least, she thought she was still on the path. Hard to tell. It was possible she'd strayed off it a few feet back.

Shit. Or several yards back.

The last thing she needed was to get herself totally lost in a thousand acres of dark woods on the side of a steep mountainside. What the hell had she been thinking, coming up here at this hour, in a torrential downpour besides?

Find him.

That's what she'd been thinking. For the past six hours, she'd been running on confusion and fear and desperation. She needed answers. She needed safety. Someone she could trust.

She needed help like never before in her life.

And she prayed she'd find it here.

Picking up her pace again, she pushed through the tangle of wet ground cover and spindly saplings. Her foot squished into the soggy pine needles and spongy earth, mud sucking at the soles of her shoes.

Rain poured off the forest canopy overhead, soaking

her from head to toe. Brush smacked her in the face as she hustled along. With each hurried step she took, the small backpack she wore under her jacket bounced between her shoulder blades. Aside from her purse, the pack held only a change of clothes and basic toiletries, but in the rain, fatigue clawing at her, the damn thing felt like it had gained ten pounds since she'd left her car about an hour ago.

Lisa wrapped her arms around herself and tried to gauge her progress. She had only been up here once before, and even though her visit had been memorable, it had been years ago. It had also been daylight, which she sure as hell would prefer right now.

Maybe she should turn around and make sure she hadn't veered off-course. Better yet, maybe she should go back to her Camry, which was stuck in a trench of sticky mud down on the pass, and wait until morning to make the rest of this trek.

Panic edged in, but she pushed it away.

Keep moving forward. The cabin is up here somewhere.

He's *up here somewhere.*

Please let him be here.

The uneven, rocky terrain was difficult enough to navigate in the moonless dark, but the relentless deluge made every step an obstacle course of thick, slippery mud and slick, matted leaves.

God, it was tempting to turn back and wait out the night and the storm.

Except time was one thing she didn't dare assume she had. Not based on the cryptic communication she'd had with her brother a few hours ago.

HIDE.

That text from Kyle—that startling, single-word

message—had sent her rushing out of her house in Cincinnati minutes later. She'd driven across three states in the rain and darkness to look for shelter in the only safe place she could think of.

All she had to do now was find the remote cabin she'd been to just once before in her life. She had to find *him*.

Find John Duarte.

It was the mantra that had begun playing in her head from the instant she received Kyle's text. John was one of his best friends, a fellow former Marine who, along with another soldier named Alec Colton, had been like brothers to Kyle from the day they'd all arrived at Camp Lejeune some twelve years ago.

Lisa hadn't been in touch with either of Kyle's friends for a long time. And after the way she'd left things with John the last time she saw him, she didn't imagine he'd want anything to do with her problems now.

But she didn't have anywhere else to go.

If anyone might be able to help her make sense of her brother's message—and help Kyle out of whatever danger she feared he was in—John Duarte was her best hope.

Regardless of how he might feel about her.

Lisa plunged deeper into the dark woods, her breath gusting through her parted lips, her heart beating a hard drum in her ears. She was soaked to the bone, shivering with the cold and an icy fear that had only taken firmer root in the time since she'd received Kyle's message.

HIDE.

What did he mean? Hide from what...or whom?

What was going on? Was Kyle in some kind of

trouble?

Was she?

Lisa had asked all those things in reply, but Kyle didn't answer back. His private cell—the number only she had access to according to him, had gone dead.

And that, more than anything else, had terrified her.

He'd always been her protector, from the time they were kids, bouncing through one foster home to another after their so-called parents had lost custody of them to the State of Ohio. Kyle had always looked out for her, kept her safe.

He'd always looked after her, even when he was on active combat duty overseas. And later, too, after his service to the country had taken on a more clandestine purpose that he'd refused to divulge to her.

All that changed about three years ago. Lisa didn't know why. She only knew that her strong, doting older brother had suddenly stopped calling to check in on her. No more emails or texts, and no replies when she tried to reach him.

There had been no more postcards from far-flung places—silly, unexpected notes that always held the power to make her feel that no matter where his duties had taken him, Kyle was still close. Still watching over his kid sister—his Little Lisa Lizard—a nickname he'd given her when they were kids and had affectionately used with her ever since.

No, the last time Lisa had seen Kyle, he'd acted strange, paranoid somehow. He'd tried to brush off her concern, but she knew him too well. He'd been involved in something mysterious. Dangerous, she'd guessed, even then.

And now this.

Fresh fear streaked through her as she picked up her pace, running now, needing to get out of the wet and cold before she collapsed. She misjudged her step across a patch of loamy ground littered with old leaves and pinecones. Her ankle twisted as the earth gave way beneath her foot.

She slid off balance and the slippery ground took her down.

She made a flailing grasp at the branches overhead, but her wet fingers closed on nothing but empty air. She fell hard, dropping flat on her ass down a shallow, sodden incline.

Dammit.

A miserable-sounding groan leaked out of her as the rain continued to pelt her and her ankle sparked with pain from the fall. Wet leaves and pine needles clung to her everywhere. And in the distance, lightning cracked, briefly illuminating the vastness of her surroundings and what might yet prove to be a massive mistake.

And as a roll of thunder set a tremor in the earth beneath her, Lisa heard the unmistakable sound of a gun being cocked from the top of the incline at her back.

"Move a muscle, motherfucker, and I'll blow your damn head off."

She froze instantly, even as the deep, dark molasses sound of John Duarte's voice and Southern accent set her pulse racing with relief. "Don't shoot." She swallowed, tried to catch her racing breath. Rain pelting her hooded head, she braved a slight glance over her shoulder. "John, don't shoot. It's me, Lisa. Um...Lisa Becker."

There was silence for a brief moment, then Duarte's curse hissed out on a sharp exhalation. She heard movement behind her, heard him disarm his weapon before he started scrambling down into the sodden trench to reach her. He gave her his hand and helped her to her feet. "Lisa. Jesus fucking Christ."

She hadn't expected a warm greeting, but his disapproving scowl stung anyway.

Her first glimpse of him took her aback. He looked very different now, even in the dark. A beard covered part of his cheeks and square jaw. His espresso-brown hair was longer, thick waves instead of the high-and-tight Marine trim he'd always worn whenever Lisa had seen him before.

But, oh God, he was just as heartbreakingly handsome as ever. Still had those dark, intense eyes that could melt a woman right out of her panties. And that line of perfect white teeth that was so devastating when he smiled, but was currently bared at her in a snarl.

"What the hell are you doing here?"

Now that she was standing in front of him, even though he couldn't look less pleased to see her, emotions rose up on Lisa like a wave. Her words tumbled out in a breathless rush. "I didn't know what to do. I couldn't think of anywhere else to go, anyone else to trust..."

His expression hardened even more as she spoke. "Tell me why you're here, Lisa."

"It's Kyle." She saw suspicion edge into Duarte's level gaze at the mention of her brother's name. Along with an instant flicker of concern. She was tempted to call it dread. "I think something's happened to him, John. Something really bad. He tried to send me a warning today. I'm scared, and I don't know what to do."

Duarte ground out another low curse. "We shouldn't

talk out here." Calm words, but there was an intensity in the way he lifted his head to scan the dark forest that surrounded them. "You came alone?"

"Yes," she said, shuddering as a chill swept over her.

He grunted, but his frown didn't lessen. "Let's get out of the rain."

She took a step and grimaced as her ankle protested the shift of her weight.

He eyed her with a scowl. "You're injured?"

She shook her head. "It's nothing. When I slipped, I twisted my ankle a little, but I'm—"

Duarte didn't wait for her to explain any further.

Hoisting her up onto his shoulder as if her hundred-and-thirty-odd pounds was no effort at all, he carried her out of the trench like a wounded soldier and didn't put her down until they had reached his cabin.

3

Duarte sat Lisa down on his couch then went into the bathroom to grab a couple of fresh towels out of the cabinet. As he collected what he needed, he stole a quick glance into the other room where she waited. Huddled in her wet jacket, she shivered on the edge of the cushion, her hair plastered to her forehead and cheeks, water dripping off the shoulder-length strands.

Christ, after all this time, it really was her.

The reality of it knocked him back. Just as it had the moment he'd realized it was her lying outside in the muddy wash down by the cabin's trail, his gun trained on her in the dark.

Lisa.

Lisa Becker, she'd said. As if he needed the clarification.

Sure, it had been a while, but she was his best friend's sister. Duarte had known her for a few years before they last saw each other, and hell, it wasn't like he was going to forget her.

No, he recalled every square inch of her... more intimately than either of them had planned on that day he'd brought her up to the cabin five years ago.

It had been a momentary loss of sanity—and control—for both of them. More so for him.

His best friend's little sister, for fuck's sake. Though even then, at twenty-three, Lisa had been plenty old enough to make her own decisions.

Looking at her sitting in his living room now, Duarte had to blink a couple of times to convince his brain that this wasn't some twisted repeat of that other time. Five years ago, she'd sat in that very same spot. Except that time she'd been smiling and happy, wearing a strapless, pale peach bridesmaid dress and high-heeled sandals, not shuddering and breathless in a sodden, leaf-littered T-shirt and jeans, and leather flats caked with mud.

On that other night, she'd waited for him there on the couch with the jacket from his dress blues draped over her shoulders, her soft, light-brown hair swept up off her neck in some kind of complicated bun that they'd wrecked moments later in his bed.

At the memory of it, Duarte's skin got a bit too tight, too warm.

Lisa hadn't aged in the least since he saw her last. She was waterlogged and pale from cold and exhaustion, but damn if the sight of her didn't kick his heartbeat up a gear.

He wanted to dismiss the sudden hammer of his pulse as leftover adrenaline from the thought of an intruder skulking up his mountainside. Or that it was just his old Marine protector instincts firing to life after learning something had scared her enough to send her racing off into the night to find him.

Anything to keep from admitting that five years and a hundred bad twists of fate later, he still couldn't look at this woman without feeling an unwanted surge of possessiveness and need.

Which was a bad idea for many reasons, then and

now. Especially now.

Duarte closed the cabinet and walked out with the towels in hand. She swiveled her head toward him, her hazel gaze hesitant, uncertain. She'd come all this way, but the look on her face said she was having serious second thoughts. No doubt, she couldn't escape the recollection of the night they had spent here together either.

Nor the morning afterward, when daylight brought them back to their senses—back to reality—and they'd parted with a shared awkward, unspoken regret. The last they'd seen of each other in all this time.

God, how scared and desperate did she have to be, to come looking for him, of all people?

Had it been anyone else on his property tonight, he would have sent them right back down the mountain. At the business end of his pistol, if need be.

He should probably get rid of her as quickly as possible, too, but he couldn't even think about doing that until he knew she was okay.

And not until she told him what was going on with Kyle.

Duarte set the towels on the arm of the couch as he approached her. "How's your ankle?"

She nodded. "It's fine. Just a minor sprain at most." Her teeth chattered as she spoke. "Like I told you outside, it's nothing."

He grunted and held out his hand to her. "Stand up, but keep your weight off it. You can hang on to me while I help you out of that wet jacket."

She obeyed, her hands warm on his shoulders as she let him pull the jacket off one of her arms, then the other. She wore a small backpack, which felt almost as soaked as the rest of her. He took it off and set it down on the couch beside her.

Dressed in a business-casual gray button-down and black pants, Lisa was quiet as he wrapped her in one towel, then dried some of the rain from her hair with the other.

Duarte worked robotically, the way he would if he was in the field taking care of a wounded comrade. Except this wasn't a fellow Marine.

Against his will, he registered the vanilla scent of her warming skin and the sweet smell of her wet, honey-brown hair. He tried like hell to stifle his awareness of her, but his body's reaction was faster than his reason.

And shit, wasn't that always the case when he was near Lisa?

Duarte cleared his throat. Definitely not the time or place to be reacquainting himself with her curves and her scent, or his instinctual response to having her so close to him again.

He put the towel aside and eased her back to a seat on the couch. "Tell me what happened." His voice was a dry growl in his throat. "You said you talked to Kyle today?"

Lisa shook her head. "I've only seen and talked to him once in the past three years. Until I got his text today."

She reached into her backpack and took out her cell phone. Turning it on, she handed it over.

Duarte read the one-word text message and frowned. *What the hell?*

The text was troubling, but that didn't mean it was from her brother. It could have come from anyone. It could be a prank or some idiot kid's idea of a joke. It could be a text sent to her by mistake.

Or it could be something else. Something worse, that he didn't want to consider when the prospect of something worse involved Lisa.

"If you haven't heard from him in so long, why do you think this is from him?"

"It came from Kyle's phone number. A number he gave me the last time I saw him. He told me it was a secret number, one only the two of us would know about."

Fuck. Some of Duarte's skepticism faded as Lisa spoke.

He didn't like where this was heading. Every covert operative in the Phoenix program had received explicit instructions to cut all ties to the people in their former lives should the highly classified program ever be compromised. Kyle knew the importance of those orders as well as Duarte did. Kyle knew it as well as the others in the program who'd all learned three years ago that its founder, Henry Sheppard, was dead and Phoenix itself betrayed by lethal, unknown enemies who intended to see the rest of the operatives terminated, too.

What the hell was Lisa's brother thinking, putting her at risk by giving her an active connection to him—even a secret one?

Duarte never would have taken that chance. Then again, he'd never had family worth worrying about, so he was the last person to try to understand that kind of bond.

"Do you know where Kyle is now?"

"No." Lisa stared at Duarte, worry filling her gaze. "I texted him back right after I got his message, but he didn't respond. When I called the number a minute later, it was out of service. It's as if he sent the message, then vanished into thin air. I'm scared for him, Johnny."

Duarte steeled himself to the sound of his name on her lips like that. No one called him Johnny. No one else would dare.

But Lisa... she'd christened him with the diminutive nickname the first day they were introduced by Kyle on the base at Camp Lejeune. He, the big badass Marine just out of boot camp, and she the bubbly, freckle-faced sixteen-year-old sister of the second-toughest son of a bitch Duarte would ever know.

"Any idea where your brother's been these past few years?"

She shook her head. "I was hoping maybe you could tell me that."

"I'm sorry," he said. "I don't have that answer."

"Would you tell me if you did?" She studied him for a moment, as though weighing her words. Torment and thinly held fear clouded her light hazel gaze. It killed him to see her so distressed, looking for answers she would be better off not knowing. "If you feel like you have to protect me from the truth, don't. I know Kyle got involved in something classified while he was in the Marines. Something covert." When Duarte neither confirmed nor denied it, she exhaled a short sigh. "How dangerous was it for him, John?"

He held his careful expression in check. "I can't tell you anything about that either, Lisa. I'm sorry."

"You can't, or you won't?" When he didn't respond, she glanced away from him. "What about Alec? Would he know how to find my brother?"

Duarte reflected on the third member of his former posse. The trifecta. The three musketeers. The bond that cemented their friendship and went beyond their service to their country. "It's been longer than three years since any of us have been in contact. Even if I wanted to, I couldn't tell you where Alec or Kyle is now, or what they might be doing."

So much had happened during that time—and before—when the three of them had been recruited into Phoenix because of their unusual, shared ability.

Shit, in light of everything that had gone down in the time since, the odds were good that Duarte would never see either of his best friends again.

Worse than that, after the program they'd served had been betrayed, Duarte wasn't certain he could trust any of his former teammates, including the two who had been like brothers to him.

And there was the distinct possibility that Kyle Becker was already dead. If that was true, and if Kyle had tried to warn his sister away from the danger following him, then she was likely in too deep already.

"Did you tell anyone about this text?"

She shook her head. "No. After I received it, I only took time enough to throw a few things in my bag, then I got in my car and left. I kept driving until I got here. I didn't know if I should try to contact someone at the Pentagon, or go to the police, or—"

"No. Fuck, no." His clipped response stopped her short. "You did the smartest thing, Lisa. For yourself and for Kyle."

Duarte could see the tension in her face. It had deepened since they began talking. He was scaring her even more, something he didn't mean to do.

He reached out and stroked his hand over her slender shoulder and arm. "We'll sort it out, all right?

Everything's going to be fine."

She didn't look like she totally believed him, but she nodded.

This sure as hell wasn't the way he'd envisioned his night playing out, but there was no going back. Like it or not, he couldn't turn her away. Her brother had made him promise more than once to look after Lisa if Kyle wasn't around to do it. While Duarte hadn't really expected to be tested on that vow, he wasn't about to back down from it—least of all when Lisa had crossed three states to reach him and was now standing in front of him, wet and trembling, desperation swimming in her eyes.

Her fear made him want to offer comfort, but that would be an even bigger mistake than before. If the timing had been bad that one night they'd shared, it was beyond bad now.

God knew it wouldn't take much to light that fire all over again. Duarte noticed belatedly that he was still touching her, still caressing her arm and shoulder long after he should have let his hand fall away.

He pulled back, an abrupt move that didn't escape her notice. He scowled. "Are you hungry?"

"Um... I don't know. I guess so." She blinked as if it took her a moment to process his question. "I haven't eaten anything since lunch at the office."

Duarte nodded as he stepped away from her. "I don't have much. Some venison stew I took out of the freezer earlier, and a couple bottles of beer."

"Sounds good," she murmured. "Anything sounds good."

He stared at her, his fingers still tingling from touching her. Other parts of him weren't faring much better. He needed time to think. And she needed to get out of her wet clothes.

"The bathroom's right there," he said, pointing down the short hallway. "Go take a hot shower and warm up. If you don't have any dry clothes in your pack, I can give you something to wear."

"Okay." She swallowed, then grabbed her backpack and the pair of towels.

Duarte didn't move. He didn't dare, not until he knew she was well out of reach.

She started to walk away from him, then paused. "John?"

"Yeah."

"Thank you."

He grunted. "Go warm up. The food will be ready when you get out."

4

The shower had been just what her freezing limbs and frazzled nerves had needed.

It also helped melt away some of the awkward awareness that had begun to swirl within her under John's lingering touch in the other room. He hadn't meant anything by his tender caress, she was sure. His abrupt retraction of his hand and deepening scowl had been indication enough of that.

She'd been a sodden, nervous wreck and he was only doing what came natural to a man who made his living protecting others.

Lisa hated that she might need anyone's protection, especially his. But whatever was going on with Kyle wasn't something she was equipped to handle alone. And John's reassurance that they would figure it all out was a life line she clung to even now.

After towel-drying her hair and dressing in the navy blue T-shirt and faded jeans from her backpack, Lisa stole a quick look at herself in the mirror and cringed. She might feel better after the shower, but her pale face and dark-shadowed eyes told a different story.

God, she looked ten years older than she actually was. The urge to dig her makeup bag out of her backpack was strong, though she doubted any amount of concealer or blush would fix the stressed-out, wan reflection staring back at her. And anyway, it wasn't as if she didn't have bigger concerns to deal with.

If it had been anyone else waiting in the other room, she wouldn't have cared at all what she looked like. But the fact that it was John Duarte made her wish she could hide in the bathroom for the rest of the night.

She walked out and was immediately rewarded with the mouthwatering smells from the kitchen. To say nothing of the sight of John standing at the stove in dark denim and a worn lumberjack flannel shirt, stirring the pot of venison stew with one hand, his other wrapped loosely around a long-neck bottle of beer.

His big, six-foot-three frame swallowed up the space in the small cabin, and when he turned to look at her as she approached, his penetrating brown gaze seemed to suck all the air from the room, too.

"Better now?" His deep voice, with its smooth Southern drawl, drew her forward like a beacon of warmth. At her nod, he stretched for the handle on the fridge on the other side of him and took out a bottle of Coors for her. "Sit down and have a drink while I serve up the grub."

Grub? Hardly. The venison stew smelled amazing. The spicy aroma invaded her senses and made her stomach growl in anticipation. She had no idea he knew how to cook. Then again, aside from John being her brother's best friend and her most incredible one-night stand, there was a lot she probably didn't know about him.

Even then, her knowledge was five years old and then some. This John Duarte seemed different in many ways. More emotionally isolated than before. Even more of a lone wolf, if that was possible.

Lisa took a sip from her bottle, but found the prospect of being waited on by him too much to bear. Instead of taking a seat at the table, she walked her beer over and set it down, then went back to help him serve the stew. "Let me take those," she said as he pulled two earthenware bowls from a cabinet. "Silverware?"

"In that drawer on the left." He gestured with his dark-bearded chin while he took the pot off the flame then grabbed a ladle from a utensil jar next to the range.

Lisa collected a couple of spoons and followed him. She watched as he scooped two generous servings into the bowls she'd placed on the table. His big hands were strong, steady. His long fingers were nicked here and there, callused from physical work. And yet, she couldn't keep from remembering how tender they could be. How delicately he'd touched her bare skin that other night that she'd been in this cabin.

"Sit," he said, glancing up at her and finding her staring. "Eat."

At his grunted command, she dropped into the chair across from him and together they fell into a strange, oddly comfortable silence as they ate their stew and nursed their beers. Lisa took the opportunity to glance around the cabin, taking in the basic, masculine furnishings and decided lack of personal effects. No feminine touches anywhere either, something she'd also taken note of while she was in his shower.

John still lived alone on his mountain. For how long and why, she could only guess.

"Sorry I don't have anything better to offer you to eat," he murmured as she spooned up the last drop from her bowl. "I don't make it down to town very often, and

I live pretty rustic up here."

"Are you kidding? This was delicious. Thank you." And she'd been so hungry, there was no chance to feign a dainty appetite now. She tipped her longneck up to her mouth, then smirked as she swallowed the bland sip. "Your cooking is impressive, but your taste in beer has definitely degraded."

There had been a time when she'd called her brother and his Marine buddies beer snobs. Nothing but small batch ales and browns, and obscure microbrews for the three musketeers when they were home on leave. Lisa had been the one who'd enjoyed her watery ultra-lights with their gleaming foil labels, and she'd caught plenty of flak from the guys because of it.

The corner of John's mouth kicked up at her jab. "Not a lot of selection out here in the sticks. Besides, I like to keep things simple now. I keep my life uncomplicated."

"Is that why there's no Mrs. up here on the mountain with you?" His expression stilled at her blurt. "I'm sorry. That was rude, and it's none of my business. You don't have to answer—"

"There's no Mrs.," he said evenly. "And yeah, that's by choice. Relationships are nothing but complicated. Wouldn't you agree?"

He was right about that. Lisa nodded, all her past mistakes playing through her thoughts. And at the head of that parade was the mistake she made five years ago in this very cabin. It had been a mistake, but not one she'd ever been able to regret.

John's gaze settled on her as she took a sudden interest in the loose edge of the label on her Coors. "What about you, Lisa?"

"Me?" She glanced up and collided with his intense stare. "What about me?"

"I heard you got married a few years back."

"Four years ago." It felt like a hundred had passed since then. Especially tonight, in this moment, discussing it with John Duarte over dinner in his cabin while her brother's life might be hanging in the balance.

John grunted, the sensual line of his mouth pressed flat for a brief second. "Kyle mentioned it to me around that time. Some kind of doctor up there in Cincinnati?"

"Pediatric heart surgeon." Lisa went back to picking at her bottle's label. "Parker and I met when I organized a charity event for the hospital. We got married six weeks later at his parents' estate."

"Sounds fancy." And John sounded thoroughly unimpressed.

"Yeah, it was. The divorce two months later was fancy, too. Lots of lawyers and engraved letterhead to sign. Lots of fancy legal agreements to ensure I didn't profit off our brief farce of a marriage."

"What happened?"

"He cheated on me."

John bit off a low curse, his dark brow furrowing. "Idiot."

Lisa shook her head. "In hindsight, I probably should've seen it coming. We were too different. From different worlds. I never should've married him."

John studied her now. "So, why did you?"

"Good question. I was asking myself that very thing a month after walking down the aisle. That's when my newlywed husband came home from a five-day seminar in Boston with another woman's panties in his pocket. I guess he forgot to check his suits before he left them for me to send out to the dry cleaner. He didn't even try to deny what he'd done. Maybe infidelity was acceptable in his world, but it sure as hell wasn't in mine."

Why had she married him? All she'd ever really wanted was to belong somewhere, to belong to someone. She wanted to feel she mattered, and that her life counted for something.

That was why she'd gotten involved in charity work. The need to feel that she was contributing to something important, while giving others less fortunate some of the care and benefits they needed.

She was still searching for that sense of purpose. That sense of belonging. Maybe she always would be.

Lisa lifted her shoulder in a shrug and went back to peeling the label off her beer. "I suppose if anyone was an idiot in my brief marriage, it was me. Like a fool, I bought into the whole knight-in-shining-armor, white-picket-fence, country-club illusion that I thought a man like Parker represented. None of it was real. You'd think I'd know not to believe in that kind of fairy tale, given how Kyle and I grew up, bouncing from one foster home to another as kids."

John grunted as he set down his freshly drained bottle. "Doesn't mean you don't deserve the picket fence and the whole nine yards. Doesn't mean you don't deserve all that and more."

He was trying to make her feel better, and his soft-spoken sympathy rubbed her like sandpaper. The last thing she meant to do was sit there whining about her pathetic childhood and equally messed up adult life, even though he already knew the basics, and from what she understood from her brother, John's early life hadn't been a bed of roses either.

She stripped off the last piece of curling foil label and crushed it into a tiny ball. "Well, I've given up looking for the fairy tale. Apparently, when it comes to men, I'm the queen of bad life choices, because the guys I date always turn out to be losers."

As soon as the words left her mouth, she winced. Glancing up, she met John's unflinching stare. "Don't think I mean you...What I mean is, you and I never dated, so..."

One of his dark brows rose. "Technically, it *was* a date."

"Okay, true," she hedged. "But I'm not sure it counts, since you only did it as a favor to Kyle."

John grunted. "Some favor. He'd have my balls—and rightly so—if he ever found out I let things get so far out of hand that night."

He had let things get out of hand? If that's how he preferred to remember it, fine by her. What Lisa recalled was a far more even-handed slip from platonic stand-in wedding date to off-the-charts one-night stand.

The details of their time together five years ago swarmed her uninvited now. John showing up unexpectedly at her apartment a couple hours away from the base in his Marine dress blues, announcing he was there to pick her up after learning that her date had gotten sick the day before and cancelled. Handsome, heart-stopping John, with his regulation-trimmed dark hair, his face tanned from time on deployment in the desert, his strong, squared jaw clean-shaven, even near the tail end of his two-week liberty back home in the States.

She'd been furious with Kyle for drafting his friend to rescue her from going stag to the wedding, but any humiliation she'd felt had evaporated the instant John smiled at her and told her she looked beautiful in her peach bridesmaid's dress and upswept hair.

They'd danced together, laughed together... and after one too many champagne cocktails on her part, she'd kissed him on the dance floor. A moment of pure spontaneity, a reckless, unstoppable impulse that had taken hold of her and given her courage she never would have had otherwise. Their kiss had been electrifying, astonishing. And too hot to contain.

They'd left the wedding to avoid the prying eyes of friends and fellow servicemen, John explaining he had somewhere private they could go. This cabin, nestled high on the side of a mountain in North Carolina, had been branded into her memory as permanently as the night they'd shared together inside it.

Followed by the awkward morning after, the silent ride of shame back to her apartment the next day, and the stinging knowledge that John shipped out a few days later without so much as a phone call or word of goodbye.

All of that was indelibly burned into her memory, too.

She and John had gone on with their lives as if the night hadn't happened, which was apparently how he'd preferred to keep it. A fact that made talking about it now all the more uncomfortable.

Of course, it didn't help that he was still the same dark, sexy warrior he had been before. Her heart still raced every time she looked at him. Her skin still felt tight and too warm, her senses far too tuned in to everything about him.

As he looked at her from across the table, she could

have sworn she saw a flicker of heat in his dark gaze, too. But it was there and gone, leaving his expression that same rigid, unreadable soldier's mask she'd seen the morning after they'd made love all those years ago.

John cleared his throat and dropped his gaze to the empty bowl in front of him. "I owe Kyle a lot, Lisa. He's pulled my ass out of danger more than one time, same as I've done for him. He was—*is*—like a brother to me, too."

The slip to past-tense hadn't escaped her. It put a fresh chill in her blood, and brought her back to reality as effectively as a physical blow. She swallowed the knot of misery that threatened to climb up her throat. "You don't think he's..."

She couldn't finish the sentence, but John didn't make her. "I don't know. That's the shittiest part of this whole thing."

"Yes, it is," she agreed. "And I need to have that answer. I need to find my brother, and I don't know how to do that alone."

He lifted his head and stared at her for a long moment. Then he blew out a long sigh, punctuated by a low curse. "What if he doesn't want to be found? Have you considered that?"

"Then why would he send me that text?" She slowly shook her head, certainty building as surely as her dread. "He's in danger. I know it. I feel it in my bones, in my heart."

"Jesus Christ." John's bleak gaze verged on pity, but she didn't let it dissuade her. She sat unfazed as he raked his fingers through his thick, coffee-brown hair. "He didn't ask you to go looking for him. Hell, we can't even confirm that text is from him in the first place."

"It is." She had no doubt in her mind at all about that. "It's from Kyle, and he's in some kind of bad trouble. He needs help."

"No, Lisa." Anger flared in those unnerving brown eyes. "If your brother sent that text to you, then all he wants is for you to obey it. He told you to hide. Not run for help from me. Not set out on some reckless course to try to find him. Just hide."

Fury sparked to life in Lisa now, too. "So, you're saying you won't help me? You won't help Kyle?"

He leaned across the table on his muscled forearms. "I'm saying you don't have any idea what you're asking. You don't know what's going on."

"Then tell me. Obviously, you know more about Kyle than I do—more than you've been willing to let on with me so far. So, tell me. You owe *me* that much, dammit."

"No, I don't." He cursed again, more vividly than before. "You're up here in my world, intruding on my life. Stirring up shit that you don't want to hear. For fuck's sake, you're asking me for answers I've sworn I'd kill to protect—"

"I think my brother is working for the CIA."

"Jesus fucking Christ." John pushed back in his chair, then stood up to pace a tight path near the table.

"I'm right, aren't I?" Lisa weathered a sharper pang of worry. "Of course, I'm right. Or is it something even worse than that?"

John didn't answer. He paused and stared at her, a tendon ticking visibly beneath the dark whiskers that covered his jaw.

"I've had my suspicions for a long time that my brother was doing some kind of covert work. Dangerous work. That feeling only got stronger the last time I saw him. I could tell something was wrong, but he wouldn't tell me anything. In fact, he tried to deny it, but I didn't believe him."

John listened without reacting as she spoke, considering her in measured silence. "You said earlier tonight that the last time you saw Kyle was three years ago?"

"On my birthday," she said. "October twenty-fourth."

Her fingers went to the silver bracelet she wore on her left wrist. Kyle had given it to her that day, a gift that had never left her sight for a minute since then. The sterling chain was hinged to a grinning, artisan-sculpted gecko.

For my Little Lisa Lizard, Kyle had said, as she'd opened the gift. It wasn't an extravagant present, but she didn't own anything she treasured more. She stroked it now like a touchstone, drawing hope from Kyle's gift, which made her feel somehow that he was still out there. That she would be able to find her big brother and make sure he was safe.

That is, if she could convince John Duarte to either help make that happen or point her in the right direction.

"What did Kyle do while he was with you that made you think something was wrong? Was it anything he said that made you worry?"

Lisa shook her head. "No, nothing specific. He seemed nervous. Paranoid, actually. He said he couldn't visit for long, that he just wanted to wish me a happy birthday and then he had to go. We had a quick lunch, then he left."

John's brow furrowed deeper. "He didn't mention

where he was living? Didn't say where he had to go when he left that day?"

"No. And when I asked him both of those questions, he was more evasive than usual. Which is saying a lot where my brother's concerned."

John grunted in agreement. He seemed lost in thought for a second, then he began collecting the empty bowls and beer bottles from the table. He didn't say anything more. Didn't even make eye contact as he cleared their meal and walked everything to the sink.

"What about you, John?"

He kept his back to her. "What about me?"

"Now you're the one evading me." She followed him into the kitchen area and got in his face, leaving him no choice but to talk to her. "What is it that you're not telling me about my brother?"

He took a slow breath, then pushed it out on a growled curse. When he swung his head in her direction, his eyes locked on her with a look she'd never seen in him before. He had been holding something back from her—something big and unpleasant, by the way he was locking her in a gaze that was both resigned and deadly serious.

"Yes, you're right. Kyle was working as a covert CIA operative." He let that admission hang between them for an agonizingly long moment, his mouth pressed flat, eyes assessing her. Was it possible he didn't trust her? Or was he afraid she couldn't handle whatever it was he planned to say next?

"Tell me," she coaxed woodenly, needing to hear the whole truth from him. "What was Kyle doing for the CIA?"

"He was part of a highly classified, counter-intelligence program."

It was a confirmation of something she'd suspected, but hearing it made her worry deepen now. John's grim expression only added to her unease.

"The operatives employed by this program all had a very unique, specialized skill. Including your brother." His gaze bored deeper into her, searching for her reaction. "He never told you what he could do? He never confided in you about his ability?"

Lisa frowned, feeling her head shake in slow denial. "I have no idea what you're talking about."

"Kyle is a precognitive. He has ESP." John said it with a perfectly straight face. He said it as if he hadn't just told her the most ludicrous thing she'd ever heard in her life. "Your brother is one of the most powerful psychics I've ever known, Lisa."

"Is that right?" She choked on a humorless laugh. "One of the most powerful, you say? And just how many other, less impressive psychics have you known?"

"More than a few. Most of them also worked covertly for Phoenix under codenames."

He wasn't laughing. Not even cracking a hint of a grin to clue her in that he was messing with her. Or that he was feeding her some epic line of bullshit just so she'd head back down the mountain and out of his life for good.

No. He was utterly, incredulously sober.

"Three years ago, Phoenix went dark. Someone murdered its founder and put the lives of all its agents in the line of fire, too. We had to scatter, go deep underground—those were our orders if anything were to happen to the program. I don't know who betrayed us, and I don't know who wants the rest of us dead, or why. Hell, it could've been someone from the inside for all I know. When Phoenix went down, we were instructed not to trust anyone, not even one another."

Her mind was struggling to process all of the astonishing things she was hearing, although not enough that she missed the full breadth of John's admission. "Are you telling me that you were a part of this program, Phoenix, too?"

"I was."

"You're telling me that Kyle is some kind of psychic covert agent—"

"A precognitive," John calmly clarified. "The same as me."

She couldn't believe what she was hearing. "You see the future."

"More or less," he said. "Precognitives get psychic glimpses of future events in their minds. Sometimes we see only pieces of those events, disconnected, erratic images. Sometimes the visions are intact and fully actionable."

"Actionable, as in—"

"As in, there is considerable power in being aware of an event before it occurs. Through Phoenix, our government shared the gift of that power. They had the ability to prevent certain events from occurring, and the power to know ahead of time and decide whether to allow various events to happen anyway."

She gaped at him, stunned. Confused. Scared as hell. And not a little pissed off, too. "If this is your idea of a joke—"

"It's no joke, Lisa."

She knew it wasn't, and in light of that, she felt a bubble of hysteria crowding in on the rest of her churning emotions. "I have to try calling Kyle again. I need to try his number again and see if he'll text me back or pick up this time."

She pivoted, glancing around the open-concept room of the cabin, searching for her phone. She found it—or rather, what was left of it—on the far end of the kitchen counter. It had been taken apart, some of the circuitry smashed to bits.

"Your cell phone was a risk I couldn't afford," John stated in an even tone. "It was a risk to you and to Kyle, too, Lisa. If he believes he's been compromised and is worried about your safety, he never should've chanced sending you that text. An assassin would need far less than that to trace him. Or they could use you to get to him instead."

Assassins. Covert CIA programs. Her brother living a double life, hiding an extraordinary ability she'd known nothing about. An ability that now might get him killed.

And John Duarte, her unwilling escort into this hidden, terrifying world she never dreamed could exist.

It was too much suddenly.

She'd never thought of herself as a weak person, and God knew she wanted to be strong now, when she needed a clear head and a steel spine to deal with whatever her brother was mixed up in. But she couldn't process anything more right now.

She leaned against the counter, numb from head to toe. Exhausted.

She didn't realize John was touching her until she lifted her gaze and met his tender eyes. He stood before her, smoothing her damp hair off her forehead and cheeks where it drooped into her face.

"I know this is a lot to take in," he murmured, the

rough pads of his fingertips gentle on her skin. "You okay?"

She managed a wobble of a nod. "I'm scared for him, Johnny. Really scared."

"I know." He caressed the side of her face, his thumb tracing over her jaw line, then slowly drifting across her bottom lip. "I'm scared for him, too. But we're gonna figure this out. We're gonna get through this together."

His reassurance pushed her over the edge. Tears stung the backs of her eyes, started to well. She kept them at bay with furious determination, but damn if one fat drop didn't spill over to run down the length of her cheek.

John swept it away, his gaze fastened on hers. "I'm going to keep you safe, Lisa. No matter what. I gave Kyle my word on that a long time ago. Tonight, I'm making that promise to you."

She nodded again, stronger this time. But she couldn't resist the comforting warmth of his palm where it rested against her cheek. She sank into his touch on a soft sigh and could only watch how John's dark eyes drifted to her mouth and stayed there.

He groaned low under his breath, and then his touch was gone. The tender protector had retreated, replaced by the rigid warrior.

"It's late. We can talk more about all of this tomorrow." He drew back, putting more than an arm's length between them. "You take my bed tonight. I'll bunk on the couch."

"You don't have to—"

He cut her protest off with a growing scowl. "Take my bed. Close the door. I'm going to be up for a while yet. I never sleep much anyway."

She recalled that about him from a long time ago. His trouble sleeping. His restless nature.

"The soldier in you never could let down his guard," she remarked quietly, trying to lighten the tension that crackled between them despite the weight of the problems they were facing.

"I think it's best if I don't," he murmured thickly.

Even though his words were heavy with meaning, his expression remained controlled. So disciplined. So unreachable. Just like he'd always been, except for that one unforgettable night when she'd glimpsed the man behind his warrior's mask.

She missed that man now, but she couldn't argue that he was wrong.

It was best that they didn't complicate the situation with a repeat of their past mistake.

And while the last thing she wanted to do was walk away from him in that moment—for countless selfish reasons—she stepped aside with a murmured "goodnight" and left him standing in the kitchen behind her.

5

Duarte lay back on the lumpy, too-short-by-half-a-foot couch in his living room. Fully clothed, with one arm bent beneath his head as a pillow, his bare feet hanging over the far end, he didn't hold much hope of sleeping anytime soon.

He'd quietly busied himself in the cabin for more than an hour since Lisa had gone to bed. The ceiling leak was stopped up for the time being. The dinner dishes were washed and stowed back in the cabinets. The remains of her cell phone had been disposed of, the SIM card drowned in the toilet and flushed away.

And yet he was still sporting one bastard of a hard-on despite the time and activity, neither of which had done much to distract him from the fact that she was just across the cabin from him behind that closed door. Asleep in his bedroom.

In his bed.

Christ.

The image sent a fresh wave of lust rolling through him. Hardened his cock even more.

He meant it when he told her it was best that he not let his guard down. That went double where she was concerned. God knew it was best for her, too, that he kept his head on straight and maintained his distance from her.

The last thing she needed was to get tangled up in anything related to the Phoenix program.

Damn her brother for not considering that fact before he risked contacting her. The in-person birthday visit after the program had been betrayed had been reckless enough, but to text her out of the blue several hours ago like he had?

Desperate warning or not, Kyle had potentially put Lisa in the crosshairs of Phoenix's enemies. Whoever they were.

Hell, Duarte hadn't done much better by her, divulging all he had over dinner tonight.

He exhaled a deep sigh. A bit too late for second thoughts on that. She was in up to her sweet ass now, thanks to everything he'd confided in her.

As much as he'd wanted to shield her from the truth and from any knowledge that could potentially put a target on her back, he'd found it impossible to lie to her. Not even about the inexplicable ability he possessed.

She'd see through him even if he tried. Those inky-lashed, light hazel eyes did things to his resolve that multiple combat deployments and years of training as a Phoenix covert operative couldn't begin to match.

No, Lisa Becker had knocked him off-kilter from the second Kyle first introduced them. With her warm eyes and easy smile, she had blasted right through his protective walls. Her honesty in all things shook him up hard, forced him to be real with her when he'd survived most of his young life by wearing one mask or another.

With her wide open heart and knockout natural beauty, Lisa had made him long for things he never realized he'd wanted. Things he had no right to want from the amazing woman who also happened to be the little sister of one of his closest friends.

And five years ago, when the revelation of all that had smacked him broadside after their mind-blowing night together, he'd run like a damn coward, back to the desert front lines. Back to the hidden life he led as one of the Phoenix, where masks and walls were not only encouraged, but required.

Duarte had never told Kyle what happened between Lisa and him. Fortunately, by some miraculous quirk of the precognitive ability they shared, Kyle hadn't psychically picked up on Duarte's failure as a friend either.

Neither had Alec. The three had bonded as friends from day one in boot camp, but it wasn't until they'd been several weeks into their first combat deployment together that they'd realized their uncommon extrasensory skills were, in fact, common to all three of them.

Seeing glimpses of the future had served their platoon well. Definitely saved a lot of lives—their own and their fellow Marines. But the trio kept their shared secret close, careful to avoid detection. Or so they'd thought.

It wasn't long before the three of them were called into a private meeting with an official from the CIA. That man had been Henry Sheppard—a good man, and the founder of the highly classified Phoenix program.

Duarte, Alec, and Kyle became covert intelligence operatives, where they were known only to Sheppard and a very select few under the codenames Ranger, Stingray, and Talon.

Like the other precognitive agents of Phoenix,

Duarte was required to report in regularly to Sheppard for various training and conditioning exercises and to divulge every occurrence of his visions, no matter how insignificant or disconnected they seemed at the time.

Insignificant sure as fuck wasn't how he would describe the vision that had been plaguing him since the program's demise.

Talking about his ability with Lisa had sent his thoughts back to the recurring nightmare he couldn't seem to escape. The vision of fire and heat and destruction was startling. Confusing. Disturbing.

Hellish.

He didn't know what the vision meant, but for three years it had been his most constant companion.

Thinking on it now made him relive the horrific sensation of melting skin, the agony of ash-filled eyes and smoking, burning hair. His own and that of the countless other people he'd been unable to save...

Duarte jerked in response, realizing only then that he'd started to doze.

Something else had woken him. A noise sounded from the other side of his bedroom door. The soft thump snapped his head up off his folded arm.

The subsequent crash of shattering glass had him on his feet and hauling ass across the room in the same instant.

He opened the door. "Lisa?"

The room was dark, but there she was. Crouched on the floor on the other side of the bed, picking up pieces of the water glass he'd left on the nightstand the evening before.

"I'm sorry. I couldn't sleep. I was going to get up, so I reached for the lamp... I didn't see the glass until it was too late."

Duarte swore in relief that's all it was. He stepped inside and flicked on the light switch. "Don't worry about the glass. You're all right?"

"Yeah." She blew out a quiet laugh. "Just clumsy as usual."

He rounded the bed to where she was hunkered down on the floor, and his mouth went dry. All she wore was her T-shirt. Her full breasts bobbed freely beneath the dark blue cotton, nipples peaked like hard buds.

Fuck.

God help him if he found out she wasn't wearing panties under there either.

He wrenched his gaze away from her and that dangerously tempting question. Broken shards surrounded her bare feet. "Don't move."

He went out to the bathroom and brought back a small trash bin and some damp tissues to pick up the smallest chips of glass. She helped him clear away the pieces, apologizing profusely even though he was the slob who'd left the glass there to be knocked over in the first place.

He wasn't used to thinking about anyone but himself. Now, with Lisa in his house for just a handful of hours, he was having a hard time thinking about anything but her.

Her warm skin. Her sweet vanilla scent. Her soft fingers brushing his as they worked together to dispose of the mess on the floor.

The dick-inflaming knowledge that she was as good as naked beneath that flimsy cotton shirt.

Yeah, he was having an undeniable, obviously very hard time thinking of anything else.

"It's all right," he muttered as her whispered apologies kept coming.

"No, it's not. I should've been more careful. Bad enough I show up here uninvited to drag you into my problems. Now, I'm hogging your bed and breaking your things..."

"Hey. Listen to me." He reached out to caress her cheek. "I don't give a fuck about a broken glass or losing my bed for the night. As for dragging me into your problems, they're mine now, too. They were mine even before you came here tonight."

She blinked up at him, frowning, her bottom lip caught slightly between her teeth. And now that the glass was cleaned up and there was nothing but heat and silence separating them, Duarte realized his mistake in touching her.

He couldn't pull his hand away from the softness of her skin.

"Shit, Lisa..."

She looked drowsy and sleep-rumpled in the dim light overhead. Just the fact that she had been in his bed a few minutes ago brought his hard-on to the verge of agony.

Against his better judgment, he looked at her—really looked at her. Christ, she was beautiful, even more so now than before. More mature, the roundness of her early twenties gone from her cheeks now, refined to a delicate, lean elegance.

She was still girl-next-door pretty, but with a devastating sensuality now.

Sexy as fucking hell.

As he stroked the pad of his thumb over her velvet skin and moist lips, the air between them crackled with a charged anticipation. He felt it in his fingers, in his bones. He felt it in every hard beat of his pulse as he tried to tell himself to back off, that kissing her right now would be a colossal mistake.

His brain knew that. Hell, even his heart warned him against complicating his solitary, dangerous existence by getting intimate again with this woman.

But neither head nor heart seemed able to convince his limbs to make the first move.

Lisa wasn't moving away either.

Leaning in closer, he cupped her face tenderly in his palms. His fingers curled around the back of her warm, soft nape, and a small sigh leaked out of her. When she licked her lips and those pretty, long-lashed eyes went dusky with desire, Duarte was done for.

He pulled her toward him and kissed her once, twice... cursing roughly against her mouth as his lust spiked white-hot with just that brief taste.

God, she tasted good. Smelled good. She felt so good and right in his arms. As if the time they'd been apart had been only minutes, not years.

That alone should have scared him shitless.

Instead it made the need for her twist tighter.

Splaying his fingers behind her head, he held her to him and ravaged her mouth with all the hunger he was feeling. She moaned and went a little boneless in his arms, everything about her telling him that she was feeling the same out of control desire that he was.

On a low groan, he broke contact with her sweet, wet mouth to trail his tongue along her jaw line, over to her ear and the satiny skin beneath. His breath was ragged, sawing out of him in hard pants as lust swamped him, took him under.

She drew in a jagged gasp as he kissed the delicate column of her throat, and each hushed sigh and purr vibrated in his body and veins like a physical caress. Every sensation seemed to radiate straight to his cock.

Arousal hammered through him, making his already stiff and straining shaft turn to heated granite in his jeans.

Lisa's hands smoothed up his arms and over his shoulders as their kiss deepened, intensified. He groaned and hauled her close, crushing her soft curves against his hard chest.

If she didn't stop him, he would be going down in flames any second.

She didn't stop him.

Clutching him tighter, she kissed him back with utter abandon. Her hot little tongue swept out and into his mouth, bold and demanding.

Oh, fuck. Not good.

All he could think about was being inside her. It didn't help that he already knew how sweet and tight and addicting she would feel. He'd been tormenting himself with that memory for the past five fucking years.

Arguments for why they shouldn't do this rolled over him one after the other. His friendship with Kyle. His affiliation with Phoenix, and the danger that brought to Duarte and anyone close to him since the program's demise. To say nothing of Lisa's current vulnerable state of distress and fatigue.

Except she didn't feel distressed or fatigued in his arms.

She felt soft and pliant and willing.

No, she felt as raw and on-edge with need as he did.

She broke their kiss on a fevered moan and withdrew

from the circle of his arms. Just far enough for her to lift the hem of her T-shirt.

Ah, Christ. She was killing him.

With her eyes rooted on his, she peeled off the dark shirt, baring her gorgeous breasts and the slender curves of her waist and hips.

Turned out she was wearing panties underneath. And fuck if simple white cotton bikinis had ever looked so goddamned hot.

She stepped back toward him, unrushed, heart-stoppingly gorgeous. The peaks of her bare nipples pressed into his chest. Then she kissed him again. Hungered. Insistent.

Leaving no room for doubt or his tarnished sense of honor.

There was no room for anything but the two of them.

And all the reasons he had for why he shouldn't want this—for why he shouldn't feel this undeniable need to be with her once more, let alone here and now—incinerated on the spot.

6

John Duarte kissed even better than she remembered.

He felt even better than she remembered. And although she was not the kind of woman to strip her clothes off in front of a man mere hours after arriving at his house in the middle of the night—unannounced and uninvited—Lisa couldn't summon an ounce of shyness around him.

They'd already been down this road once before, so he was hardly a stranger. God knew he didn't kiss like one. His tongue invaded her mouth with a possessive demand, and she opened to him, eager and hungry, as wildly turned on as he clearly was.

His hands roamed over her bare breasts before moving around to the column of her spine as his kiss deepened to a fevered pitch. Heat followed his palms as he traced them down onto her ass where his strong fingers flexed and clenched at the sensitive mounds of flesh scantily covered by her simple cotton panties.

Wet need surged between her legs as he clutched and fondled and stroked her. Her sex ached for something to hold on to, the fine muscles pulsing, clenching with every deep thrust of his tongue in her mouth.

Good as this was already, it was probably a bad idea.

She wasn't looking forward to another awkward morning after, once they both came to their senses. But she was too far gone to worry about that now.

Not when she was practically naked and they both had their tongues down each other's throats.

She wanted him naked, too.

Reaching up, she found the first button on his soft flannel shirt and struggled to work it loose. Her fingers were shaky from the power of her need for him. When she moved to the next button, John stopped her, his large hands engulfing hers, stilling her. He broke away from kissing her, his expression grim and serious.

Oh, God. If he had suddenly found the will enough to put the brakes on now, she was going to die from embarrassment. Either that, or from imploded lust.

But he didn't seem ready to kill the moment at all. Instead, he lifted her hands up to his mouth, dropping a tender kiss on one then the other, his dark eyes smoldering, hooded and heavy on hers.

"On the bed," he told her, his voice dark and rough.

She scrambled onto the disheveled sheets as he made quick work of his shirt, casting it away.

Lisa feasted her eyes on the sight of him. Broad, powerful shoulders and strong, muscled arms. His chest was amazing, harder than before, even more defined with roped sinew and pecs that looked like shields of velvet-covered steel. His trim waist was leaner now, iron-hard ridges and smooth slabs of lethal strength.

She licked her lips, her mouth suddenly gone bone dry while other parts of her body pooled with liquid heat.

Her gaze drifted lower, down the trail of crisp dark hair that disappeared into the waistband of his jeans. The outline of his erection was massive, and she knew from past experience that it was even more impressive unclothed.

When he stepped forward without taking his pants off, she couldn't bite back her small groan of disappointment. Sliding his warm palms under the backs of her knees, he drew her legs to him, pivoting her onto the edge of the bed. Then he leaned down and kissed her, driving her wild for more.

He caressed her naked breasts, rolling her taut nipples between his fingers in sweet torment. His body pressed her backward onto the soft mattress and he followed her there, moving over her as he laid her out beneath him.

He kissed her lips and chin and throat before beginning a sensual descent down her body. She could hardly take it, his unrushed exploration of her bare skin. His tongue trailed lower, his wet, warm lips dragging onto her breasts while need for more of him boiled deep and molten inside of her.

Then he descended farther, taking his time as he kissed his way to her hip bones. She cried out when his hot mouth latched onto her mound over her panties. The heat of his lips and rough breath, the startling graze of his teeth as he closed them over her clothed sex, nearly made her come on the spot.

She caught her lip on a gasp as he slipped his fingers beneath the thin cotton on either side of her pelvis and drew her panties down. Freed of them, she didn't resist as he put his palms on her inner thighs and spread her for his gaze.

He stroked her wet slit and the swollen bud at its crown. "Just as pretty as I remember. Damn, you kill me, girl. You know that?"

She couldn't answer. She could only stare in mesmerized fascination as he lowered his head between her legs and took his first taste of her. She sucked in a shallow breath when his tongue cleaved her folds. Wet. Hot. Mind-numbingly good.

As he suckled her, he slipped a finger into her body. Her walls clenched around him, tremors already starting to build as he teased her with his touch. For each thrust, he sucked her clit deeper into his mouth, tonguing her into a state of pleasured frenzy.

Before long, she was arching and writhing beneath him, panting for more. She reached for him, caught her fingers in the soft, thick waves of his hair. "Please," she gasped. "I need to have you inside me when I come the first time tonight."

He glanced up, his mouth glistening with her juices as he cocked a wicked smile. "The first time?"

"Just come up here, dammit," she commanded him, clutching at his shoulders.

He didn't argue. Shucking his jeans and boxers, he moved up on the bed. Lisa sat up, her gaze riveted to him. She couldn't resist taking hold of his erection. She stroked his length and cupped his balls, reveling in the powerful feel of him in her hands.

His breath shuddered as she explored him. When she dipped her head to cover the engorged head of his cock with her lips, he exhaled a ragged curse and set his hand on the back of her head while she sucked him.

She loved the taste of him on her tongue. Salty and hot, silky and strong.

The scent of his sex and his skin was instantly familiar, felt instantly right. As if he'd been branded into her senses.

He was so hard, so big. She could barely wrap her fingers all the way around his girth as she held him.

He dropped his head back on a groan as she sucked him deeper into her mouth and stared up at him, his reaction giving her encouragement, making her burn hotter for even more of him. Tendons strained in the sides of his neck with each pull of her mouth. His big body twitched and tensed with every slow suction and teasing flick of her tongue against the underside of his thick shaft.

On an abrupt curse, he bent toward the nightstand beside the bed and fumbled the top drawer open. He dumped a small box of condoms and took one out.

Now it was his hands that shook.

He nearly dropped the thin packet, but recovered on a harsh chuckle. He grinned down at her and shrugged. "I've clocked thousands of hours with my finger on the trigger of a hundred different weapons in the heat of battle, yet look at me. All thumbs around you."

Lisa drew back with a smile. "Let me help—"

"Oh, hell no." His sandpaper growl cut her short. "You touch me right now after what your sweet mouth just did to me, and I'm done for."

His confession warmed her. The idea that she could make the stoic, steady John Duarte tremble a little was a wild turn-on. She watched as he rolled the condom onto his length, then scooted back to make room for him on the bed with her.

He moved between her legs, nudging her thighs open with his knee as he came down on top of her. He resumed kissing her, his warm hands on her face and tangling in her loose hair.

She moaned at the pleasure of his weight and the

need to have him inside her. "I can't take much more, Johnny."

"That makes two of us," he uttered thickly, guiding himself to her slick cleft.

The blunt head of his cock slid between her folds, demanding entrance. Seated at her opening, he began to push inside, inch by glorious inch.

Lisa gasped at the fullness invading her. "So good," she murmured as he stretched her, filled her. Made her yearn for more of him. "You feel so good."

"Ah, fuck, sugar... so do you." His molasses-rich voice and sexy Southern drawl made her heart flutter even more behind her ribs. "You feel too damn good. Just like that first night. Too fucking good."

He took her in a hungered kiss as he rocked deeper into her, leaving her quivering and electrified with pleasure. He rolled his hips forward and back in long, powerful strokes, his eyes blazing as he watched her arch and rock with him.

Then there were no more words. Just skin rasping against skin, breaths mingling. And need burning hotter as their rhythm picked up, turning urgent and fevered.

John's low curse was a snarl against her ear as he drove deeper, faster, harder.

Nothing about him was gentle now, and that lack of control sent her own sanity reeling. She couldn't hold on any longer. Her climax built toward a dizzying crest, swelling like a tidal wave.

He was right, it did feel too good.

They felt too good.

While the rest of her life had careened out of control a few hours ago with her brother's disturbing message and apparent involvement in things she still struggled to understand, this moment with John—in his arms again, in his bed—felt so good and right it terrified the hell out of her.

Yet as her orgasm washed over her, she could only hold on to him for dear life and let the pleasure take her blissfully down.

~ ~ ~

He'd never known anything as sexy as Lisa moaning his name as she orgasmed in his arms. His own climax roared up on him in response, a wild thing he could barely control.

She'd had him so ready when she'd sucked on him. The satiny glove of her mouth on his naked cock had almost made him spill before they'd even gotten started.

Now this, the sanity-robbing feel of her channel walls rippling against his shaft as she came. Her tiny muscles milked him toward a massive release, and he chased it with greedy abandon.

He knew it was selfish, acting on his need for her tonight. But right now, with Lisa writhing and arching with the onslaught of another orgasm, he couldn't regret it.

His senses filled with her. The feel of her warm, soft skin against his body. The wet, erotic sounds of their sex combined with her little moans and gasps as he filled her, stretched her, gave her every inch of him. The pleasured look on her face was heaven, making him want nothing more than to cage her beneath him all night and watch her break on him over and over again.

Christ, this woman could become a swift and merciless addiction. He'd recognized that five years ago.

He'd walked away to save himself—to save them both—for all the good it had done now.

Desire consumed him. His own climax coiled tight and pulsing as he lost himself to a more urgent tempo. He thrust harder, knowing he was taking something he didn't deserve, at the worst possible time in both their lives. Yet he was unable to deny himself the want of it. Of her.

All that mattered was Lisa beneath him and the pleasure exploding between them.

He drove deep as a violent shudder racked him, and his orgasm ripped out of him on a raw shout. The release seemed endless, mind-blowing.

So fucking good he could hardly bear it.

"Jesus," he muttered hoarsely, his face buried in the curve of her neck as the aftershocks finally began to subside. He smiled against her sweat-dampened, vanilla-scented skin. "Can't move. Crushing you?"

"M-mm." Her voice vibrated through him, as warm as her skin. "I don't want you to move."

"Have to," he groaned, hating the need to pull out and dispose of the condom.

All he wanted to do was rock into her some more, stay inside her all night if she let him.

Bad idea, but his dick was already rising in agreement.

Before he could lose the argument with himself, he withdrew and moved to toss the used protection in the trash bin next to the bed.

Lisa's hands were soothing on him as soon as he returned to her side. She smiled, sultry and spent. "That was..."

"Yeah," he agreed. "Incredible."

She nodded, looking satisfied and too damn sexy lying naked on the rumpled sheets. He couldn't resist another kiss, then another. Stretching out alongside her, he stroked her hair, traced an idle pattern on the gentle curve of her shoulder. She curled up next to him, one bare thigh slung across his.

For a long while, they simply lay there together in a quiet peace.

And although his thoughts were churning over a hundred troubling issues—not the least of which being the reason for her arrival at his cabin tonight—he stepped away from all of that and let himself relax into the rare feeling of contentment that enveloped him as he held Lisa in his arms.

7

To his complete astonishment, Duarte slept five-plus solid hours, clear through to daybreak. So much for his chronic insomnia. Apparently, all he needed was a good fuck and the warmth of a good woman in bed beside him—the latter more than he cared to admit.

Lisa was still sound asleep, curled up like a kitten in the tangled sheets, her loose honey hair fanned across his pillow.

The soldier in him wasn't accustomed to soft nights and slow mornings, but he was in no rush to leave her side. For a brief moment, he imagined waking up every morning to that vision. Unbelievable that she'd been married to a man who'd been stupid enough to let her go. Then again, Duarte himself had once been that stupid, too.

Ancient history. Except last night had brought their past back to life in living, breathing color. And this morning, reality slapped him awake with the reminder that it was time to start thinking with his head again.

He twitched with the need for movement, for exertion, for action. Before his body decided to work out those impulses indoors with Lisa again, Duarte eased out of bed and got dressed.

The rain had passed overnight. He thought about her

disabled car she'd told him she'd left down on the mountain road. He didn't like the idea of leaving a vehicle out to be discovered in the daylight. Three years living off-grid had worked for him because he'd been cautious, inconspicuous, unfailingly private. Deliberately closed off from the rest of the world as much as he could be.

Now he had a Phoenix operative's sister lying naked in his bed and her car abandoned practically in his front yard. He should have made a point of going down to retrieve it or hide it last night.

Yeah, he should have done a lot of things differently last night.

Scowling at himself as he left the cabin with the key fob to Lisa's Toyota in his pocket, Duarte tucked his pistol into the back waistband of his jeans as was his habit any time he stepped outside. A shortcut took him through the acres of woods he knew like the back of his hand, and down to the dirt road near the base of the mountain.

Her silver Camry had made it a few hundred yards up the muddied tract before getting stuck. Duarte ran a hand over his beard-grizzled jaw as he eyed the deeply entrenched rear tires. They were spun down to the rims of their hubcaps in the thick mud. And with the rain stopped hours ago, the drying mud had turned to concrete.

Shit. No way the puny little two-wheel-drive, four-cylinder was going to have the horsepower to plow out of the deep rut. Gonna have to dig it out.

Using a sturdy stick from the surrounding forest, he went to work freeing the vehicle. It took a lot of elbow grease, and he had to hunker down to chip away at mud encasing the tires. As he dug out the last rut, his gaze strayed to something odd clinging to the underside of the rear bumper.

A small black magnetic GPS tracker.

Holy hell.

He wrenched it off on a harsh curse, his blood running cold.

Someone had been watching Lisa. Thanks to her brother's careless text, Duarte didn't have to guess at who might have put the damn thing on her vehicle. Phoenix's enemies, tracking her.

For how long?

Long enough to know her activities and movements.

Long enough to know where she was now, and whoever it was could easily follow her to the mountain. If they hadn't already.

And Duarte had just left her all alone, unprotected, at the cabin.

As the dread seized him, a sudden chilling image flashed into his mind's eye: Lisa in the hands of a killer, a gun jammed against her temple.

It was there and gone in an instant, like glimpsing a single frame from a rolling film. Nothing to tell him where or when it would happen, only the stark vision of Lisa's pretty face contorted in terror as the nose of a SIG nine-millimeter pressed tight at her head.

Fuck. For all he knew, it could be happening right now.

Icy panic froze his veins at the mere possibility.

Duarte drew his pistol and bolted back to the shortcut, adrenaline pouring through him like acid. His boots chewed up the uneven terrain. Branches slapped at him as he cut a frantic path through the bramble and over the rocky, root-tangled forest floor.

All the while he ran, he tried to reassure himself that she was okay. He'd only been gone a few minutes, and the chances that any of Phoenix's enemies had trailed her to this remote stretch of North Carolina wilderness were slim at best.

But even slim odds were too much for his liking. Especially when his soldier's instincts were clanging in high alarm.

Something felt off about the mountainside as he tore up the incline, racing to reach Lisa. Someone was in these woods with him now. He'd bet his life on it.

He knew it the same way his instincts had served him well on combat patrols.

A bogey was somewhere on his land right now with his sights set on Lisa. Closing in on the cabin... armed and ready to kill.

Son of a bitch.

Duarte's chest squeezed as if caught in a vise. If anything happened to Lisa because he'd let his fucking guard down, he didn't know how he would live with himself.

And then he heard it.

A single gunshot. Up ahead of him through the woods. Where the cabin was.

No. It wasn't happening. It couldn't be.

He couldn't already be too late to save her.

He ran faster, his heart about to explode in his chest. *Goddamn it, no!*

~ ~ ~

Yanked from a pleasant drowse, Lisa bolted upright.

Was that a gunshot?

Holding the sheet to her naked chest, she shook off her sleep and blinked to clear her eyes. She was in the middle of John's bed. His empty bed.

And that sharp, echoing crack outside had definitely been a gunshot.

"John?" No answer. No sound at all from anywhere in the cabin. "Oh God, where are you? John!"

She flew off the mattress. Got dressed as fast as she could, forgoing her bra, which had evidently gotten lost somewhere on the bedroom floor a few hours earlier. No time for shoes, she tore out of the cabin and into the dewy, early morning forest outside.

She spotted him a couple of yards ahead of her, near the ditch she'd stumbled into the night before.

"John!"

He wasn't alone. Another man stood in front of him, his back to Lisa. A mane of shaggy, sun-streaked dark blond hair fell to his shoulders in beach bum waves, but there was nothing else soft about him. He was dressed in a camo shirt and olive cargo pants that made him blend in with the foliage around him. A big man, he was tall and muscular and intimidating, nearly the size and bulk of John.

And, like John, he also held a pistol down at his side.

They both looked her way as Lisa hurried toward them. John's dark eyes were grave, but he didn't warn her away as she ran toward him with her heart in her throat.

The other man's face was equally sober, and... vaguely familiar.

Confused, Lisa tried to process the tanned, angular cheeks and sharp blue eyes that stared back at her from this stranger with a gun in his hand. Then realization settled in.

She knew him. The third member of her brother's trifecta.

"Alec?"

Instead of greeting her as she reached them, he did a quick visual scan of her, from bed-mussed head to barefoot toes. Then he turned a questioning look on John. "I'm not gonna ask."

John grunted. "Good. Because I'm not about to explain."

"I heard a gunshot," Lisa said. "Someone want to tell me what's going—" Her breath caught in her throat. She pointed to the large, unmoving lump in the bottom of the ditch. "That's a dead body."

"It is," John said, his low voice guarded.

"Did you shoot him?"

"I did," Alec answered, his baritone drawl equally cagey.

Lisa glanced between the two men caught in their unspoken standoff. Then she glanced down at the body and the nasty looking pistol beside him. The man wore plain clothes, but his trimmed hair and athletic physique screamed military to her. "One of you two please tell me what just happened. What's going on here? Who the hell is that guy?"

"An enemy of the Phoenix program," John replied. "Or someone working for the program's enemies."

Alec cursed low under his breath. "You told her about Phoenix? Jesus fucking Christ, Ranger."

Lisa frowned. "Who's Ranger?"

"I am." John didn't take his eyes off Alec. "It was my codename in the program."

Alec blew out a sharp exhalation. "She shouldn't be out here, man. She's in danger."

"No shit," John ground out. "The question is, what are you doing here?"

"You mean, besides saving both your asses just now?" Alec gave a slow shake of his head. "Maybe I need to be more concerned about you now. What are you doing up here with Talon's little sister? Other than the obvious, that is."

"That's between me and her. How did you know where to find me?" John drew a small black object out of his jeans pocket and held it in his palm. "This belong to you or the dead guy, Stingray?"

Ranger. Talon. Stingray. Codenames and dead guys, and...

A chill swept over her when she realized what John was holding. "Is that some kind of tracking device?"

"I found it on your car. Then I had a vision of some asshole holding a gun against your head."

Oh, yeah. Let's not forget the whole ESP thing either.

She swallowed hard, eyeing the dead man in the ditch. "You're saying this guy followed me here to kill me?"

"I had the same vision," Alec said, still looking grimly at John. "A week ago. I've been having a lot of visions lately."

"You're clairvoyant, too?"

Amazing how calmly she was able to ask that, given that before last night, she'd attributed claims of psychic abilities to people with overactive imaginations or a desperate need for attention. Neither John nor Alec fit those molds. For that matter, neither did her brother, if everything John told her last night about Kyle and the Phoenix program was true.

62

Which it certainly seemed to be, considering there was a corpse armed with a pistol lying three feet away and Kyle's two best friends discussing the whole thing as if there was nothing strange about any of it.

"The tracker isn't mine," Alec said. "I followed Lisa here last night from Cinci. Been staked out in the woods all night, waiting to see what she was doing up here. And with whom. Now I know."

"What about him?" John asked, ignoring the jab and cocking his head toward the ditch.

"He showed up a few minutes before you came crashing through the woods like an elephant on the charge. Lucky for you, I already had the son of a bitch in my sights."

"More like convenient." John's tone and expression were filled with suspicion.

Alec scoffed. "This fucker would've killed you both if I hadn't been here."

"I wouldn't have given him the chance," John growled back. "How do I know you're not part of the problem, too, Stingray? You working for the dark side since Phoenix went down?"

Alec gave a slight shrug. "I could ask you the same thing."

Lisa couldn't take the sudden overdose of testosterone rolling off the two men. And she also had about a thousand questions swarming in her head.

They started pouring out of her in a rapid stream. "Why would this guy want to kill me? Is it because of Kyle? Do you think he might've known where my brother is? Oh, God... do you think he might've killed Kyle, too?" She looked at Alec then. "And what do you mean you followed me here? Why would you do that? I haven't seen or heard from you in years, so how do you even know where I live? You two need to tell me what the hell is going on, right fucking now."

John's narrow glare stayed rooted on his former comrade. "Yeah, Alec. You start. What the fuck are you doing creeping after Lisa?"

"I told you. Last week I had a vision that she was in danger. Didn't think I could live with myself if I just sat back and let it happen, so I decided to check things out. She wasn't hard to find through public records, the DMV." Alec glanced to Lisa. "Once I had the info, I went to your place just to make sure you were okay. I've been keeping an eye on you ever since."

"Spying on me?"

"I prefer to think of it as stealth body-guarding," he said, some of the wry humor she knew him for edging his deep voice. "I didn't want to scare you, and it was crucial that you continued to act naturally in case anyone else was watching, too."

She thought back to the past couple of weeks, and to one instance in particular, when she'd come home from work and couldn't shake the feeling that someone had been there. No evidence at all to support it. Not a single thing out of place, but she just... *knew*. "Someone broke into my house last week. They must've spent some time nosing around in stealth mode, too. I suppose that was you?"

"No, ma'am," Alec replied. He and John exchanged a look. "But if it was someone else..."

John blew out a curse. "Kyle texted her yesterday. Told her she needed to hide."

Alec seemed surprised, and not pleased. "You've been in touch with your brother recently? Where is he?

What else has he told you?"

She started to answer, but John did it for her. "We don't know any of that yet. The communication cut off right after she got the text."

Alec cursed, frowning as he considered. "I need to see her phone. It could be tapped. Or traced."

"Already disabled it," John said. His fist swallowed up the GPS tracker and he put it back in his pocket. "Obviously, she's on the radar now. So is this mountain. Which means so am I."

"It's my fault," Lisa murmured, hating that she was at the center of John's problems. She was terrified for her brother's wellbeing—her own as well, especially after realizing an armed assassin had come after her today— but that didn't mean she had to put anyone else's life in danger. "I shouldn't have come here, John. I'm sorry. It's not your problem to fix for me. I should go before anything worse happens."

"You're not going anywhere," he said, stepping closer and pulling her under his arm. "Not without me. Got it?"

The intimate gesture and softly worded order sent Alec's brows up a degree, but he didn't comment. "You both need to get out of here," he advised soberly. "The sooner, the better."

"Agreed," John said. His muscled arm flexed around Lisa as he met her upturned gaze. "Alec and I need to dispose of the body and take care of some other business out here. Be ready to leave when I get back, all right?"

"Okay," she murmured.

"Take this." He put his pistol in her hand, his voice quiet and deadly serious. "Don't be afraid to use it if anyone shows up at the cabin before I come back."

She took the gun, catching his meaning as he curled her fingers around its grip. If she needed to use the weapon in the next few minutes, then very likely the only person who would be on the business end of it was Alec Colton.

8

Twenty minutes later, Duarte stood next to Alec on a narrow curve of mountain pass where they had driven Lisa's car and parked it. The dead guy was in the trunk, his nine-millimeter pistol in Duarte's safekeeping.

"You still don't trust me, do you?" Alec said as they walked around to the back of the Camry to pull the body out.

Alec took the corpse's feet, while Duarte grabbed the arms. "Sheppard warned us to cut all ties with our pasts, not to trust anyone—not even another Phoenix operative—if the program ever got compromised. That advice has kept me alive these past three years."

"Same with me," Alec said as they hoisted the dead weight out of the trunk and carried it around to the open driver's side door. "Yet here I am, not killing you. Helping you. Trusting you, in fact."

"Yeah." Duarte grunted, watching the former Marine sniper with more than a little caution. "The question is, what for?"

"*Semper fi* and all that shit, I guess."

After they positioned the dead man behind the wheel, Duarte stood back. "Go get the gas."

Alec gave him a cautious look, but the cocky bastard had balls enough to grin at the same time. "You're not gonna throw a match on me now, are you?"

"Not today." Duarte smirked in spite of himself. "*Semper fi* and all that shit."

Chuckling, Alec swaggered back to the trunk for the container of gasoline they'd brought along from the cabin. He opened the cap on the red plastic can and gave the Camry a good dousing, shaking some of the gas out inside the vehicle and onto the body as well. Once the can was empty, he tossed it in the backseat and came over to stand beside Duarte.

"So, you've been living up here this whole time, I take it?"

Duarte nodded. "You?"

"Got a place down near the beach in Miami."

"Let me guess. One of those sleek high-rise condos with glass walls and ocean views for miles?"

It was no secret that Alec Colton came from money—very old, very established East Coast money—even if he was the unabashed black sheep of his well-heeled family. He'd joined the Marines soon after the Trade Center attack, just like Duarte and Kyle Becker had, but Alec had also admitted he'd done it to escape the yoke and disapproval of his family.

Now, there was no going back. None of the former Phoenix operatives could go back to what they'd once had.

"Nah, nothing like that," Alec said. "That never was my style, man. I'm renting a sweet little Airstream in a trailer park a few blocks from the water. I keep my head down and my ear to the ground, online and otherwise."

"What's your cover down there? Doing anything for work?"

"I pick up the odd job here and there. Nobody to

answer to, nobody telling me how to live my life, which is how I prefer things these days." He paused for a long moment. "So... you and Lisa."

"Yeah," Duarte said. "Me and Lisa. Long story. Private one, and I'm not of a mind to get into it with you at the moment."

Alec nodded slowly, studying him now. "You trust her, though?"

"I trust her."

"Well, that's good, because that dead guy we're about to toast isn't the last of her problems. Not the last of ours either, my friend."

Duarte had a feeling he knew where Alec was heading with this. The same thing had been bugging him since they'd dragged the would-be assassin out of the ditch. "The pistol he was carrying—"

"Isn't a SIG," Alec finished. "It's not the one I saw in my vision."

Not the one Duarte had seen either. Which meant that whatever this man had intended by tracking Lisa up the mountain with a weapon drawn, even though he was now dead, her life was still in danger. The thought put a knot of fury and dread in Duarte's chest. "I'm not going to let her get hurt. Anyone tries, and they'll have to come through me first."

"Even her brother?"

Duarte narrowed his eyes. "What do you know about him?"

"Like I said, I've been having a lot of visions lately. One of them involves Talon."

"As in?"

"As in, him working with the bad guys. Giving them intel, using his ability to help them put hits out on other

Phoenix operatives." When Duarte cursed, Alec went on. "The vision first came to me a couple of months ago, but it was hazy. I wasn't sure what I was seeing."

"Then maybe you were wrong. Hazy could mean you're mistaken."

"I've seen it a few times now, each one clearer than the last. Enough to know that it's real." Alec's expression was as sober as his tone. "Once the premonitions started, I dug into Becker's sister online, began keeping a covert eye on her from a distance, in case she might lead me to him. But nope. Not even a blip of activity on that front. Then, last week, I got the vision of her being held at gunpoint and I decided it was time to move in for a closer look."

Duarte raked a hand over his jaw. He'd been having his own share of disturbing premonitions, too, but the news about Kyle Becker was difficult to reconcile.

None of the three of them was a saint, but Talon a traitor to Phoenix and his comrades? If that was true, it was going to devastate Lisa. And if it was true, then Duarte would have to take the double-crossing son of a bitch out personally. "You sure about all this?"

Alec nodded. "Wish I wasn't, man, but I know what I saw. He's working with Phoenix's enemies. I would bet my life on it. I just don't know where the son of a bitch is, or who's calling the shots above him."

"We need those answers," Duarte murmured.

"Right. And now that Lisa's heard from him, there's a chance she can help us find them—"

"No fucking way." A spear of possessiveness—of white-hot protectiveness—surged through him at the thought of using Lisa to prove, or disprove, her brother's guilt. And Duarte wasn't about to put her anywhere near the fallout, if Alec's vision turned out to be true. "She stays out of this, you got that?"

Alec eyed him soberly and gave a mild shake of his head. "Like it or not, Ranger, she's already in. You and I both know that. And sooner or later, before this is all done, she's gonna have a SIG nine cocked and loaded up against her pretty head."

The reminder chilled Duarte to the bone. It also solidified his resolve. "I'll die before I let that happen."

"Let's hope it doesn't come down to that, my friend."

"I need to take her someplace safe," Duarte said. "I want to keep her close by while you and I figure out what's going on with her brother. And then decide what we need to do about it."

"Right," Alec agreed. "As for where to go, I have some connections that may be able to help with a temporary safe house."

"What kind of connections?"

"Trustworthy ones," he said. "Let's just say I have a business colleague who owes me a favor or two and won't balk at being asked for payback. There won't be any questions, and the place is guaranteed secure."

"You talking military security?"

Alec smirked. "More or less."

"Why do I get the feeling it's much less?"

"Guess you're just gonna have to trust me, Ranger." The Marine comrade who'd had Duarte's back since boot camp held his gaze now from under the fall of a shaggy mane of surfer dude waves. Crystal blue eyes held Duarte's stare, measuring him, too. "Guess we're both going to have to trust each other now."

Duarte nodded, and suddenly it felt a bit like old

times. Like being back in the platoon in the sandbox, preparing to head out on a combat mission.

Except this time, if Alec was right, the enemy on the other side of the wire could be one of their own. Duarte didn't want to consider that possibility, but he was too jaded by war and betrayal to believe it could never happen.

And his years in the Phoenix program had taught him another thing, too. The visions never lie.

"Come on," Duarte said. He took the GPS tracker out of his pocket and pitched it into the woods. Anyone else monitoring the signal would have to search a thousand acres of wilderness before they realized Lisa's car was no longer attached to the beacon. "Let's start the barbeque and get the fuck out of here."

Leaning into Lisa's open car, he put the transmission in neutral. Then he closed the door and together he and Alec went around behind the Camry and pushed it off the narrow dirt road and over the steep ledge.

9

They cleared out of the cabin and hit the road as soon as the guys returned. Leaving her car smoldering at the bottom of the cliff along with the gunman who'd come to find her, John explained that the diversion would likely only buy a day or two lead time before someone else came looking for her.

They needed to put miles between themselves and the cabin, and they needed to do it fast. John had packed a duffel with a change of clothes and some additional firearms. Lisa had the few things she brought with her from Cincinnati in her backpack.

With it likely that whoever was tracking Lisa now also had John on their radar, his old pickup would have been as useless to them as her car. Alec's Jeep, parked down at the base of the mountain since he'd arrived last night, made for a cramped road trip option but they had few choices.

Lisa didn't know precisely where she and her pair of grim companions were headed now. Before they left North Carolina, Alec had made a call to a friend who'd agreed to provide them with a temporary safe house somewhere. Now, as the sun began to set over I-95 South some eleven hours later, Lisa watched from the Wrangler's small backseat as the highway signs indicated they were approaching Miami.

Alec exited the highway and drove through a maze of side streets and back alleys, skirting the tropical vibrancy of the downtown for a more industrial section of the city. The salty scent of the ocean and aromatic, spicy foods carried in through the Jeep's open windows as they traveled deeper into Miami's back channels.

Alec seemed to know the area well. He navigated with a sure hand, eventually rolling the Jeep to a stop at a gated entrance to a large dock-front warehouse.

A mean-looking security guard came out of the small gate shack to approach. He was swarthy and thick-trunked, his dark brows furrowed over black-lensed sunglasses. At his hip, a holstered pistol bobbed with each stride he took. Behind him came an even bigger guard to circle around the other side of the Jeep.

"Jesus Christ," John muttered under his breath as the armed men stalked toward the car.

The surly guard's face lost some of its aggression as he ambled forward, but the whole thing still left Lisa on edge. She could sense John's unease, too, as the second man strolled slowly up to the passenger window, his hand resting on his weapon. From the way John's muscled shoulders tensed, there was little doubt he was prepared to draw his own pistol any second.

"It's cool, relax." Alec lifted his finger off the wheel in a casual wave of greeting as he cranked the driver's side window down. "Hey, Luis, *qué más?*"

The guard on Alec's side cracked a broad smile and chuckled. He thrust his big mitt into the vehicle to clasp Alec's hand in greeting. *"Qué has hecho, parce?"*

They launched into a brief but congenial conversation in some form of Spanish. Alec was fluent, almost familial, with the men. As they were with him. Even the second guard's face slackened into an expression that was almost friendly. Then the guard talking with Alec nodded to his comrade, who clicked a button on a remote he wore on his belt. The gate swung open, permitting them through.

Alec gave the two men another smile and a salute, then he drove inside the warehouse yard.

John slanted him a suspicious look as they rolled away from the guard shack. "My Spanish is rusty as fuck, but I'm guessing that was Colombian?"

"My friend and his associates are from Bogotá," Alec said as he drove toward the large square building up ahead and the deepwater docks behind it.

"Your friend and his associates." John grunted. He swung a glance at the warehouse and cursed. "Just what kind of safe house did you arrange for us, Stingray?"

Alec flicked an arch look at Lisa in the rearview mirror. "He always this growly and ungrateful?"

John glared. "Some people just bring out the best in me."

Lisa smiled in spite of the apprehension that rippled through her. John's caution was understandable, after all. In coming with Alec, they were putting their lives in his hands. She and John—Alec, too—were putting their lives in the hands of people he said could be trusted, yet who seemed to be more than a little dangerous in their own right.

"That's our ride over there," Alec said. He nodded ahead of them, to where a sleek helicopter stood. "The safe house is a short flight from here. The pilot will take us the rest of the way."

As they collected their things and climbed out of the

Jeep to approach the helipad, John caught Lisa's hand in his. The gesture was as unexpected as it was intimate and reassuring. She didn't try to pretend she didn't welcome his warmth as they embarked on this strange new leg of their journey together.

Alec greeted the pilot with the same fluent Spanish and easy charm. Like the guards at the gate, this man was also armed with a holstered pistol and a don't-mess-with-me demeanor. After a few words with Alec, a few moments to allow them to get settled and buckled in to their seats in back of the cockpit, they were off.

The chopper lifted up over the azure water and strip of white sand, then banked into a southerly course. The Florida keys lay up ahead, a chain of green islands of varying sizes and populations. They spangled like dark jewels in the setting sunlight.

Lisa watched the scenery pass below, then realized they were heading for a small island set by itself about a quarter-mile off shore from a larger key. The beach-fringed clump of green foliage was home to a single residence—a sprawling tropical mansion with a pool on one side and a helipad on the other. A pair of wooden boat slips stretched out into the blue water, and circling the entire diameter of the residence was what appeared to be a hand-dug moat.

The helicopter began to descend. As they touched down on the concrete pad, two pairs of guards waited nearby.

Lisa was apparently getting used to the idea of being greeted by heavily armed Colombians, because she hardly flinched when one of them gestured to take her backpack inside for her while Alec chatted up the leader of their detail and casually shook hands with the others.

The guard who'd taken Lisa's backpack went to the helicopter and retrieved a medium-sized silver suitcase. When he started carrying it inside with her backpack, she stepped in and shook her head. "Wait, that one's not ours—"

"He knows," Alec interjected smoothly. Smiling, he gestured to the guard to continue on. "My friend on the mainland sent along some other cargo with us."

Duarte slowly shook his head. "We're not staying."

Alec frowned. "What?"

"We're not taking favors from some fucking drug dealer, Stingray."

"You got a better option, Ranger?" Alec met him stare for stare, every bit as hard-headed and clearly just as accustomed to being the chief alpha in charge. "Like I told you, we'll be safe here. Those men in there and the one they serve may operate outside the law, but they're good people. And so long as we're here, they'll guard us like they would their own family." He pivoted away from John and Lisa, and started walking. "I smell dinner cooking inside. You two coming, or what?"

~ ~ ~

Duarte had his doubts about Alec and his so-called friend's provision of a safe house, but even he had to admit the accommodations didn't suck. Neither did the dinner they'd all enjoyed an hour ago in the main house. Turned out one of the rifle-toting Colombians who'd greeted them on arrival was also a gourmet-caliber cook.

After feasting on marinated grilled mahi with melon and citrus salsa, spicy roasted vegetables, followed by a sweet coconut flan for dessert, Duarte's doubts about their private island hosts had lost some of their edge. The generous pours of hundred-year-old scotch he and Alec had enjoyed after the meal hadn't hurt either.

As for Alec, some of Duarte's reservations about trusting him had smoothed as well, despite the numerous questions Duarte had when it came to his old friend's current dubious affiliations. The two of them had shot the shit over dinner, falling into an easy camaraderie that made Duarte miss the old times. It had made him miss the tight friendship their one-time trifecta had enjoyed.

And it had made the specter of Kyle's possible defection loom all the more ominously. Especially when Duarte had been seated at the table with his arm draped intimately around Lisa's shoulders while the three of them relaxed after dinner.

Now, Duarte found her standing outside on the open-air veranda of her guest room. She'd excused herself from the table about twenty minutes earlier to freshen up, and it had taken just about all of his willpower not to insist on going with her.

He told himself the impulse was a protective one, but seeing her now, standing alone in the moonlight beneath a canopy of swaying palm trees, looking out at the dark water as he approached her from behind, the feeling that gripped him wasn't simple concern for her wellbeing and a need to know that she was safe. It wasn't even basic lust, though there was plenty of that going on.

No, what he felt when he looked at Lisa Becker went deeper than he wanted to acknowledge.

And he'd been carrying this feeling around for longer than he was willing to admit.

Hell, she'd gotten under his skin well before they'd

fallen into bed together that first time. From the start, she'd gotten under and stayed there. He just hadn't realized it until fate sent her back to him again last night.

Not good, Duarte. Turn the fuck around and let it go. If not for your own sanity, then for hers.

Too late. Lisa must have sensed she wasn't alone.

She pivoted around and her soft eyes found him standing in the open room behind her. She was still wearing her clothes from that morning at the cabin. Duarte had left his shoes and flannel shirt behind in his own room a minute ago, and now wore only his jeans in the warm night air.

Lisa smiled hesitantly. "Hey."

"Hey," he said. For a moment, he stood there, his bare feet rooted to the cool tile floor. Still time to about-face and not complicate things any further with her. "Just wanted to check on you. Make sure you had everything you need for the night."

"I do now." Her shy smile warmed, became a welcoming beacon in the moonlit darkness and dim light of the room. She glanced back out at the night sky and endless expanse of glittering black water. "Pretty spectacular, isn't it?"

Duarte stalked forward, all thoughts of doing the right thing—the uncomplicated thing—blown away on the tropical breeze. He stood directly behind her, their bodies' mingling warmth heating his bare chest like a furnace. He couldn't resist sweeping her silky hair away from the side of her neck to make room for his kiss. "Spectacular," he murmured against her satin skin. "Never seen anything more gorgeous in my life."

Her soft moan vibrated through him as she leaned back, into the cradle of his arms. "Is that you or the single malt talking?"

God, he wished he could blame the scotch. "Just me, and I mean every word. You are..." He shook his head slowly, still trying to make sense of everything she was to him—back then, and especially now. "You always have been... a surprise."

"In what way?" She sounded curious, but he could hear the smile in her voice as well.

"In the best way. Shit, in the worst way, too." He caged her loosely in his arms, taking another taste of the sweet softness below her ear. "I've made my living always knowing how to respond to any situation, how to approach and attack any kind of problem. Nothing knocks me off course. I'm prepared for anything because I have to be. It's how I survive. But damn if I've ever known how to handle myself around you."

"Oh, I think you do all right." She caressed his arms as she continued to rest against him. "And sometimes it's okay to shut all that other noise out. It's okay for you to just *be*, Johnny. Especially when you're with me."

Duarte held her and watched the moonlight dance on the water beyond the island's shore. For a moment, it was easy to believe they'd escaped to some secluded haven together. Someplace warm and pretty and tranquil, like she deserved.

Someplace where the Phoenix program never existed and they weren't running from armed killers on their trail or dependent on a minor drug lord to provide them shelter. For just a moment, he wanted to ignore the nightmare premonitions that plagued him and the dread that he might not be able to protect Lisa from the danger his vision and Alec's predicted.

For now, holding her like this, it was all too easy to

imagine none of that could touch them.

Feeling Lisa going warm and pliant in his arms made him wish the illusion could be real.

She slowly shifted, turning around to face him. Her touch was feather light on his cheek and whiskers. That gentle caress alone nearly undid him.

"I hoped you'd come to find me here," she confessed softly. "I wasn't sure you would."

The night breeze lifted the fine tendrils of her golden brown hair, sent it dancing around her beautiful face. Dusky hazel eyes stared up at him from under the fronds of her lashes.

He saw desire there, raw and unmistakable, and it sent an arrow of need into his veins. "I shouldn't stay..." He trailed off on a low, muttered curse. "You look too good out here in the moonlight. It's been a long, fucked up day, and you've got to be tired. The last thing you need is me pouncing on you again when I'm supposed to be protecting y—"

She silenced him with a kiss. A very hot, take-no-prisoners kiss. Her bold tongue pushed past his teeth and invaded his mouth, turning his cock to fire-forged steel. His pulse quickened and the growl that rolled off his lips was ripe with need.

"If you don't stop now," he warned thickly, "I won't be able to."

She licked her lips. "Do you want to stop?"

Fuck no. He managed a vague shake of his head before he took her mouth in a hard, claiming kiss of his own. His erection pulsed with each heartbeat banging in his chest. His hips rocked forward, seeking the friction and heat of Lisa's body.

"I want to be inside you, right now. Christ, I want

that more than you can know." He groaned. "All my stuff's in the other room. No condoms on me."

Unfazed, Lisa wrapped her arms around the back of his neck, pressing herself against him in delicious torment.

"Stop thinking every problem is yours to solve, John Duarte." Her mouth curved in a wicked smile. "Now shut up and kiss me again."

10

Lisa pulled John into another slow, passionate kiss.

He was right; she was tired and exhausted. And it had been a long hell of a day. But the one thing she needed most at the end of it was him.

She lost herself in their kiss, let her hands skim over his strong bare shoulders and into the thick waves of his hair. His soft beard rasped against her cheeks and neck as his mouth roamed over her in a fevered path, igniting sparks of heat everywhere he kissed her.

It didn't matter that they were in a strange place, under troubling circumstances. Her heart needed this man, just as much as her body needed him now.

John's low voice vibrated through her. "Damn, woman... what you do to me."

"Then let me do it," she whispered breathlessly. Twining her hands in his hair, she crushed her mouth to his again, thrusting her tongue past his teeth.

He met her with equal ferocity, then tore his mouth away on a growl. "You sure? Right here?"

She nodded, too swept up in him to reply.

They weren't alone on the island, not even alone in the sprawling house, but it was warm and secluded on the veranda. The last guard to walk past on patrol of the perimeter hadn't been back in a long while. So, with the warm breeze off the ocean sifting through the palms overhead, and nothing but the moon to see them, Lisa kissed him deeper as she reached down to unfasten his jeans.

She slipped her hand inside, moaning at the heat and power of his shaft. The velvety strength of him surged even harder, even hotter, as she caressed his length and teased the juice-slickened, broad plum at its crest. Her palm and fingertips glided over his shaft in smooth, wet strokes, each long pull drawing ragged breaths and delicious shudders from his immense body.

His hips thrust with the increasing tempo she set, and his kiss took on a wildness she reveled in.

She wanted him to let go with her.

She wanted to feel him lose control, and know that she had given him that freedom.

She wanted...

God, she wanted everything when it came to this man.

Hunger building, she broke their kiss to focus on pushing his jeans and boxers down to give her fingers better access to him. His erection sprang free, heavy and heated in her palm.

She couldn't get enough.

Sinking down onto her knees in front of him, she helped him step out of his clothing and pushed it aside. Then she cupped and stroked him with one hand, the other trailing down to his balls and back again, praising him with her fingers. Beautiful. That's what he was. Beautiful and strong and magnificent.

And he was hers, even if he didn't know that. She wanted him to know tonight.

Yeah, their lives were tangled up in chaos and

uncertainty now, but John Duarte had always belonged to her. And she to him.

Tonight she wanted—*needed*—to hear him say it. If not with his words, then with his body.

With the surrender of his hard-held, iron control.

She licked the crown of his cock as her hands continued their worship of him. The salty, hot taste of him intoxicated her, made her suckle him deeper into her mouth on a soft moan. He hissed as she drew him in and out with the suction of her lips and tongue. His big hands came down onto her head, fingers spearing into her loose hair.

On a throaty sigh, she swallowed him nearly to the root, relishing the surge of his pelvis as she descended on his length. His balls were tight in her palm, his thighs spread apart, quivering as she pulled back, then pushed down once more. Again and again, her own arousal mounting from the delicious friction of his cock filling her mouth.

"Jesusfuck... Ohyeahsugar..." The words rushed out of him, short, strangled whispers as she sucked him deeper, harder, into her mouth.

She loved the feel of him on her tongue. She loved the way his powerful body tensed, how his breathing gusted out of him, ragged and rapid, each time she slid along on his shaft. The head of his erection knocked against the back of her throat and a shudder wracked him.

He groaned, let out a harsh curse. "That sweet mouth of yours... you're killing me here. So wicked... so fucking hot."

She purred at his praise, every bit as frenzied as he was. His hands roamed wildly in her hair, messing it all up, winding the tresses around his fists while his body bucked and shook with each stroke and lick and nip she lavished on him.

Another groan ripped out of his throat. "Ah fuck... baby, you gotta stop now. You gotta—"

"Not a chance," she murmured, glancing up at his pleasure-contorted face.

To demonstrate her intent, she took him deep and slow, all the way to the base. He dropped his head back, sucking in a hissed breath as she tightened her lips around him and pivoted her mouth on his cock.

Her name was a thick whisper on his exhaled breath as she worked him to the point of no return. She felt his body ratchet further, every strong muscle and tendon going tight as bowstrings. He held her head to him, fists tangled in her hair. His hips jutted forward in a hard thrust, and she smiled when she felt his leash begin to slip.

"Lisa," he uttered again, though whether in warning or plea, she didn't know.

With another fierce pump, his release spilled into her mouth, scorching and erotic. She lapped at him greedily, taking everything he had to give, savoring the moment.

Right now, nothing else could touch them.

Right now, they belonged only to each other, and to this moment.

The blazing look in his eyes left no room for doubt.

~ ~ ~

"Come up here." Duarte could hardly croak out the words.

He drew her up from her knees and slanted his

mouth over hers in an unhurried tangling of lips and tongues and panting, mingled breaths. His entire body was electrified, a tinderbox of raw, combustible need, even after the incredible orgasm that Lisa had wrenched from him.

Sucked from him without mercy or hesitation, like a cat with the cream.

Holy fuck, had she ever.

The thought alone rendered him rock-hard, instantly ready for another round. She tasted sweeter than ever, and the fact that his own juices lingered on her kiss only made him crave her more.

He needed to be inside her. He wanted to be the one delivering the sweet torture now, turning her inside out with pleasure until she couldn't bear another second of it. He wanted to feel her body detonate on his cock in an orgasm she'd never forget.

Except he'd been the dumbass to walk into this without a condom.

He snarled a curse at himself for letting things slip out of control here. *Ought to be getting used to that by now.* Lisa Becker was the one woman who'd ever been able to make him crack.

Broke him wide open, and not just because she was the hottest thing he'd ever laid eyes or hands on.

He turned her around so she was facing the dark, moonlit water beyond the veranda. As she stood at the railing, bent slightly forward to brace herself, he moved in behind her. Swept her hair aside so he could nuzzle his mouth in the curve of her neck and shoulder. "Now I'm going to taste you, sugar. Every sweet inch of you."

She tipped her head back on a sigh as he kissed her. Shivered as he ran his hands down her back, then onto the sweet flare of her denim-clad hips. She moaned as he took hold of her and pulled her ass against his erection. He thrust into her rounded curves, desire stabbing him like spurs as she met his tempo, grinding along with him.

"You're overdressed," he murmured. He should be grateful for her clothes, probably the only thing keeping him from slamming his cock home inside her heat where it wanted to be. Even so, his hands were already moving to remedy the situation.

Reaching around to the front of her, he unbuttoned her jeans and tugged down the zipper. He pushed the faded denim off her hips. Her panties went with them, down her long, gorgeous legs to her slender ankles. Duarte skimmed his palms over her soft skin. Her naked backside was a thing of indescribable beauty, firm and round and enticing. He caressed her, squeezed her possessively in his greedy hands.

On a ragged breath, he slid his hands to her inner thighs and guided them wider apart. Her ass thrust higher with the shift in her stance. The seam of her body glistened with her juices. The scent of her arousal was honey-sweet, and far too tempting to resist.

His hands on her hips, he crouched down behind her, holding her steady as he moved in for the first taste. The instant his mouth made contact, her body jerked in response. He held fast, pushing into her satiny flesh and licking a slow path up the full length of her core.

"Oh God," she bit out, hissing as he dragged his mouth lower and opened her folds to his questing tongue.

"I'm not gonna go easy on you, baby," he warned as he continued to lick and suckle her. "Not after your little power play with me."

She didn't seem worried. Her pleasured moan vibrated into his bones, rocketing straight into the pulsing stalk of his erection. He reveled in the way she writhed and rocked against his mouth. He strummed her clit with his tongue, flicking the swollen bud mercilessly, just to feel her shudder with pleasure and need. Her juices felt like liquid velvet against his fingers as he brought his hand up to her sex and teased the delicate flesh.

With his mouth still busy on the tight bundle of nerves at her core, he delved inside the wet heat of her sheath, penetrating her with one finger, then another. Her walls clamped down on him as he picked up his pace and thrust deeper, mimicking what he wanted to do with his cock.

"John..." She gasped his name, her spine bowing.

Oh, yeah, she was close. He smiled against her quivering little bud. Pure male satisfaction surged through him when he felt the first tremor begin to shake her. "No mercy, sweetness. I meant it."

She swayed with his building rhythm, her small pleasured sounds filling the air as he caressed her into a thrashing, whimpering madness with his hands and mouth. Her orgasm boiled out of her on a hoarse cry. Violent shudders traveled over her limbs, but he steadied her, held her and petted her as she crested the peak of the wave, then began her spiral back down to the here and now.

"Oh, my God," she whispered brokenly, her slender arms locked in front of her, hands gripping the veranda's railing.

Duarte stood up, his naked body still fiercely aroused as he pressed himself against the back of her. Guiding her face to the side to meet his, he took her mouth in a long, claiming kiss. He shifted until he could slide his fingers back into her drenched sex.

Tiny spasms raked her at the invasion, but she didn't deny him. Not this woman. She was still hot and wet, still ready for more. Ready for him.

His cock jumped in eager response, blood coursing through him with the hard beat of a drum. "I've got to be careful here," he told her, his voice rough, thick with desire. He broke their kiss and held her dark-lashed, sex-drowsed eyes. "I've got to be real careful, my sweet, beautiful girl. Because what I want more than anything right now is to bend you over this railing and fuck you under the stars. I want to be inside you, fuck you until you shout my name across those dark waves when you come for me again."

Her gaze glittered in the moonlight. A small smile spread over her lips. "That's what you want?"

"Fuck yeah. More than I should. More than you can know."

The smile became a grin. "Okay." She backed away and pulled off her T-shirt. Unclasped her bra and let it drop to the veranda floor.

"Lisa, wait." Did he actually have the strength of will to deny her? To deny himself? "We can't—"

She put her finger to his lips. "I'll be right back."

Before he could ask where she was going, she darted back into the guest room, stark naked. The bathroom light flicked on. Rummaging sounds and the clatter of small items rolling across a countertop filtered out to the evening air.

The bathroom light went out and she strolled back out, holding her prize between her thumb and forefinger. "It was in the bottom of my makeup bag. It's been in there for a while...Well, a long while... but I think it's still good."

Duarte gaped. Then he chuckled, marveling at this woman and her endless ability to surprise him. Guess she had plans of her own when she told him not to worry about the protection he left behind in his room. He shook his head as she joined him on the veranda. "Look at you, solving problems like a boss."

She laughed, then tore the packet open with her teeth.

Duarte reached for her, snagging her by the arm. He swallowed her quiet shriek with a long, unrushed kiss. Then he hauled her back into his embrace to make good on his threat.

11

The nightmare woke him before dawn.

Duarte sat on the edge of the bed, his heart hammering, a sheen of cold sweat coating his naked back. *Breathe. In, out. In, out.* Simple task, but it was always a struggle after the terror of the vision.

Feet planted on the cool floor tiles, head braced in his shaking palms, he blinked into the predawn darkness of the guest room, trying to purge the horrifying images from his brain. The stench of burning flesh. The shock of a searing, mass obliteration that engulfed everything in its path.

Just a dream. A vision, not reality. Not yet, anyway.

He worked to concentrate on reality. On the quiet tranquility of the here and now. Not the hellish premonition of fire and decimation that had been haunting him for most of the past three years.

Behind him on the bed, Lisa slept soundly. He glanced back at her, thankful that he hadn't disturbed her. She rested so peacefully, so innocently. The urge to return to bed and gather her in his arms stirred inside him, but he tamped it down hard. He'd be damned before he'd put the terror and ugliness of his premonition anywhere near her.

Being with her last night had been a vision of its own

kind, too. A far too pleasant one. It had coaxed him into believing there might be a future for them somehow. That he might actually be able to have a normal life.

With her.

Christ, with Lisa in his arms, he could almost believe anything was possible.

The nightmare vision had been a wakeup call in more than one way. His life would never be normal. And this vision only made him recall the other disturbing premonition he'd had—the one that had left him equally shaken.

Lisa at the business end of a SIG semi-auto held at the side of her pretty head.

A chill washed over him at the reminder. He'd die before he let her stand in harm's way. And he would kill anyone to ensure her safety. Including her brother, if his actions had put Lisa in danger from Phoenix's enemies.

Duarte stood up and got dressed in his jeans, careful not to wake Lisa as he stepped out onto the veranda. It was quiet, and it was early. The first pink hues of dawn were barely a glow on the watery horizon. He headed down toward the beach, in need of fresh air and space to think.

He wasn't the only one up early. Alec stood outside the main house, talking casually on one of the decks with a couple of the island's armed guards. All three men glanced in Duarte's direction, Alec giving him a nod of greeting and a salute with the steaming mug in his hand.

If it was an invitation to join them, Duarte wasn't taking it. He'd never been the most social person in the best of times. He sure as hell wasn't up for the morning's drug dealer coffee klatch, no matter how much he could use the caffeine.

He strode to the water's edge and took a seat on the cool sand. It didn't take long before Alec came over to meet him. He'd brought a second mug, and held it out to Duarte.

"Thanks." Duarte closed his eyes and inhaled deeply as he drank, letting the black coffee aroma chase away the ghosts of the smoke and ruin that still lingered from the fiery premonition. It almost worked.

Alec dropped onto the beach beside him, elbows draped over his bent knees. "I don't sleep for shit either. Too much time on deployments, grabbing shut-eye in twenty-minute increments between engagements, probably. Can't remember the last night I slept all the way through. What about you?"

Duarte grunted, recalling much too vividly the deep sleep he'd been enjoying the past two nights with Lisa. Or rather, *after* Lisa. Amazing what sexual depletion could do for insomnia.

Alec took a drink of his coffee in the silence. "'Course, the nightmares don't help either."

"You, too?" No need to ask if his former Phoenix comrade was talking about combat terrors or something else. The grave look on Alec's face said it all. "The explosion?"

"More like a fucking annihilation."

Duarte nodded. "I started seeing it within days after Phoenix went dark."

"Yeah, me, too. It's always the same vision, always in the form of a dream. I know how it's going to play out, but I can never make it in time to stop it."

There was little comfort in that confirmation. If either of them had wanted to deny the nightmare was attributable to their precognitive gifts, that hope evaporated now.

"The vision, the outcome... it's always the same," Duarte murmured. The images were still fresh in his mind. They replayed now in rapid speed, like the flickering frames of an old projector film. "The building. The heat and flames. It consumes everything."

Alec listened in knowing silence, his head bobbing faintly in agreement with everything he was hearing. He exhaled a curse under his breath. "It's the sight of those kids that shreds me the most. Even more than when I feel my own face melting off my skull."

"The kids?" Duarte's thoughts ground to a halt. He turned a confused look on his friend. "What do you mean?"

"The ten kids playing basketball when the explosion detonates."

"No. That's not right." He set his coffee down in the sand beside him. "There aren't any kids in my vision."

Now Alec was staring at him in doubt. "I try to warn them to get out of the way, but they don't seem to hear me. So, I start running toward them. And that's when everything blows apart."

Duarte shook his head. "The explosion goes off right after I find the guns in the cabinet. There are three of them—military rifles. I grab one, but then I realize it's all fucked up. Rusted, corroded. Useless. When I reach for another one, I hear the first rumble in the building outside. It's already too late by then. I run out to try to stop what's going to happen, but it's too late..."

Alec said nothing, but then he didn't have to.

"No guns in your vision." Duarte rubbed his hand over his forehead. "So, the premonitions aren't exactly the same—"

Alec's expression was grim. "Other than the end result."

Death. Destruction. Mass-scale obliteration.

Duarte stared out at the Atlantic, and the muted light now reaching over the horizon. "Do you think we're the only Phoenix operatives having this vision? It seems odd—too coincidental—that it started after the program went down."

"You think there's a connection?" Alec blew out a short sigh. "Jesus Christ, Ranger. If that's true..."

"Then the past three years that all of us have been on the run and in hiding was only giving Phoenix's enemies the chance to grow stronger. To make plans." A curse erupted out of him. "They drove us underground when we needed to be on their asses, hunting the bastards down instead of looking over our shoulders."

"They knew we'd scatter after Sheppard was killed," Alec murmured. "Somehow they had to know what his instructions had been to all of us if the program was ever compromised."

"Assume the worst. Cut all ties. Run and hide." Duarte recited the founder's orders, fury beginning to boil in his veins. *"Trust no one. Not even one another."*

Alec nodded soberly. "If they knew how to get us out of their way, then someone had to tell them. Someone who's been working from the inside for a long time. Maybe the entire time."

Duarte didn't want to acknowledge it. The possibility grated, not only because Kyle Becker was Lisa's beloved brother, but because he'd been a close friend. Duarte's best, most trusted friend. Alec's too.

"He's got more honor than that," Duarte said.

"Christ, let him have more honor than that."

Alec stared at him. "I know what I saw, man. He's on the wrong side of this."

"And all I know is what you've told me. You say you had a premonition Talon's turned. Maybe you did. Maybe you didn't." He searched the face of his former comrade, looking for cracks in the friendly facade. "How do I know you're not on the wrong side, too? Spying on Lisa, following her up to my place, hanging around with drug dealers and their armed thugs like they're your fucking family? Far as I can tell, you're nothing but suspicion and secrets, Stingray."

"They *are* my family."

Duarte felt his brows crash together. "What?"

Alec shrugged. "Diego Zapata owns this place. He deals in weed mainly, with the occasional side-deal in guns. He operates out of Miami, and before you ask, yeah. I've done a few jobs for him these past three years. I'd kill for the man... *have* killed for him. And he would do the same for me, because he considers me a son. Son-in-law, to be exact."

The news was unexpected to say the least. "You're telling me you're married—"

"Was married," Alec said quietly. "To his daughter, Maria. She died eleven months ago. Inoperable brain tumor."

"Fuck... I'm sorry." He couldn't even imagine that kind of loss. Didn't want to imagine it. "How long were you together?"

"Not long. Three months."

Not long at all. Duarte never would have taken Alec for the whirlwind type, but then again, all bets were off when it came to the right woman. He'd only seen Lisa a handful of times at the base before she eclipsed any other woman in his eyes.

If she hadn't been Kyle's little sister, Duarte would have put the move on her right away. Instead, he'd played it cool. Played it safe. Told himself she was off limits and no matter how much he wanted to look, he'd never touch.

Until the night of that stand-in wedding date and subsequent trip up to his cabin.

And now?

He didn't want to acknowledge what she meant to him now. Nor how much it would wreck him to lose her. But to lose her to death as Alec had lost his wife?

He didn't think he could survive that.

Alec stared out at the ocean, contemplative. "I knew she didn't have long when I asked her to marry me. We'd been messing around in secret for a few weeks, flirting with each other for a lot longer. When I realized she wasn't healthy, I didn't want to just keep playing games with her. She deserved better than that, you know?"

"When you say you knew she wasn't healthy..."

"I knew about the tumor," Alec confirmed. "Thanks to my so-called gift, I watched her die in my arms twice. Once in the premonition, then again on the day I lost her."

"I'm sorry, man," Duarte murmured, staggered by what his friend had done, and by what he had endured. "Sorry for the way I pushed you to tell me about her, too."

"No apology needed." Alec lifted his shoulder, gave a mild chuckle. "No one ever counted on you for your diplomacy, anyway. Asshole."

Duarte smiled at the light jab, relaxed immediately.

It felt good to look at his old friend—his brother-in-arms—and think maybe he wasn't alone in this fight anymore. Risky or not, he believed Alec Colton. He trusted him—with his own life and with Lisa's.

As for her brother?

"Tell me again about the vision you had about Talon. What was he doing?"

Alec cleared his throat. "I saw him sitting in a room, telling someone about the program and the file he had with intel on the operatives. Giving them names and location information. Real names, John. Not just our codenames. He was giving them everything they asked for."

"Fuck." Duarte scowled. "Did you see who he was talking to?"

"No."

"Kyle's ability was off the charts, always has been. Easily the strongest of the three of us, anyway. It wouldn't surprise me if he was one of the strongest of all the operatives. If Phoenix's enemies have him on their side, they couldn't ask for a more powerful tool to use against us." At Alec's nod of agreement, Duarte exhaled sharply. "For all our sakes, I hope to hell you're wrong."

"So do I. But if I'm right?"

"We have to find him," Duarte said. "We need to have that answer, no matter what it is."

"Agreed. Because when we find Talon, we're one step closer to finding the murdering bastards he's working for."

"Assuming Kyle's still alive," Duarte suggested. "That text he sent to Lisa seems like the act of a desperate man. A terrified man. You first saw him in your vision two months ago. He may have outlived his usefulness."

"If he hasn't, and we find him first, he's gonna wish he was dead," Alec growled. "If he's turned traitor, we can't let him live. You know that, right?"

Hard as it was to consider it, much less deal the punishment should the time come, Duarte nodded his head in agreement. "Yeah, I know. There'd be no coming back from that kind of betrayal. No forgiveness."

Alec was quiet for a moment. He pitched the last of his coffee into the surf. "What about Lisa? You tell her anything about this?"

"No." Duarte felt a stab of guilt for that. "Not yet. She's been through a lot these past two days. Hard to find the right time to drop that kind of bomb on her."

Particularly when he'd been too busy losing himself in her body, in her sweet smiles and tender gazes. He'd been lost in the fantasy, letting himself imagine they could ever have something real and lasting when he'd never had roots anywhere for long. Even now, he knew there was no going back to his cabin again. He was without a home, so what did he have to offer her, even if she wanted to be with him?

And what could he ever hope to do to cushion the anguish he would inflict when he had to explain that he and Alec were now hunting a personal enemy of their own in her beloved brother?

"You gotta tell her, man." Alec's voice was sober. "She needs to know about Kyle."

"What do I need to know about Kyle?"

Lisa's voice came from behind them.

Duarte's heart sank, as cold and heavy as a stone in

his chest. He pivoted around and found her standing at the crest of the beach, just off the guest room veranda where they'd made love the night before. She wore an oversized terry bathrobe, her hair twisted up in a towel as though she'd just stepped out of the shower.

Her eyes were questioning on him now. Searching and uneasy. "What do you need to tell me, John?"

12

The fact that he didn't answer made her breath catch in her throat.

But it was the bleak look in John's eyes as he stood up to face her—the unmistakable guilt and dread she saw in him—that made Lisa's heart stutter, suddenly frozen in her breast.

"What's going on?" She glanced to Alec as he got to his feet now, too, but it was John she looked to for answers. She looked to him for honesty and trust, two things that seemed missing from the unreadable expression on his face. "Do you have information on Kyle? Do you know where he is?"

"No."

"Then what is it you need to tell me about him?" Her voice rose along with the acid of her mounting fear. "Is he hurt? Is he... oh God, is he dead?"

John shook his head. "We don't know any of that—"

"Then what?" She couldn't take his maddening, careful calmness. "Tell me what you do know about him, dammit!"

John swallowed and glanced at Alec, who looked equally reluctant to give her the truth. "We don't know where he is, or if he's alive, Lisa. But we do think there's a chance Kyle's working with the other side."

The other side? It took her a second to realize what she was hearing. "Are you saying my brother is a bad guy? Because that's not possible. It's absurd. For crissake both of you, he's been your best friend for more than a decade—"

"I had a vision," Alec said, his voice grave, more sober than she'd ever heard him before. "The first time I saw the premonition was a couple of months ago. I've seen it half a dozen times since, and it's always the same. I see Kyle giving up classified intel on Phoenix operatives. He's betraying the program. The only question is, for how long?"

She shook her head. "My brother's one of the most patriotic, devoted people I know. Just because you think you saw something in a vision, doesn't make him guilty."

Even so, she felt sick with the information. Miserable with the very idea, and the fact that John seemed to know about Alec's premonition, yet hadn't felt the need to talk to her about it.

And then, as she looked at the two men, at John in particular, a deeper concern took hold of her.

"There's more, isn't there?" She could see the weight of it in his somber brown eyes. She saw the other painful truth he'd been shielding her from in keeping Alec's vision a secret. "If Kyle's the one who betrayed Phoenix, then you intend to hunt him down. You intend to go after him like your enemy."

John cursed, low under his breath. "Lisa, if the vision is true, then we don't have a choice."

"Will you use me to do it?" She barked out a raw, humorless laugh. "Have you already been using me? Letting me think you care, letting me think you were going to help me find Kyle... God, letting me throw myself at you like an idiot while you and Alec make plans behind my back—"

"It wasn't like that at all," John said sternly. "Don't say it. Don't even fucking think it."

When he walked toward her, she backed up several paces. "When were you going to tell me about this? After you fucked me a few more times?"

He bit off a sharp denial, but she was already pivoting away from him. She couldn't talk to him anymore. She didn't want to hear anything more, could hardly breathe through the tumult of confusion and outrage and hurt that held her in its grasp.

Storming back into the guest room, she began picking up her clothing. John came in behind her, his presence sucking even more of the air from around her. Her skin tingled in reaction to him, all of her senses instinctively drawing toward him even while she struggled to ignore him.

"It isn't like that," he said gently at her back. "I didn't mean to keep it a secret from you. I just knew it would hurt you to hear it, and I didn't want to be the one to do it."

She spun a pained look at him. "Do you think it hurts me any less to find out this way? To be blindsided by the fact that you and Alec are conspiring against my brother?"

John huffed out a curse. "We weren't conspiring, damn it. We were hashing things out, trying to make sense of it all. You think Alec and I want to believe Kyle's guilty any more than you do?"

Tears pricked her eyes, but she held them back with fury alone. "Tell me what you'll do to him if you're able to find him."

"Make him tell us the truth. Give him the chance to convince us we're wrong."

"And then what?"

A tendon ticked in John's bearded jaw. "That will depend on Talon."

"Stop calling him that! His name is Kyle. He was your best friend, John. He thinks of you like a brother. I know because he's told me so. You and Alec both are like family to him."

John nodded soberly. "You're right. Kyle Becker was my closest friend, a brother I'd never had. But when the three of us joined the Phoenix program, we all took an oath—to put the program ahead of anything, and anyone, else. We left our pasts behind us. We devoted our lives to it, Lisa. Our futures, too. That's how important our work was. We all believed in that, but someone betrayed us. Someone betrayed that oath."

"Not my brother." Her voice sounded small, wooden. As if even she was beginning to doubt.

Kyle was her only family. He was all she had in the world. For that reason alone, she would cling to her faith in him.

"I hope you're right," John murmured. "Alec and I both hope you're right. But understand, we have to find out."

She stared into his handsome face, heartbroken by the solemnity of his expression. "Then I hope you understand that you'll be doing it without me."

Turning away, she walked into the bathroom to take the towel off her head. She finger-combed her damp hair and met John's reflection in the large mirror over the sink. "I want to leave. Right now."

"No, you don't. You want to run away. From me. From us." He shook his head slowly. "But I can't let you do that."

"Why not?" she shot back. "Isn't that what you did five years ago?"

A direct hit. She could see it in the way his mouth pressed into a flat line, his dark eyes piercing her in the glass. "Yeah, I did. And if you think I haven't spent a lot of those years regretting it, then you'd be wrong about that, too."

God, she didn't want to be swayed by his tender words right now. She didn't want to believe the raw honesty in his deep voice, or the way it made her melt inside.

She wrenched her gaze away from him and busied herself with the makeup and brushes left on the bathroom countertop where she dumped them out last night in search of the condom. Just the thought of making love with him made her legs go a little weak beneath her. Worse, it made her anger lose some of its edge.

She dropped a handful of cosmetics into the cloth bag, then gathered up the scattered brushes. "I can't do this, Johnny. Please... just go tell Alec and his thug friends I want to get off this island as soon as possible."

"It's not that simple, Lisa. I can't let you go. If anything were to happen to you—" He broke off abruptly, and in her peripheral vision she saw him cross his arms over his broad chest. "I need to keep you close to me, where I know you'll be safe."

"Safe? With you?" She crammed a couple of eyeliner pencils into the little bag and glanced up at him in the mirror. "I'm not feeling very safe with you right now,

John. I'm feeling used. I'm feeling sick with myself that I came running to you as soon as I got Kyle's text. Too bad I don't have the gift of precognition, too, or I might've saved us both a lot of trouble."

With the last of her things stuffed into the cosmetic case, she tugged on the zipper to close it. The lining had a small tear in it near the top, and the loose thread was caught in the zipper's teeth. Frustrated even more, she yanked on it again, but it didn't give.

Then she realized why.

The lining wasn't torn.

It had been cut. A small, carefully opened slice.

She might have never noticed it...

John moved into the bathroom to stand beside her. "What's wrong?"

She slipped her finger between the lining of the bag. Something small and flat and round was inside. She pulled it out on a gasp.

Her blood ran cold in her veins.

The tiny black disk was a thinner, more compact version of the GPS tracker her pursuers had placed on her car.

13

Duarte's heart still felt clutched in a vise a few minutes later, as he and Lisa met up with Alec in the empty kitchen of the main house.

"They know she's here." Duarte put the GPS tracker down on the white marble countertop, barely resisting the urge to smash it under his fist.

"Holy shit." Alec's brows went up in shock. "Where the hell did that come from?"

"My makeup bag. It was hidden inside the lining," Lisa murmured. She wrapped her arms around herself, looking small and vulnerable—frightened—in her T-shirt and faded jeans. "Now I guess I know what they were doing in my house a week ago. God, I *knew* someone had been inside my home. They traced my car, probably traced my phone, too. Now this..." She trailed off on a small shudder.

Duarte wanted to pull her into his embrace, but he didn't expect she'd welcome his comfort. They'd left a lot unresolved back in the guest room, and this new emergency meant they would have even less alone time to talk things out and try to patch things up.

If that was even a possibility now.

He met Alec's serious gaze. "It's not safe for Lisa to stay here. We have to get her off this island ASAP."

Alec nodded. "Agreed. You got an idea where you want to go, or should I arrange for another safe house somewhere?"

Duarte considered his few options. Time would be working against them. Hell, it already was. They'd been on the radar since the minute they had left his cabin. "Another safe house would be best. Your pal Zapata got a place to spare down in Colombia, by chance? The farther away, the more remote, the better."

"No." Lisa's quiet but firm interjection drew both their gazes. "No more running. No more safe houses. I'm not going to live like this. I can't."

"You don't have much of a choice right now," Duarte told her, as gently as he could. "You have to keep moving. You can't let these people get their hands on you. Damn it, *I* won't let that happen."

He sounded possessive and overbearing, but fuck it, he didn't care. So long as he was drawing breath, he meant to keep this woman safe. Whether she felt he had that right or not.

Lisa's jaw tensed as she stared searchingly into his eyes. "Kyle wanted me to hide. You're telling me I need to run. But if I do either of those things now, when will I be able to stop?"

"I'll make it safe so you can stop." A promise he would uphold with his life, if it came down to that. With her brother's life, too, even though he knew that price would come with Lisa's hatred. "I'll make it safe. You have to trust me, and give me that chance."

She slowly shook her head. "I can't do that, John." The fear he'd seen grip her just a few moments ago began to fade into a subtle, but stubborn determination. "I'll never have answers if I don't go after them. I need to know where my brother is, and if he's in trouble, I need to know why. Even more than you or Alec or anyone else in the Phoenix program, I need to find him. I can't do that if I'm on the run or in hiding somewhere."

She was right. He knew in his heart that she couldn't hide forever. She couldn't run far enough if the men trying to reach her had any part in Phoenix's demise.

Hell, he and Alec and the rest of the program's operatives had been running and hiding for too long already. It was time to put an end to that, too.

"Whoever put that tracker on Lisa knows she's here. They don't know we've found this." Duarte picked up the small disk. As much as he wanted to smash the damned thing to dust, he wondered if it might serve them better to keep the tracking device operational. "And since we took out the first guy who followed her to my place—"

"I believe you mean since *I* took out the first guy. With a flawless shot, I might add," Alec said, arching a brow. "Credit where credit's due, man."

"Whatever." Duarte didn't try to bite back his smirk. "Since their first guy's at the bottom of a cliff in North Carolina, they may not know he's dead yet. And they may know Lisa's on the move now, but that doesn't mean they know who she's with."

Alec nodded, conspiracy glinting in his eyes. "So if someone comes looking for her here—"

"We'll be waiting," Duarte said. "We'll be ready. I don't think they'll make us wait too long."

"What if they send more than one next time?" Lisa asked. Her anxious gaze bounced between the two of them. "What if they do know their first man is dead? I've been carrying around that tracker all this time. Someone else could have tailed us to Florida. What if they know exactly who I'm with and they decide to send a full team armed to the teeth next time?"

She was smart, thinking strategically, like a partner. *His* partner, even though he knew she still didn't fully trust him when it came to her brother.

Duarte wanted to tell her they'd sort it all out—the same promise he'd made to her the night she'd shown up at his cabin, rain-drenched and terrified, pleading for his help. He wanted to explain to her that five years ago, he'd been an idiot to let her leave his place thinking the night they shared hadn't meant anything to him... that she hadn't meant anything.

Right now, when she was standing beside him yet never further away, he wanted to tell her that they'd find a way to make it work between them this time.

But the truth was, he wasn't sure if that could happen. He wouldn't be sure until the questions surrounding Talon were answered and the threat pursuing Lisa was eliminated.

Duarte cleared his throat. "We'll be ready."

"The two of us and the four men guarding this house will be ready," Alec said.

"Are you sure about that?" Lisa frowned at him, lowering her voice. "Isn't it just as risky to put your life in the hands of a bunch of drug dealers?"

Duarte grunted. "He's sure. Long story."

He set the GPS tracker back down on the counter, his tactical mind already running through various attack and ambush scenarios. None of them were without potential problems. Then again, the same could be said for every other battle he and Alec had lived to talk about. "So we're agreed? We sit tight for a while and see what turns up on the other end of our hook?"

"Agreed," Alec said, grinning like the fearless bastard he always had been. He gestured for Duarte and Lisa to follow him. "Let me show you what we've got in our tackle box."

He led them out of the kitchen and down the main artery of the big house to the spacious great room. At the far end of the space stood a massive built-in bookcase filled with countless volumes from the classics to commercial potboilers. Alec strode up and ran his palm down one section of the hand-carved wood. There was a small electronic beep, then the bookcase popped open to reveal a hidden room.

As Alec stepped inside ahead of Duarte and Lisa, lights snapped on inside the cool, climate-controlled room. Guns of various types and calibers lined the walls of the space. Gleaming hunting knives and blades of every size bristled on shelves, ready for action. There were enough boxes of bullets to supply a small army.

"Holy shit." Duarte had seen some sizeable weapons caches in his day, but this was impressive. He walked farther inside, taking note of the pump-action rifles and Russian semiautomatics that made his hands itch to hold them. "Which ones can we use?"

Alec shrugged. "Any of them. All of them. Whatever we need."

John nodded and continued with his mental cataloguing of the tools at his disposal should he need them. He was aware of Lisa moving alongside him as he strolled past one collection then another. This wasn't her world—dealing in violence and death. He didn't want it ever to be her world. But to her credit, she didn't shrink away or flinch at the sight of so many lethal instruments.

She was virtually unshakable, except when it came to her beloved brother.

And for what wasn't the first time, Duarte found himself wishing things were different. Wishing *he* was different. Just a man, not a soldier. Not a precognitive freak whose life had been defined, then forfeited, by the power of his gift. Not the former Phoenix operative whose duty and commitment to the program now stood in the way of what he felt for Lisa Becker.

She drifted past him, taking a sweeping look at a case filled with sniper sights and night-vision equipment. "What's in this cabinet?" she asked Alec, already heading toward it.

"Ah, those are Mr. Zapata's favorite rifles."

A knot of panic lodged in Duarte's chest as he glanced up and watched Lisa reach for the door handles on the tall gun cabinet. The familiarity of it froze his blood.

All at once, his nightmare vision seized him in a cold fist. The opened gun cabinet. Three rifles inside. Then the explosion that obliterated everything in its path. He lunged for her. "Lisa, no. Don't—"

She pulled the doors wide, throwing a questioning glance over her shoulder at the same time. "What's wrong?"

Nothing.

He stood behind her, panting as if he'd run a marathon, his entire body coiled in horror. Terrified for what might have happened to her. To all of them.

But the gun cabinet wasn't the one from his premonition. Half a dozen rifles stood inside it, not a single one of them anything less than pristine. There was no derelict weapon. No earth-shattering roar of obliteration. No hellish fire and heat that he could never prevent.

Lisa's hands were tender on him when she turned to face him. She held his shoulders, touched his face, smoothed her fingers into the sweat-dampened hair at his temples.

"John, are you all right?" Genuine care and concern shone in her sweet hazel eyes. "What just happened?"

"Nothing. It's nothing." The words were a raw croak on his dry throat.

Alec eyed him gravely. "Not the vision again? While you're awake this time?"

"No," he said. "I thought... Forget it, it's cool now. Wasn't the same as in my vision."

"What vision?" Lisa searched his gaze. "What are you two talking about? Another vision about Kyle? About me?"

"Nothing like that." Duarte caught her anxious hands and brought them to his lips. He kissed her fingers gently, then stepped out of her embrace because holding her felt too damn good.

He wanted her arms around him, and he wasn't going to be satisfied with having just her sympathy if she kept on touching him so tenderly and looking at him so... affectionately. Lovingly.

"John, tell me what you've seen." Her voice and gaze were soft, but he could tell from the angle of her chin that she wasn't going to let him off until he leveled with her. Not after today. Not about anything anymore.

He cleared his throat. "I've had a recurring nightmare since Phoenix went down. Alec's been having the same one, too."

She glanced briefly at Alec before looking back to

Duarte for confirmation. "You mean a premonition? Something awful."

He gave a sober nod. "A massive explosion. Catastrophic. When it happens, it obliterates everything. In the vision, I know I have to stop it... I know what's coming every time the damn thing starts, but I'm too late. Every fucking time, I'm too late."

She absorbed the information in silence for a long moment. "And when I opened the gun cabinet? Is that part of the vision, too?"

"The cabinet, yes. The detonation happens right after I see it. In the vision, it's me who opens the cabinet, but when you reached for it..." He trailed off, unwilling to speak the words.

The dread he'd felt when she had started to pull open those doors still gripped him. Seeing her in harm's way—imagined or not—was a terror that still raked him with icy claws. And the danger for her *was* real in other ways, from the men who had her in their sights now, and from the other vision he and Alec shared. The one that predicted Lisa being held at gunpoint, the nose of a pistol resting at her temple.

Chilling, hideous thoughts, all of them. His gut clenched, and it took every bit of his self control to resist dragging her into his arms now, just to feel her against him, safe and sound.

He cleared his throat, needing to get a hold of himself and his thoughts. "Alec's recurring vision is different from mine. He doesn't see the gun cabinet or the three rifles inside. But the end result is the same."

"Total annihilation," Alec confirmed grimly. "My hair ignites. My skin melts away. The heat and fire leaves nothing behind. It's a destruction that can't be stopped."

She looked to Duarte in question and he nodded. "The same for me."

"My God..." Her voice was reduced to a whisper. "You've both been seeing this vision—living it—how many times for the past three years?"

"Hundreds, easily." Duarte had lost count a long time ago. "I didn't know Alec was having the same premonition until we met up again yesterday."

"It's possible other Phoenix members are having it, too," Alec suggested.

"And if they are?" Lisa asked. "Maybe there's something more to the vision. Maybe if you work with the others, there could be a way to prevent it from happening."

Smart girl. She was just coming up to speed that moment, and she was already on the same page as Alec and him. "It's something we need to find out, yes."

"First we'd have to locate them," Alec said. "And there's no telling which of them we can trust."

"Including my brother," she murmured.

Neither Duarte nor Alec could deny it. It killed him to see her soft gaze on him shutter now, but he refused to reassure her with what he felt in his heart would be tender lies.

She crossed her arms over her chest in the heavy, uncertain silence that followed Kyle's mention. Her lovely face was pinched with worry, with regret. And with fresh hurt as she looked at Duarte. "I need some time to think," she said quietly. "I need to process... everything."

When she turned to leave the weapons room, Duarte took a step after her. He reached for her hand, took it gently in his. "I'll come with you. We still need to talk."

"Please don't." Her head shook slowly and she withdrew from his loose hold. "Don't come with me, John. I don't want to talk anymore. Right now, all I need is for you to leave me alone."

14

Although she'd told him she refused to run or hide anymore, Lisa knew that's exactly what she was doing behind the closed door of her guest room the rest of that day and into the evening. She'd ventured out once, only to eat. To her relief, John had been off somewhere else on the property with Alec, the two of them no doubt planning and preparing their next move.

Seeing them working together, undertaking a new personal mission, kindled something warm inside her. Pride, she thought. And a sense of reassurance, that no matter how dark and dangerous they believed Phoenix's enemies to be, no matter how grim the fiery premonition John and Alec shared, these two men would not rest until their world was set to rights.

The problem was trying to imagine that her brother could ever willingly stand on the wrong side of his friends and his former operatives in the program.

To believe that would mean she had never really known Kyle.

The same way she'd never known about his gift of precognition.

And then there was the fact that he'd been acting so strangely the last time she'd seen him. Anxious. Paranoid.

Guilty.

The word whispered in the back of her mind as she idly rotated her bracelet from him around her wrist. She never would have let the idea of Kyle's possible duplicity form in the least, if not for her conversation with John today. Her argument with him. The one that had left a wedge between them that she wasn't sure how to mend.

He'd hidden the truth from her. He and Alec had suspected Kyle of a terrible betrayal—they had all but condemned him—and yet John had chosen to hide that information from her.

It was as bad as a lie. And it had left her angry and hurt, feeling like a fool.

She was still nursing that emotional sting when she heard the firm rap on her guest room door.

"Lisa." John's deep voice sounded weary from where he stood in the hallway outside. "You planning to avoid me forever? Open up. We need to talk."

She knew he was right, but it was difficult making her feet move when her heart was still a heavy weight in her breast. Slowly, she went to the door and pulled it open.

As always, the sight of John Duarte stole her breath.

Tonight, aside from looking broody and sexy as usual, he appeared tired, hesitant. His shaggy mane of dark hair was tousled, as though he'd been repeatedly raking his big hands through it. His beard-covered jaw was rigid, ready for a battle. But his eyes... God help her, his chocolate eyes were intense with a bleak, private torment.

All of it focused on her.

He glanced pointedly at the fact that she was blocking the doorway with her body, not moving aside to let him in. "There are things I need to say to you, Lisa. Things that can't wait anymore." His full lips quirked into an uncertain smile. "You gonna make me do that standing out here in the hallway?"

She exhaled sharply, refusing to be charmed. "I think we both know what's liable to happen if I let you in."

The way he looked at her said he knew damn well and didn't think it was a bad idea. His dark eyes seared her, penetrated her. And as his faint smile faded into a sensual line, her own mouth began to water a bit. She crossed her arms in front of her as if she could physically ward off the primal effect he had on her.

It wasn't working. Even her heart was beginning to warm to the sight of him.

"What do you want, John?"

"To check on you, make sure you're okay."

She frowned. "You're not my bodyguard or my keeper, so there's no need for you to feel responsible for me. I can take care of myself."

"I know you can. Not what I meant." He paused for a moment, an unreadable emotion flickering across his handsome, troubled face. "Are you okay? I don't like how we left things today."

Neither did she. But that didn't mean they could change any of it. "I'm confused right now... about everything."

He nodded once. "I've had better days, too. I know you said you didn't want to talk to me. Hell, I get it. But not talking to you is driving me fucking mad, Lisa. Knowing you're in here upset, disgusted with me. Hating me..."

"I don't hate you." She could never do that, especially not after these past two days. Not even five years ago when he'd broken her heart the first time.

No, it would never be hate where he was concerned. What hurt so badly right now was that she loved him. She always had.

"I owe you an apology for today," he murmured. "For not being totally honest with you about what Alec told me about Kyle. I should've told you right away. I should've trusted you to handle it. I owed you that much."

"Yes, you did."

"I said the reason I didn't tell you was because I didn't want to hurt you." He shook his head, his gaze solemn, contrite. "I said that, but it wasn't really true. Not the complete truth. The complete truth is that I didn't want to tell you what I knew about Kyle and see you looking at me the way you did this morning. The way you're looking at me right now."

She stared at him for a long while, her emotions tangling with her confused thoughts. "I can't do this with you again, John."

"Do what?"

"Let you into my heart when I know you won't stay. I did that five years ago. I started making that same stupid mistake three nights ago when I came looking for your help." She swallowed past the regret that was caught in her throat. "I may not have the gift of precognition, but I can see the heartache coming, and I can't do it again with you. Not now."

John said nothing, not for a prolonged moment. She thought he might turn around and leave as she'd pretended she wanted him to do. But he didn't go.

His eyes stayed tender on her, and his deep voice was as soft as velvet. "I told Kyle *no* twice, you know. When he called and asked me to stand in for your date that weekend. I didn't want to do it."

Lisa swallowed. She didn't know that. Hearing it now made her feel awkward... as embarrassed as she'd felt when she had first heard John was going to rescue her from attending her friend's wedding alone.

John didn't show her any mercy now, holding her in his penetrating gaze as he spoke. "I knew if I went on a date with you, even a pretend one, I was playing with fire. And then when I got to your place to pick you up... Christ, you looked so beautiful."

Beautiful? She felt heat creep into her face at his praise. Her throat wasn't working anymore. She went utterly still, watching his handsome face as he spoke.

"You were wearing a peach strapless dress and matching sandals. Your hair was done up all pretty. Swear to God, Lisa, you looked like an angel that night."

She couldn't bite back her nervous laugh. "That dress was awful. Maybe guys don't know this, but it's an unwritten law that bridesmaids' dresses have to be hideous."

"It wasn't the dress that stopped my breath," John said. "It was the girl wearing it. You stop my breath every time I look at you, Lisa Becker."

Without warning or asking permission, he stepped in close and kissed her. He kissed her like he couldn't go another second without it. As though he couldn't get enough.

His hands came up to cradle her head as his mouth claimed hers possessively, reverently. She felt him guiding her backward and she didn't resist. When they were both inside the room, John reached back and closed the door behind them.

His hands left searing trails everywhere he touched her, and his mouth was quickly burning up all her defenses. As wounded and scared and angry as she was with him today, she couldn't deny—at least to herself—that she felt better in his arms than away from him.

When John drew back, his eyes hadn't lost a bit of their solemnity. When he spoke, his voice was thick and raw. "I suck at relationships, Lisa. As a rule, I don't do them. Never seen them end up in a good place, so I never wanted to try. You changed all that." He stroked her cheek. Ran the pad of his thumb over her kiss-swollen lower lip. "The first day he introduced you around the base, Kyle made sure everyone knew his little sister was off limits. I tried to respect that. No man wants to violate that code. Truth is..." John exhaled an airless chuckle. "Truth is, I was already half in love with you when he insisted I take you to that wedding."

Was he serious? She couldn't find her breath to speak now. Joy and disbelief and confusion crashed together inside her. And as much as his admission astonished her, it also infuriated her.

"No," she said, her scowl deepening. "No, you can't do this, John. You can't say that to me. I wanted to hear those words five years ago, not now. Not when we don't know where my brother is. When we don't know who's been tracking me or what they want. You can't stand here and be the man I needed you to be back then, when right now we don't even know if either of us will survive past tomorrow or next week or next year."

Unless he knew that answer already...

Was he baring his soul to her now because he knew something more that she didn't?

She drew out of his arms. "Back on the mountain,

you and Alec said you both had a premonition that someone was holding a gun against my head. But the man who tracked me there didn't do that. There was no gun to my head. It didn't happen..."

And then she knew.

A coldness crept into her, an ache started blooming in her chest. "What you and Alec saw didn't happen then... It hasn't happened *yet*."

"No," he said, somber with the admission. "Not yet."

"Oh, my God." She closed her eyes as the understanding settled on her.

"The visions don't lie, Lisa. But they can be altered. That's the power of precognition. And I'm not saying any of this because of what I saw. I'm telling you how I feel because I should've done it that first night we spent together. Or three nights ago, when you showed up on my mountain again." He stepped closer, his hands moving gently on her face, over her hair. "I don't want to let another night pass without letting you know what you mean to me. What you always have meant to me, if I'd been willing to admit it, even to myself."

He framed her face with his large, careful hands, holding her with a fierce reverence. "I'm not going to let anything happen to you. Not ever." He growled a low curse. "I've had five years to think about what I let go of—what could've been, if I'd been honest with myself... and with you. I didn't want to betray my friend's trust in me, so instead I betrayed yours by letting you leave my place thinking you didn't matter to me. You deserve white picket fences and fairy tales, Lisa. I can't give you any of those things. At this point, I'm not even sure I would know how."

"I never asked you for any of that," she murmured.

"But you deserve someone who can give it to you." He caressed her cheek, his dark eyes searching, tender. "Five years ago, I was scared shitless to even try to be that man. And now... *damn it*. Now I want to try, but I'm afraid I'm losing you before I even get the chance."

She wanted to hold on to her anger from earlier today. She wanted to hold on to her anger from five years ago, too. More than anything, she wanted to deny that she could trust this man, *love him*, after just a few days and nights together and a handful of pretty words.

But this was John Duarte. And if he'd been half in love with her at one time, she'd been all in for just as long.

She had no fight left in her when he drew her into his arms. His mouth came down on hers in a tender, yet claiming kiss, leaving no room for anything but the two of them. She kissed him back, melting into his embrace, losing herself to the moment, and to him.

It took her a few seconds to feel the tension—the alarm—seep into the strong muscles that held her. John broke their kiss and pulled back, his eyes stark... distant.

He blinked, and when he glanced down at her a shiver of dread snaked through her.

"They're coming now." His voice was quiet, so grim it shook her to the bone. "I just saw them—a flash of precognition. The men who're after you... ah, fuck. They're close. They're heading here now."

15

Duarte took Lisa by the hand and ran with her out to the main house. Alec was in the kitchen finishing a sandwich and drinking a beer. A pistol lay on the table in front of him. A long-range rifle outfitted with a silencer rested against the wall in easy arm's reach.

"Look alive, Stingray. Things are about to get interesting."

"You had a vision?"

"Only a flash of one. Just now," Duarte told him. "I saw a pair of bogeys in wetsuits swimming over from Marathon. Three more paddling behind them in a dark Zodiac powerboat. I can't be sure, but everything about them says military, black ops. They're on the approach as we speak. I'm sure of it."

Alec's face immediately took on a familiar battle-primed intensity. He stood up, stuffed the pistol down the back of his jeans. "How far out?"

"Not far." Duarte shook his head. "Could be right on top of us any minute."

No sooner had he said it than the first gunshot rang out.

Fuck. Ready or not, showtime. Duarte reached for the nine-millimeter at his back while Alec grabbed the rifle. Both men locked and loaded, ready to unleash hell, just like old times.

Duarte glanced at Lisa. She'd gone pale and silent with the first sound of gunfire. As urgent as the situation suddenly was, he stole a moment to brush his fingers along her stricken face. "We've got this. That's a promise, yeah? No one touches you without going through both of us." At her nod, Duarte turned to Alec. "We need to secure her while we—"

"Tackle box. She'll be safest in there. And armed if needed."

Without missing a beat, Alec hit a switch on the wall, instantly killing the house lights. And just like that, the former sniper was gone, absorbed into the night as he slipped outside.

"Come on." Plunged into darkness, Duarte raced with her for the bookcase hideaway.

He glimpsed a flash of shadow at the window in the great room. Had less than a second of time to push Lisa down before the glass exploded with the gunman's shot from outside.

She screamed. Searing pain tore into his left shoulder.

The hit staggered him, but as he started going down, Duarte steadied his aim and squeezed off two rounds at the assailant outside. The guy dropped like a stone. Chest shot would have killed the son of a bitch, but the head shot made sure.

"John!" Lisa scrambled back to him in the darkness. She ran her hands over him in a panic, freezing when she reached the sticky wetness on his chest. "You're bleeding! Oh my God, you've been hit!"

The metallic stench of spent bullets and spilled blood hung in the air around them. Outside the house, the sounds of combat continued in a chaotic blur. More gunfire. Pounding boots. In the distance, a curse went up in English, followed by abrupt silence. Wasn't Alec. Which meant one more bad guy down. Someone shouted in urgent Spanish near the house. Rapid shots ripped in a sudden burst as a body came tumbling off the roof into the bushes.

"Get in the weapons vault. Go now!"

"What? No. I'm not going to leave you—"

"God damn it, go!" His pistol still gripped in his right hand, he tried to lift his left one to push her into motion. Pain lanced him from his injury, but he ignored it. "Don't worry about me. Go while you have the—"

Words dried up in his throat. Because at that same moment, the light from a red laser sight hovered on Lisa's forehead.

The bastard holding the weapon on her stood behind Duarte now. His feet moved silently except for the crunch of broken glass. She saw him now, too. Lisa's eyes went wide in the darkened room.

The bad guy held steady as he stepped farther inside. "Set the pistol down, motherfucker. Nice and slow. Push it out of reach."

That fiery red dot was the only reason Duarte laid his gun down. If Lisa hadn't been in the room—if she hadn't been a trigger squeeze away from death right now—he would have told the asshole to get fucked and forced him to eat a lot of lead.

But fear had a stranglehold on him so long as she was in danger. The risk was too great. He shoved his weapon away.

"Lisa Becker," the gunman said. "You need to come with me."

Duarte braved a look over his shoulder at the man in night raid tactical gear and infrared goggles. No doubt about it, the team was military. Or former, more than likely.

"Stand up now, ma'am. My orders are to bring you in alive. Don't make me hurt you."

Duarte growled at the thought. "Who the fuck are you? Who sent you?"

The guy ignored the questions. "On your feet and walk to me, unless you want me to pop your boyfriend here."

Like hell he would. Duarte's fingers itched to reach for his pistol, but Lisa was already starting to comply. "Okay, okay. Please... don't hurt him."

Beneath his night-vision glasses, the gunman sneered. "He killed our captain. I ought to blow his fucking head off, but that's not what I was hired to do. Now, move it, lady."

Lisa got to her feet. "What do you want with me? Where are you going to take me?"

As she spoke, she inched almost imperceptibly backward, toward the far wall, her hands trembling at her sides. Her steps were hesitant, carrying her farther out of his reach.

He had to make a move. He had to chance it, or watch her end up in enemy hands. Not gonna fucking happen.

Outside the house, a sudden hail of gunshots blasted in the night.

He saw Lisa's hand reach up along the wall in the instant her assailant's head flinched toward the sound. She hit the light switch.

Hell yeah, clever girl.

Duarte rolled for his pistol at the same moment.

The room lit up, blinding after so much darkness. Especially for the asshole in the infrareds.

Duarte had his gun in hand and fired two rounds into the bad guy's torso. He aimed to injure more than kill, because despite his fury, he knew he needed answers more than revenge. He'd have time for that later—on this man and whoever contracted him and his comrades to come after Lisa.

"John!" She ran to him as he came up on his feet and kicked the assailant's rifle away from him.

The gunman writhed on the floor in anguish. Outside, silence had fallen. Alec appeared in the great room a second later. He glanced at the mortally wounded attacker as if eyeing fresh roadkill, all of his concern on Duarte and Lisa. "We're clear outside. Lost Emilio, one of the guards. Another one got clipped in the leg. Everyone good in here?"

"John's been shot," Lisa said, her face stricken with worry.

He gave a dismissing shake of his head. "Shoulder wound. It's nothing."

Alec grunted. "Hell, I've self-dressed worse scrapes than that after a wild weekend. We'll get you sewn up."

Duarte wasn't concerned with his own injury right now. He let go of Lisa to stalk over to the gunman who was still thrashing and groaning on the floor.

He aimed his pistol at the guy's bloodless face. "If you want to keep breathing, I suggest you start talking." But shit... even as he said it, he could see it was already too late for the man. They would have a few minutes at most to question him before he bled out. "Who are you working for?"

Defiant eyes glared up at him. He spoke around a wheezing moan. "Wouldn't tell you... if I knew..."

Duarte chambered a round. "Who hired you? Who sent you after Lisa Becker? Trust me, asshole, I've got more time to do this than you do."

"Don't know who. Don't... care who it is." The guy coughed, a wet, raking sound. "Cap knew... he's the only one... They only talked to the captain."

Fuck. At Alec's questioning look, Duarte gestured to the body slumped over the window sill in the great room. "The one who clipped me in the wing."

The talking dead man gave a raspy chuckle. "Too bad you killed him..."

"Yeah, it is. Too bad for you." Duarte put the nose of his nine between the guy's eyes. "Where were you going to take Lisa? What were the orders once you had her?"

His eyelids drooped as he struggled to breathe in and out. They weren't going to have much time to do this. "Thirsty. Need... some water."

"Answers first." The drink wasn't going to do him any good anyway. "What were your orders? Where were you taking Lisa?"

He licked his dry lips. "Temporary drop-off point... Someone was gonna collect her and... pay us for the job..."

Lisa made a small noise in the back of her throat, no doubt as sickened as Duarte was to hear there was a price on her head.

Duarte looked over at Alec, before glowering back down at the dying soldier. "I figured you for former military. That's obvious. So, you're fucking mercenaries?"

"Hell no." He scowled, or maybe it was a wince. "Private security... hired about a week ago."

"To do what, exactly?"

"Tail her. Report her movements..."

"You assholes broke into her house, planted the GPS trackers on her."

No need for confirmation, but the man nodded. He closed his eyes, his breathing labored. "Three days ago... orders changed. Supposed to close the net, bring her in." He groaned, face pinched with pain. "Shoulda been a one man job... Tate, our guy on task... he went missing, lost contact..."

The guy Duarte and Alec encountered at the cabin, no doubt. "So then what? What were the orders?"

"Get the girl... take out anyone in the way." A violent shudder swept over the man. His color was bad, deathly white. "Jesus... so cold in here... water now... please?"

Duarte gave a tight nod and gestured for Alec to help him out. "Where was the drop-off point?"

"Don't know." He gave a weak shake of his head. "Jensen... he was supposed to report in. Text his contact..."

Duarte relaxed his hold on his pistol. No need for force anymore. His subject was getting more forthcoming now that death was pulling him under. "Jensen. He's your captain?"

"Yeah." The guy's eyes rolled back in his head, lethargy settling over him. "Is he... Do you think he's gonna be okay?"

"No, I don't think so," Duarte answered grimly. "Tell me about the drop-off arrangement. Captain Jensen texts his contact and lets them know you have Lisa Becker. Who's waiting for her at the drop? I need a name, a description, anything."

He got no answer, just fading light in the unfocused gaze blinking up at him. Damn it. Futile or not, Duarte kept his questions coming. "Does the word Phoenix mean anything to you? Your captain or anyone else ever mention it to you or the other men? What about Kyle Becker or Talon? These names, do any of them sound familiar?"

Alec returned with the water, but there was no point. The dying man's breathing had slowed drastically now. When he closed his eyes, Duarte knew they wouldn't open again.

As far as intel went, they still didn't have much. "Whoever's waiting for that all clear from the captain is going to know something's wrong pretty damn quick here."

Alec stared at him, and Duarte could practically see the wheels turning. "So let's give them the all clear."

"I know where you're heading with this and I don't like it."

Alec pressed his case. "Their captain was the only one in contact with whoever hired them. Except, oops, he's dead. Hazard of the job. So we tell them that. We call in the all clear like we're part of the surviving team, we get the drop location, and we bring this fucking fight to their doorstep."

Duarte wanted nothing more than to follow this lead to wherever it took them. But the plan wasn't without problems. "Calling in the all clear and getting the drop location is one thing. They won't let us near the doorstep when they see we've come empty-handed."

"No, they won't," Alec agreed. "They'll demand proof of life. We'll have to show it to them."

Alec's sober expression made a curse explode out of Duarte. "No. No fucking way. Leave her out of this."

"We wanted to see what was on the other end of this hook, Ranger. This is our chance."

"With Lisa as the bait? Fuck you very much, Stingray. I should kick your ass just for suggesting—"

"Alec is right, John."

When he glanced at Lisa, he didn't see fear or confusion in her eyes. He didn't see any of the things that were riding him at the mere idea of bringing her into the fray.

No, he saw a fortitude, and a bravery that staggered him.

"The only way we'll get close—the only hope we have of getting to the truth about any of this—is by giving these assholes what they want. If that's me, I need to know why as much as you do." She drew in a breath, then pushed it out on a resigned sigh. "If this will get me closer to the truth about Kyle, whatever that truth ends up being, I need to know that now, too."

He wanted to refuse her outright. Hell, every fiber of his being rejected the idea with violent repugnance. Not that she would have let him overrule her.

And damn it all to fuck anyway, he knew she was right. They might only have one shot at this, and they needed to take it while they had the chance.

Duarte went to her. The fact that she was unharmed after tonight's attack eclipsed even his cold need for justice. It was a fierce relief he wouldn't even attempt to hide. That she would willingly walk right back into battle terrified him, but it also made him love her all the more.

And yeah, it was love choking his heart right now.

Not halfway, like he'd been from the day he met her.

Nothing halfway about anything he felt for her. He was all in, and he couldn't let his miserable past or current enemies stand in the way of what he hoped to have with this woman.

My woman.

He lifted her beautiful face with the tips of his bloodstained fingers and kissed her. Heat zinged through him, everything he felt for her burning brighter than ever in the wake of this ordeal and the one that still lay ahead.

When their lips parted, Lisa's gorgeous hazel eyes glimmered with determination. "No more running. No more hiding. Not for either one of us, John. If you're in, then so am I. Together."

Fuck, yeah.

This was his woman.

This was their fight.

This was their future, waiting on the other side of whatever went down tonight at the drop location.

Pulling her close, he kissed her again. Then he turned to Alec. "Let's go do this."

16

An hour later, Lisa sat in the backseat of a moving Escalade beside John. Alec was at the wheel, speeding them toward the appointed drop location somewhere north of Miami.

After regrouping at the island house, the three of them motored back to Marathon Key in the raiding party's Zodiac. The big black SUV parked near the shore woke up and unlocked when John clicked the remote they had taken off the captain's body back at the house.

The plan was to arrive at the drop-off point looking every bit the part of two security team survivors returning with their prize. To that end, John and Alec now wore the bloodied tactical gear and black fatigues of the dead. They were both clean-shaven with fresh buzz cuts that completed their transformations to startling effect.

Looking at John Duarte now, Lisa couldn't help but recall the stony, hard-to-read Marine she'd first met on her visit to Camp Lejeune.

He'd owned a piece of her heart then, but now what she felt was far beyond that white-hot crush she'd had on him. Seated next to him now, with his strong hand idly caressing her arm and his serious brown eyes holding her with such intense affection, her heart ached with devotion.

Three nights ago, she couldn't have imagined her life would be entwined with his again. Now she couldn't imagine her life any other way.

All they had to do was survive tonight.

"We're about ten minutes out from the drop location," Alec advised from the driver's seat. "Time to suit her up, Ranger."

"Right." John's deep voice was quiet, sober. "Jesus, I hate like hell to do this."

Lisa put her hand over his. "We have to make it believable. That means me, too."

A tendon ticked in his smooth-shaven jaw before he bit off a low curse. He reached into a duffel bag they'd retrieved from the Zodiac. Inside was a dark hood, zip ties, and duct tape. He pulled them all out and set them on the seat.

Then he reached into another duffel that contained weapons they'd taken off the dead security team and a few more items he and Alec had collected from the cache back at the house.

John held a large semiautomatic pistol in his hand. "This one is unloaded," he said. "I took the magazine out, and you can see there's nothing in the chamber either." He pulled the slide back and put his finger inside to show her it was totally empty. "Shit. I didn't notice this until just now..."

"What's wrong?" Lisa asked.

"This gun. It's a SIG Sauer. Nine-millimeter."

Alec glanced in the rearview mirror. "The weapon in our premonitions was the same model."

"Yeah," John said. "Same one."

Hope bloomed suddenly and brightly in Lisa's

breast. "Maybe that's what you saw in the vision, then? Oh my God, John... Maybe that's what you and Alec both saw. You holding the gun on me, not someone else."

He stared at her for a moment, considering. "Yeah. That could be it."

"This is our exit," Alec said from up front. "We're five minutes to go-time, guys."

John nodded, his expression solemn. "All right. So, like I said. The gun is empty. It can't hurt you, but when we roll in there I need you to play along, pretend you're terrified."

A bubble of nervous laughter escaped her. "Who's pretending?"

He set the gun down and palmed the back of her head, dragging her toward him. His mouth met hers in a powerful, breath-robbing kiss. He rested his forehead against hers, just holding her close for a long moment. "I love you, Lisa. No matter what happens in there, know that. I love you. More than anything else in my fucked up life. You're it for me. You're everything."

Her heart wanted to explode from joy. And from frustration. "I love you, too. I always have." She brought her hands up to his handsome, earnest face. "But your timing really sucks, Duarte. Anyone ever tell you that?"

He chuckled and kissed her again, deeper this time. As if nothing else existed. As if nothing could touch them, not even the danger that waited less than five minutes up the road.

From the front seat, Alec cleared his throat. "Ranger, stop molesting the captive. There's our drop location up ahead. White building on the right."

It didn't look like much, particularly in the dark. No

signage out front. Extremely private. Lights were on inside the building, but blinds obscured every window. Three stories high, set back from the main road, it was the kind of place that didn't invite casual visitors.

Lisa weathered a chill as they approached the turn for the entrance. "What is it, a lab of some kind?"

John gave a grim nod. "The government kind. The worst kind." Frowning, he picked up the zip ties in one hand. With the other, he lightly stroked her cheek. "You sure you're okay about this?"

No, she wasn't. Not really. She was only realizing that just now. But the only way out of this nightmare was through it. "I'm sure. I'm ready."

She pivoted to give him access to her hands behind her back. He secured her wrists, then tore off a strip of tape and placed it over her mouth.

John's lips pressed warmly behind her ear. "Okay, baby. Last part. Here we go."

He blew out a low curse. Then he placed the black hood over her head.

~ ~ ~

An armed security guard came out of the shack at the entrance gate as Alec slowed to a stop at the barricade and slid his window down. And as Duarte expected, the man approaching the SUV with a holstered firearm at his side was indeed on the government payroll.

"Got a delivery for this address," Alec told the U.S. Army soldier.

The guy motioned for him to roll down the back window. Lisa was already struggling and whimpering, playing her role like a pro, as the dark glass glided down. Duarte held the pistol against her hooded head.

The guard gave him a curt nod, then glanced back to Alec. "Deliveries around back. West loading dock."

As soon as the windows were up and their wheels were rolling through the checkpoint, Duarte caressed her shoulder. "Good job, sweetheart. We're heading around to the back of the building now."

He talked her through each second of their approach, needing her to hear his voice, to believe they were going to make it through this ordeal. They had to. He'd let her go once before; he wasn't about to make that same mistake again.

And if fate had other plans, fate was welcome to get fucked.

"We're approaching the west loading dock," he murmured. "Someone's waiting for us at the door. He's motioning us into the bay now, Lisa."

The tall, athletic looking man in the white lab coat stood in the open door as Alec parked the Escalade and killed the engine. Duarte barely resisted the urge to check the weapons he wore on his person, some in plain view as would be expected, others concealed in his pockets and strapped to his limbs.

"Let's rock n' roll," Alec said, his face lowered to conceal the movement of his lips from the man observing them in the open doorway. He got out of the vehicle and walked back to open Lisa's door.

Duarte gave her thigh a tender squeeze. "Here we go, baby. You're gonna be just fine. I promise you."

Holding the pistol to her head as she climbed out with him behind her, Duarte weathered the stabbing pain of his shoulder injury. The bullet hole that had ripped through his flesh still hurt like a bitch, but what killed him even more was the feeling that his heart was carrying an open wound.

As much as he wanted to pretend the SIG he and Alec saw jammed up against Lisa's temple was the unloaded one he held in his hand now, Duarte knew it wasn't.

And he couldn't shake the sense that the reality their vision had predicted now waited for them inside.

He and Alec walked Lisa up to the door. The man waiting there stared at them in clear distaste as he gestured for them to step in. Once inside, he used the access card hanging around his neck to secure the door behind them.

Without permission or preamble, their unfriendly greeter pulled the hood off Lisa's head. She moaned behind the tape that silenced her, and her eyes were wide with terror—real or for effect, Duarte didn't need to know. He could hardly stand there, all of his protective instincts at war with the need to play things cool.

The guy looked her over from head to foot, his tongue darting out to wet his thin lips. He grunted in leering approval and Duarte had the fierce and sudden urge to kill the bastard on the spot.

"Come with me," the man instructed them. He started leading them up an empty corridor, his side glance taking in Duarte and Alec's bloodied clothing. He chuckled. "Thought you guys were supposed to be professionals. Looks like you had your asses handed to you tonight."

Duarte growled. "Thought you guys said it would be an easy smash and grab. We had to take out half a dozen armed men to get to her. Lost Captain Jensen and two other teammates back there."

"Tell it to the boss when you see him. I'm just the doorman."

"We'll be glad to," Alec snarled. "Someone needs to tell him how fucked up this op was. Hope the bitch is worth it."

The guard chuckled, a sadistic rumble of humor. "I hope she is, too. For her sake... and for his."

As he said it, he indicated the room they were approaching. A room with half-glass walls and a lone occupant inside. The man lay in restraints on a narrow bed, almost skeletal. Gaunt nearly beyond recognition.

Kyle Becker.

Lisa screamed, but the tape throttled her broken cry.

Now Kyle saw them, too. He lifted up off the mattress as best he could, wild-eyed, miserable. The instant his dark-ringed eyes lit on his sister, he bellowed with animal fury. "Nooo!"

He started thrashing on the bed, bringing a male attendant in from a connected room.

Duarte and Alec exchanged a knowing glance. Things were about to go to hell. Time to make their move.

The man in the lab coat swiveled his head to say something and Alec plugged him with a nearly silenced bullet to the forehead.

Meanwhile, Duarte was freeing Lisa from her tape and bindings. Frantic to get loose and reach her brother, she burst out of Duarte's hold as soon as Alec had yanked the dead man's access card off his neck and sliced it through the slot on Kyle's room door.

"Lisa, wait!"

She was too overcome to hear him, already lunging

into the room as soon as the door was open.

It happened in less than an instant, but Duarte saw everything in virtual slow motion. Lisa just out of his reach. Racing toward her brother. The big male attendant snatching her in midstride. Pulling her off her feet. One muscled arm wrapped tight around her waist as she screamed.

And now, jammed up against her temple, the nose of a deadly nine-millimeter pistol. "Nobody fucking move!"

Duarte didn't need to see the gun up close to know that it would be a SIG.

Lisa's eyes were wide, her face shocked and bloodless. Her body was utterly still except for her rapid breathing. She stood there at gunpoint, gripped in abject terror.

Just like in the premonition.

God damn it. No!

Duarte and Alec both had their weapons aimed and poised to fire, but neither of them pulled the trigger. The risk to Lisa was too great. *Unless...*

From the same door the first attendant emerged, another one now crashed into the room, shouting in confusion and alarm. "What the fuck is going on in—"

The interruption was brief, but that's all Duarte needed.

The gunman holding Lisa took his attention away from her to glance over at his colleague.

Two silenced shots popped at the same time—Alec's round, which blew away the newcomer, and Duarte's, a fatal headshot to Lisa's captor.

"I'll get the body from the hall," Alec said, springing into action to drag the other dead man into the room to delay its discovery.

Duarte meanwhile dropped the shades and jammed the lock on the adjacent room door to bar anyone else from pouring in to confront them. Across the room, Lisa was drifting over to Kyle's bedside on unsteady legs, her face still blanched and now speckled with her captor's blood.

There wouldn't be much time for the siblings' reunion, no matter how hard-won it had been for Lisa. They'd have maybe a handful of minutes, tops, before the rest of the building caught on to them and the situation really went to hell. They had to clear out ASAP. And as Duarte saw it, they only had a couple of options.

Free Talon and try to get him to safety along with Lisa...

Or break her heart when they eliminated another of Phoenix's enemies here and now.

17

Her own ordeal just a moment ago was all but forgotten as Lisa neared the bed and saw the full scope of her brother's condition.

Emaciated and pale, he was restrained to the bedframe by steel cuffs on his wrists and ankles. All he wore was a pair of torn and filthy gray sweatpants, marred with dried blood and heaven only knew what else. His skin was waxy, bruised in more places than not. Reddened welts peppered his torso and limbs. Injection marks. Easily several dozen of them.

She covered her mouth to keep her ragged sob from erupting. She hadn't cried when John and Alec's premonition had become reality, but she couldn't hold back her tears now. They streamed down her cheeks in hot, wet trails. "Oh, Kyle... Oh, my God, what have they done to you?"

"Lisa?" He stared up at her with wild, confused eyes. "Ah, Christ... It *is* you. Hoped I was wrong. Hoped it was another bad dream..."

"It's me, Kyle. We're here to help you."

"No, you can't. You can't be here. You have to get away! Get out now, before they find you!" He bucked and fought against his bindings, though he didn't seem to have much energy in reserve. A few more thrashes and he collapsed onto the mattress with a long, anguished moan. He closed his eyes, his head thrashing on the stained pillow. "I told you to hide... Wanted you to be safe. Why... why didn't you listen?"

"Because I knew you were in trouble." She reached out to touch his sweat-soaked, unwashed hair. It killed her to see her strong, handsome brother reduced to this broken, pathetic shell of a man.

She brushed her fingers over his pinched brow, wincing at the clammy feel of him, the sickening sight of the sores that rode his cracked, dry lips. Her tears kept coming, and she swiped at them with her free hand. "I knew something terrible must've happened to you, Kyle. I had to find you."

His lids opened as she spoke, and she saw his bleary gaze catch on something. He smiled wanly. "You still have it... the birthday present I gave you."

"Of course." She touched the silver gecko that had been on her wrist since the day Kyle came to see her. "I'll cherish it always."

His weak smile lingered for a long moment. "My Little Lisa Lizard," he murmured. He chuckled, but it was a sad, regret-filled sound. "My *Loyal* Lisa Lizard, that's what you are."

His head lolled to the side, eyes drooped shut. Lisa gave him a slight shake to rouse him. "Kyle, you can't sleep. Please, you have to stay awake. We need to talk to you. We're here to help you."

"We?" He lifted his eyelids and found John standing beside her now. Alec stood at the room's large window, peering into the corridor from behind the blinds with his pistol at the ready.

"We aren't going to have much time," Alec warned

them. "What are we doing here, Ranger? Let's get it done."

Kyle's gaze fixed on John. His eyes widened in surprise, confusion. Then recognition...

And guilt.

"You know, don't you?" he asked his best friend. "You know what I've done."

Lisa's heart cracked open at his airless whisper. At the damning words. She hadn't wanted to believe what John and Alec had suspected—what they'd known—but she couldn't deny her brother's betrayal now.

His gaunt face sagged. "I can't ask you for forgiveness."

"Don't think we could give it to you, Talon." John's voice was toneless. "Who've you been working for?"

"No one. Not for a long time." His chest sawed with the sigh that heaved out of him. "Been trying to get out... Trying to get away. They won't let me go, Ranger. Won't let me die either."

Lisa crossed her arms over herself, feeling cold and empty as she looked at her brother and heard the resignation in his thready voice.

"I broke loose a few days ago," he said, his dim gaze drifting over to her. "I tried to reach you... tried to warn you. But they caught me again, brought me back here."

She nodded. "I got your text, Kyle. It scared me to death—for you, I mean. I didn't know what else to do but try to find you."

At her side, John radiated a dangerous fury. "Bad enough what you've done to Phoenix and everyone who was a part of it, Talon. You've put Lisa at risk now, too. Why do they want her?"

Kyle groaned. "To make me talk. Been giving them

bad intel for a while now. They caught on. They've beaten me, drugged me... only one thing left. They need something I care about."

"Who's behind this?" John demanded. "Who'd you sell Phoenix out to?"

"I don't know. They've kept me isolated. I talk to lieutenants, no one else." He blinked slowly, glimmers of his former intellect still there beneath the drugged haze. "Figure that means someone high on the food chain's pulling all the strings."

"Tell me something we couldn't already guess on our own," John ground out harshly. "You never heard a name? All this time you've been giving them intel on the program and its operatives, you never used the power of your gift to look behind the curtain?"

"Tried," Kyle murmured. "Couldn't do it. Couldn't get through."

"What do you mean, couldn't get through?"

"Hit a wall. Every time I tried to see who it was..." His shoulders went up in a feeble shrug. "A wall went up, like I was being blocked."

"Why would you do this?" Lisa asked, heartsick and disgusted despite his apparent remorse. "How could you betray your friends? People trusted you, Kyle. I trusted you, too. You've betrayed us all."

He looked at her, regret heavy in his expression. "They promised me things. They gave me things... money, girls, expensive toys. Everything I asked for."

John growled now. "You traded people's lives for all that shit, Talon. What did it get you in the end? Look at you. You traded your fucking soul."

Pain swam in his dull gaze. "I know that now. I know... a lot of things now."

"Do you know about the dream?"

Kyle looked up at John, stricken. "The explosion."

"Fuck." John and Alec exchanged a troubled look. "What about the guns? The kids?"

Kyle frowned, shook his head. "I don't know what you mean. There's only the fire. Only heat and flames. Then... nothing. The fire... it destroys everything."

John scowled, studying him. "You don't see the gun cabinet with three rifles in it? Or ten kids playing basketball?"

"No. None of that."

"What's it mean?" Lisa asked, seeing John's confusion and distress. "If Kyle's vision is different, do you think he can help you and Alec make sense of what you're seeing?"

"I don't know, but I think we need to find out."

Alec's sharp curse at the window drew their attention. "We don't have time to sit and chat about all of this right now. We've gotta get the fuck out of here."

"Yeah, we do. But we can't leave Talon behind."

"Like hell we can't," Alec replied. "He betrayed us once, Ranger. What says he won't do it again?"

"We're going to have to take that chance. We're not leaving him behind."

Lisa's heart ached with tenderness for what she saw in John's eyes as he spoke. He loved her, but he loved her brother, too. He wouldn't give up on Kyle, no matter how heinous the betrayal. She reached up to touch his smooth-shaven cheek, needing to feel his warmth. She needed him to know how much this gift meant to her. "You're a good man, John Duarte."

He pressed a quick kiss to her palm. "You can tell me all about that once I find the keys to those cuffs and we're out of here."

He stalked over to the dead attendant and started searching the body.

"Come on, man," Alec warned from his post at the window. "The clock is running out. We got guards at the far end of the corridor now. I hear a lot of boots heading this way."

"I used you, too, Lisa." Kyle's voice was so quiet, she almost didn't hear him. She looked down at her brother and smoothed his limp hair from his face. "When I came to see you on your birthday... I left something important with you. Thought I'd come back for it one day... my backup plan, in case I needed a way out of all... this. Too late for me now. Maybe you can use it now instead. You and Ranger and Stingray."

Lisa frowned. "What are you talking about?"

"The bracelet. Find Fox. Give it to him. He'll know what to do."

"I don't understand." She glanced at her gift from him and shook her head. "Who's Fox? What's my bracelet got to do with any of this?"

John came back with the keys and started unlocking Kyle's restraints. He saw her confused face. "What's wrong?"

There was no time to answer. He likely wouldn't have heard her anyway.

In that same instant, security alarms started blasting from all directions in the building.

~ ~ ~

"Haul ass, everybody! Shit just got real." Alec's shout was barely audible over the ear-splitting whine of the building's alarm system.

Keys in hand, Duarte went to work freeing Kyle from his restraints. As he leaned over his old friend to uncuff his wrist, Kyle's urgent voice grated near his ear. "Forget about me, Ranger! I'm beyond anyone's help. Just get Lisa to safety. She's all that matters."

"We agree on that," Duarte told him. "But she'll never forgive me if I don't try to save your sorry ass, too. Now, get up. Let's get the fuck out of here!"

The unlocked restraints fell loose, but getting Lisa's brother to his feet posed even more of an obstacle. He was shaky on his legs, whether from the prolonged torture he'd obviously endured or the narcotics his handlers had addicted him to, Duarte wasn't sure.

On a curse, he wedged his wounded shoulder under Kyle's arm and hefted him into a run across the room. Lisa was right on the other side, doing her best to hold her brother up as they made their way to the door.

Alec yanked it open, but held them back as he peered out to the corridor. Security lights flashed like strobes all along the L-shaped corridor. Over the blare of the alarms, men's voices sounded from nearby, shouting orders to one another, getting closer by the second.

"We're gonna need cover," Duarte said. "Lay down some smoke and bullets. Lisa and I will get Talon out to the vehicle."

Alec nodded. "Right behind you, brother."

With his pistol held in one hand, he dug into his vest pocket and pulled out one of the backup items they'd brought from Zapata's tackle box. He pulled the pin on the small smoke grenade and let it loose, tossing it toward the far end of the corridor. Another one followed, both erupting in a billowing shield of thick white plumes.

Kyle was finally moving on his own, but his steps were sluggish as Duarte ran for the receiving bay exit with Lisa and him. Behind them in the corridor, Alec fired off a spurt of gunfire into the smoke to hold back the approaching crowd of security personnel. It wouldn't hold them for long. They'd bought themselves precious seconds at most.

Duarte grabbed Lisa's hand as Kyle dropped behind. Even though he'd do his damnedest to save her brother, Duarte wasn't about to let go of his woman. "Come on, baby. We're almost there."

Duarte swung a glance behind them as they neared the exit. Alec had just emerged from the smoke, his long legs carrying him swiftly toward the group. But Kyle wasn't moving anymore. He'd stopped completely, watching Duarte sweep Lisa farther away from him, toward their escape.

Alec barked an order at him. "Move it, Talon! Those assholes are gonna be on us in two seconds."

Kyle slowly shook his head. "I'm not going with you."

Duarte had his hand on the opened exit door when he realized what was going on. Lisa realized it now, too.

Halfway to freedom outside, she pivoted to look back at her brother. Her voice cracked with panic. "Kyle, what are you doing? We have to get out of here!"

His regret-filled gaze found her through the drifting smoke and rising commotion in the corridor. "I'm sorry. I can't go with you." He looked to Duarte. "You always told me you'd look after her if I wasn't there to do it."

"And I will. No matter what." It had been a battlefield promise to his brother-in-arms. Now it was an unbreakable vow to the woman Duarte intended to spend the rest of his life with, if she'd have him. "You don't have to worry about her. She's my life now. But you don't have to do this. Come with us."

Lisa let out a soft, despairing cry. "Kyle, please. Don't do this. Come with us."

His eyes were tender on his sister. "You be strong, baby sister. Be happy." He wrenched his gaze away from her to look at Alec. "Give me your weapon, Stingray. I can hold them off long enough for you all to get away."

"Jesus Christ," Alec hissed. "It's suicide and you know it."

Kyle didn't flinch. "I can't change anything I've done. I can't expect forgiveness. Let me do this. There isn't much time."

Alec cursed again and swung a questioning look on Duarte. Neither man was eager to give their friend permission to die.

But Kyle didn't wait for it. He wrenched the pistol out of Alec's hand. "Go. Get her out of here now!"

And as Alec ran to catch up with Duarte and Lisa, Kyle Becker walked to the exit behind them and jammed it closed. Then he turned and strode away, vanishing into the roiling clouds of obscuring white smoke.

~ ~ ~

Sounds of gunfire exploded the instant he walked away.

"Kyle, no! Come back!" Lisa knew there was no stopping her brother from doing what he felt he had to, but the anguish of watching him disappear from sight— from her life this final time—broke her heart wide open.

There had been no time to convince him to stay.

No time to mourn his loss now that he was gone.

She would never understand how he'd been seduced into betraying the program he'd sworn to serve and the people who served along with him. But that had been a choice he'd admittedly made freely.

As was the price he chose to pay today.

"Come on, sweetheart. We have to go." John's voice was soothing in the midst of her grief. Calming in the midst of the chaos that still surrounded them.

And as they ran through the darkness and climbed back into the waiting vehicle, his arm around her was warm and strong.

John's love was a comforting shelter as Alec sped them all away from the building...

Away from the carnage inside.

18

As the sun began to rise a few hours later, Duarte walked out onto the oceanfront patio of Diego Zapata's heavily secured Miami mansion. Lisa was there, looking out at the horizon.

She'd been at his side most of the night since their arrival at the estate and through his gunshot wound treatment by Zapata's personal physician, who'd been summoned for a discreet house call long after midnight.

Lisa had stayed with Duarte the whole time, but she'd been quiet, reflective. Mourning her brother in private. Almost in shame. He'd wanted to give her all the time and space she wanted to process Kyle's death, but the need to be near her was more than he could bear. Especially after all they'd endured—and narrowly survived—tonight.

He walked up without speaking, his footsteps the only sound as he crossed the stone tiles to where she stood. She knew he was there, neither of them needing words right now. Duarte placed a kiss in the curve of her neck and shoulder.

He held her in front of him for a long while, both of them watching the sun come up. Listening to the waves breaking against the shore. Finally, Lisa let out a soft sigh.

"Do you think you'll ever be able to forgive him?"

He couldn't give her anything less than honesty. She'd always have that with him now. "I don't know if I can. His betrayal cut deep. Cost lives. The damage he's done to Phoenix by helping our enemies could be irreversible."

"I know," she murmured quietly. "I'm sorry, John. For what he did. For the fact that I didn't want to believe you and Alec that Kyle might be capable. I'm... sorry."

He kissed her soft skin again, breathing in her sweetness. "What your brother did tonight to help us get away, *that* was the old Kyle. The one I knew. That was the friend I could always count on. The one I miss already."

She turned in his loose embrace. A fat tear slid down her cheek. He swept it away on the rough pad of his thumb, then leaned down to press his lips to her forehead. "I'm sorry for what you're going through. I never wanted you to get hurt. Christ, I hate like hell that you're hurting like this now."

"I hurt because I loved him." Her breath caught as she spoke. "I hurt because I always will love him, despite what he's done."

"I know, babe." Duarte stroked her lovely face, his heart squeezing tight at her capacity to feel, to forgive. To love so unconditionally. He could only hope she might feel that way for him one day. He'd devote his life to proving himself worthy of her love.

"Do you hate him, John?"

He frowned, shook his head. "I can't hate him. Because for all his betrayals, he also brought you back to me." He brushed his lips over hers in a reverent kiss. "Stay with me this time, Lisa. It won't be white picket fences and fairy tales, but I love you. Wherever I am, I want you in my life. Forever, if you can stand it."

She smiled. "There's nowhere else I want to be. There never was." She kissed him now, long and slow and deep. "I love you, John Duarte."

He growled, pleasure and relief pouring over him. "Christ, I like the sound of that. I want to hear you say that every day for as long as I live."

She laughed softly, but her eyes were full of emotion. "I love you."

They were still kissing when Alec cleared his throat behind them. "Are you two going to be making out every time you're within a yard of each other?"

Duarte grunted, smiling against Lisa's mouth. "Get used to it or get lost."

Lisa put her fingers to her wet lips and glanced in Alec's direction. "Everything all right, Alec? How are you doing?"

"I'm cool," he said, ever the nonchalant one. "I just spoke with Mr. Zapata. We can stay here at the mansion as long as we need to. Obviously the safe house isn't the best choice, and anyway, it's in bad need of housekeeping."

Alec strode over and glanced out at the early morning for a moment. "You know, that was straight up heroic, what Kyle did last night. I doubt we'd have made it out of there cleanly, if at all. He probably saved our lives."

Lisa smiled sadly. "I only wish he'd had the chance to tell us more. I know he regretted what he'd done. He said he tried to get away. He didn't want to help them anymore."

"Too late for that," Duarte said. "Whoever's behind

this isn't playing games. They've got a plan and they'll stop at nothing to achieve it."

"I think Kyle knew that, too." She frowned, going pensive now. "He said something strange to me... that he left something important with me."

"What do you mean?"

"Some kind of backup plan, he said. He left it with me the last time he came to see me."

"On your birthday," Duarte recalled.

"Yes. When he gave me this bracelet." She held up her wrist and the quirky gecko bracelet she'd been wearing since the night she arrived at his cabin. "Kyle said it was his way out if he needed it. He said we should give my bracelet to someone named Fox and he'd know what to do with it."

The name gave Duarte more than a moment's pause. Alec, too. "You sure he said Fox, babe?"

She nodded. "Does it mean something to you?"

Alec ran a hand over his close-cropped, dark blond hair. "It's a Phoenix operative codename. I've never met him, but I've heard he's some kind of computer genius."

"Got any idea where to look for someone like that?" Duarte asked.

Alec raised a brow. "I can think of a few places to start."

Duarte still wasn't sure they could trust Talon, but at the moment, they didn't have many better alternatives. "Assuming we can locate Fox, that still doesn't tell us what he would want with the bracelet. Did he say anything else about it, Lisa?"

"No. Maybe he would have, but then the alarms started going off and then... then he was gone."

"Can I see it?" Alec asked.

"Sure."

She took it off and handed it to him. He inspected it for a long moment, turning it this way and that, his shrewd gaze scouring the silver chain and lizard emblem. "That's odd," he murmured. Then he chuckled low under his breath. "God damn Talon. That crafty son of a bitch."

"What is it?" Duarte and Lisa asked in unison.

"I think I've found what will be of interest to Fox." Alec looked up at them. "What we still need to know is, why?"

The trio exchanged glances. Then Lisa raised a slender, but determined brow. "So, what are we waiting for? Let's go find out."

~ * ~

ABOUT THE AUTHOR

LARA ADRIAN is a *New York Times* and #1 international best-selling author, with nearly 4 million books in print and digital worldwide and translations licensed to more than 20 countries. Her books regularly appear in the top spots of all the major bestseller lists including the *New York Times*, USA Today, Publishers Weekly, Amazon.com, Barnes & Noble, etc. Reviewers have called Lara's books "addictively readable" (Chicago Tribune), "extraordinary" (Fresh Fiction), and "one of the consistently best paranormal series out there" (Romance Novel News).

Writing as **TINA ST. JOHN**, her historical romances have won numerous awards including the National Readers Choice; Romantic Times Magazine Reviewer's Choice; Booksellers Best; and many others. She was twice named a Finalist in Romance Writers of America's RITA Awards, for Best Historical Romance (White Lion's Lady) and Best Paranormal Romance (Heart of the Hunter). More recently, the German translation of Heart of the Hunter debuted on Der Spiegel bestseller list.

With an ancestry stretching back to the Mayflower and the court of King Henry VIII, the author lives with her husband in New England.

Visit the author's website and sign up for new release announcements at **www.LaraAdrian.com**.

Find Lara on Facebook at
www.facebook.com/LaraAdrianBooks

SEEK

Tina Folsom

1

"Gotcha!"

Nick Young pumped his fist in the air and let out a triumphant growl while continuing to stare into the computer screen. A red dot was blinking on a map of Washington, D.C. Next to it, an IP address flashed.

"You bastard! Did you really think you could outwit me? Looks like I'm smarter than you after all."

Because the guy had made a tiny mistake, whether out of stupidity or laziness, Nick didn't know, nor did he care. What counted was that now Nick knew where to find him.

He felt a genuine smile curve his lips, the first in a long time. For over a month now, he'd been playing cat-and-mouse with an online adversary who was trying to keep him out of the servers that held crucial data Nick had been looking for ever since the secret CIA program he'd been part of had been compromised three years earlier.

Nick memorized the address the dot was pointing to and logged off. He flipped the lid of his laptop shut and stashed it in his backpack. Then he pulled an old keyboard out of the drawer, hooked it up to the dinosaur PC that he kept as a decoy and connected a mouse to it.

Should anybody find him and try to trace what he'd

been doing, the files he'd planted on the hard drive of the old desktop he'd bought second-hand would lead any pursuer on a wild goose chase. With a little luck, nobody would be looking for a second computer, and he'd be long gone before they were on his tail and could kill him like they'd killed Henry Sheppard, his mentor and the leader of the Phoenix program.

The same fate was waiting for him and his fellow operatives—CIA agents selected not for their physical abilities but their unique mental skills. Each of the Phoenix, including Henry Sheppard, possessed the gift of premonition. Three years ago, somebody had decided that the Phoenix presented a danger and killed the leader of the program.

When Nick had received Sheppard's mental call, his world had collapsed.

"Phoenix down."

He could still hear the alert echo in his mind. He'd left everything behind and gone into hiding. But the need to know what had happened to Sheppard and the other agents had driven him back to Washington D.C. Back into the lion's den.

"Keep your friends close and your enemies closer," Nick murmured to himself now. It had become his mantra since Sheppard's death.

It had been easy to create a new identity. His skills as a hacker had proven to be invaluable. His new identity was ordinary. No family, no special skills, a low profile all around. He kept himself afloat by creating websites for small businesses around the world.

He lived in an apartment in a run-down house the absentee landlord was renting to him for cash so he wouldn't have to tax the proceeds. Every month, Nick deposited the money in a mailbox. Fine with him. He wasn't exactly keen on the government right now.

He'd served his country as a CIA agent for many years, and they'd failed to protect him and his colleagues. He was on his own now, responsible for his own life, and out for revenge. One day, he'd make sure the men who'd killed Sheppard would pay for what they'd done.

And the person at the other end of the IP address he'd traced would help him find the responsible party. Whether he wanted to or not.

Nick knew of many ways to persuade another person to do whatever he wanted him to do. His favorite toy to elicit such cooperation was his Glock. The cold metal never failed to convince the other party that loyalty was overrated and life was a fleeting thing.

At first sight, people always assumed that Nick was merely a computer geek and not to be feared. Maybe his boy-next-door looks and his quiet demeanor were responsible for that misperception. But those people who cared to give him a more thorough look would discover what he really was: a man who knew how to handle himself and the weapons at his disposal. Sheppard had made sure of that. All the men he'd selected for his Phoenix program had to undergo rigorous training at The Farm, just like all other CIA agents, though it wasn't necessary for their ultimate work. But maybe Sheppard had known all along that one day his protégés would have to rely on those very skills to survive.

Nick inspected his gun, pulled the magazine from it, and made sure it was fully loaded, before inserting it back into its chamber. Then he stashed it in the secret, padded compartment in his backpack. Lifting his foot onto the chair, he pulled up one pant leg and slid a knife into the hidden pocket in his boot. Sometimes a little knife was all he needed to come to an agreement with an adversary. It was less conspicuous than a gun, and much less noisy should he need to use it.

There wasn't much else to do. Nick let his gaze wander around the room. The shredder bin was empty. The little mail he received was solicitations addressed to *current resident.* Any mail related to his website business went to a P.O. box, anything related to any bank accounts he received in electronic form. Only the utility bills came to the house, and those he paid promptly and then shredded. For all intents and purposes, Nick Young didn't exist. But Fox was still alive. It had been his codename while in the Phoenix program. And the few other Phoenix members he'd met—since Sheppard had always insisted on keeping them apart as much as possible—only knew him by that name.

He'd been proud when his mentor had given him the name. It showed that Sheppard understood him. Because Nick *was* like a fox, cunning and clever. And he would need these skills now to ferret out the computer genius who'd been fighting him online. Now Fox would bring the fight to his doorstep and up the stakes.

Showtime.

2

A parking garage? Really? How *Deep Throat* could this guy get?

Michelle Andrews shivered despite the fact that it was sweltering hot in D.C. Her tank top and short skirt had been just fine at the coffee shop where she'd spent the morning, but the massive concrete walls, floors, and ceilings of the dark underground garage kept the air surprisingly cold.

She hadn't expected this meeting. When she'd received the text message on her burner phone, she'd panicked. It was the reason she'd spilled coffee on the table and rushed to the barista to ask for a rag to clean it up. Unfortunately, those few seconds of inattentiveness had caused her to disconnect much later than planned from the online trace she'd been running.

She replayed the incident in her mind once more. Was there any chance that the hacker she'd been trying to get a lock on had instead gotten the drop on her? Michelle shook her head. No. Nobody was better than her. Since she hadn't been able to catch him, he wouldn't have had enough time to catch her either. She'd taken ample precautions to remain hidden. Still, with all that had happened in her life lately, she was on edge and had started doubting herself and her abilities.

Nervously, she twisted her pendant between her fingers, an old habit that died hard. The little memento from her time as a member of Anonymous, the worldwide hacker cooperative, always lent her strength—and reminded her of what had gotten her into this mess in the first place.

Nevertheless, she would get through this, no matter what the shady *Deep Throat* character who'd requested this meeting threw at her now. Whether he was FBI, CIA, or NSA, she didn't know. Nor did it really matter. Any of those government agencies had sufficient powers to lock her up for the rest of her life if she didn't do their bidding. They held all the cards. She held none. She'd become a pawn in whatever game they were playing and would have to play along until she found a way out.

When she heard footsteps echo against the bare concrete walls, she made a motion to turn.

"You know the drill," her handler said.

Michelle froze, facing away from him. "Mr. Smith." It wasn't his real name. When he'd first contacted her and she'd asked him who he was, he'd paused for a long while before saying, "How about Smith? Does that sound good to you?"

She'd never seen his face, though from his accent and speech pattern she assumed he was well-educated and middle-aged. There was a nasal quality to his voice that made her picture him as a short, balding guy with a beer belly and pale skin. Of course, she could be completely wrong, but didn't everybody like to picture their enemies as ugly and unattractive?

"I'm very disappointed in you, Miss Andrews."

Instinctively, she pulled up her shoulders, tensing.

"You've had a month now, and what have you got

to show for yourself? Nothing. My employers are not very happy with you." He sighed. "And neither am I."

She contemplated his words and chose her own with care. "I've done what you've asked me to." *Asked* was not exactly the right word. *Coerced* was more like it.

"Really, Miss Andrews? I have the feeling you haven't given it your all yet. Or do I need to remind you of what will happen if you don't comply?"

She needed no reminder. "Mr. Smith, I've used my skills—"

"When we caught you," he interrupted, his voice sharp and cold, "your skills seemed to be much more refined. I find it odd that you can't get a trace on a hacker when you yourself were immersed in that community for so long."

"It would help if I knew what this guy is after, so I don't have to keep wasting my time on hackers that you're not interested in."

A low growl came from behind her, and she realized that he'd come closer without her noticing. A cold chill raced down her spine and made her blood freeze in her veins.

"You know too much already, Miss Andrews." He inhaled. "It's dangerous to know too much. Haven't you learned anything?"

She shivered, her palms beading with sweat.

"You were a very bad girl. Do you remember?"

Michelle didn't answer, knowing he didn't expect her to.

"Hacking into servers you had no business being in. And your friends at Anonymous, they couldn't help you either, could they? Because now that we have you, nobody can help you. You work for us now, or you'll go to prison. It would be a shame. A pretty girl like you. You know what they do with somebody like you in prison?"

She didn't want to know. "I'm doing what you've asked me to do."

"Do it faster. I'm getting impatient. How hard can it be to find a hacker who's been trying to get into our servers, hmm? Aren't you the best? Or was that a lie?"

"I am the best," Michelle insisted, not because she was arrogant, but because admitting that she wasn't would surely get her killed.

"Good, then prove it. Give me something I can work with. You want to keep your freedom, don't you?"

She nodded automatically.

"The hacker in exchange for your freedom. You know I'm not bluffing. Tell me you understand."

"I understand."

"Good, then here's what you do: find him, but don't spook him. If he finds out that you're onto him, he's gone. Do you get that? You have ten days. If you can't deliver him by then, our deal is off, and you'll be prosecuted. Not as an American, but as a terrorist. You should have thought twice about what you were getting yourself into when you hacked into the Department of Defense's servers. You committed an act of terrorism." He clicked his tongue. "Very despicable indeed."

"I never—"

His hand on her shoulder made her swallow her words. The urge to turn around to look into the face of her tormentor was strong, but she suppressed it, knowing it would earn her a bullet in the head.

"No more excuses."

Her heart raced, and her pulse thundered in her ears.

Rage made her clench her teeth. She wasn't a terrorist, far from it. She and her fellow hackers at Anonymous had been trying to uncover documents about the United States' involvement in the latest Middle East conflict and the real reasons behind their support for a regime that tortured its own citizens. She'd wanted the American public to know the truth. That wasn't terrorism. It was freedom of speech. She hadn't hurt anybody by hacking into government servers.

Nevertheless, she was paying for it now. They'd tried to get her to give up the other members of Anonymous who'd taken part in this project, but she'd refused. She was no snitch. Besides, Michelle hardly knew who the others were, only knew them by their screen names.

The sudden silence made her pause in her thoughts. She listened intently, but there was nothing. Not even the sound of breathing.

"Mr. Smith?"

There was no reply. Michelle spun around. She was alone in the dark underground parking garage. Alone, except for a few parked cars.

Clutching her messenger bag that held her laptop, she walked toward the elevator. Ten days was all she had left. Judging by the little she'd accomplished in the previous four weeks, she had a snowball's chance in hell of delivering the elusive hacker Smith was looking for. Without any clue as to what the person was actually after, she couldn't narrow down her search. Did Smith have any idea how many hackers attacked governmental servers every single day? Despite that obstacle she'd come across one particular individual who'd piqued her interest, but she hadn't been able to get a lock on him yet.

Essentially, she was looking for a needle in a haystack. A needle she couldn't afford to search for any longer, because if she didn't get away before the ten days were up, she'd be as good as dead.

It was time to plan her escape while continuing to pretend that she was following Smith's request, so he wouldn't catch on to her deception until it was too late.

3

This wasn't going to be quite as easy as he'd thought at first.

For starters, the IP address Nick had traced had led him to the Foggy Bottom neighborhood of D.C., an area that not only housed George Washington University, but also the George Washington Medical Center and numerous government buildings ranging from the World Bank and the International Monetary Fund to the Federal Reserve Building and the Department of the Interior.

In addition, the address wasn't a private home, or even an office. It was a coffee shop with free WiFi access. Anybody with a laptop could hook into the coffee shop's free internet and be on their IP address. An extremely odd choice for the computer genius with whom Nick had been at odds during the last few weeks. Why would somebody risk working on an open internet connection where others might be able to listen in? Or was it pure genius, hiding in plain sight?

Nick glanced around the coffee shop. At least two dozen students, young doctors, and suits were hunched over their laptops, working, surfing, and reading. At first glance, none of them looked like a hacker, but then, what exactly did a hacker look like? He knew that appearances could be deceptive.

Was he the scruffy student, who was balancing his laptop on his knees while eating a muffin with one hand? Or the young woman in the white doctor's coat and the dark circles under her eyes, eyes that kept falling shut while she stared intensely into her computer monitor? Maybe the heavy-set black guy in the gray suit was the man in question, trying to divert any suspicion by looking all businesslike with his manicured nails and trendy haircut.

In short, it could be anybody.

This would take some time. He might as well get comfortable and find a corner from which to watch the comings and goings. Sooner or later, his CIA training would kick in, and he'd pick up on the tells his suspect was giving off. He'd learned that nobody could hide his true nature forever. Particularly once they relaxed and let down their guard, their true self emerged, and Nick would be there, waiting for him to make a mistake. He'd waited three years to get this close to the information he needed; he could wait a few days longer.

Behind the station where the baristas were taking orders and preparing fancy custom coffee drinks, it was buzzing like a beehive. Like a well-oiled machine, the employees shouted drink orders to each other: single shot this, no-foam that, half-caf the other. Even one of the employees could be his guy. They all got breaks during their shifts. Anyone of them could go in the back where they kept supplies and spend a few minutes on a computer. It would be a great cover. And who would suspect a minimum-wage barista?

"Double shot, no-whip mocha for Nick."

Upon hearing his drink called out, Nick pivoted and

snatched his overpriced coffee from the bar.

"Ouch!" he hissed and set it back down.

"Sleeves." The employee behind the counter pointed to a basket with cardboard cup protectors, before calling out the next drink. "Triple shot, grande latte for Michelle."

"Thanks." He slipped a sleeve around the hot paper cup, took his drink, turned on his heel—and instantly froze.

Only his extremely fast reaction saved him from colliding with the young woman who'd approached the counter for her latte. Instead, Nick jerked backward, hitting the counter with his back. The impact made him involuntarily tighten his grip on his coffee cup. The plastic lid popped off and the hot mocha splashed over the rim, spilling over the front of his T-shirt.

"Shit!" he cursed as the hot liquid touched his skin.

Instinctively jerking back from the burning coffee, his elbow hit something behind him. Nick shot a look over his shoulder just as the latte the barista had called out for the next customer spilled onto the counter.

"Well, great!" the woman he'd nearly crashed into grumbled beneath her breath. "I really needed that latte."

Yeah, and he needed not to be making a spectacle of himself.

Way to stay under the radar, Nick.

Setting his half-spilled drink onto the counter, he flashed the barista who was already cleaning up the mess a quick smile. "So sorry, I'll pay for it, of course."

"No worries, I'll make another one." She looked past him. "Michelle, just a minute, okay?"

"Thanks," the female customer—Michelle presumably—answered.

Nick nodded. "Much appreciate it. But I'll pay for it."

He turned around to face the woman the barista had addressed and froze once more, when he caught something flashing silver. Instinctively, he focused on the pendant around her neck. A spotlight from the ceiling reflected off the shiny surface, giving it emphasis when at any other time Nick wouldn't have given the item a second glance. It was probably not even made of silver, maybe just of steel or aluminum. But its shape was undeniable: it was a tiny Guy Fawkes mask, the same kind the hacker cooperative, Anonymous, used as their symbol.

This couldn't be a coincidence. What were the odds of somebody wearing this type of keepsake in the same coffee shop he'd traced the hacker to? Nick was no betting man, but he would put his money on this woman.

Slowly, he lifted his eyes and looked at her for the first time.

His breath hitched, air fleeing his lungs. Red lips was the first thing he saw. Full and plump, slightly parted, showing perfectly straight, white teeth. Her skin was olive as if she came from the Mediterranean. There was a golden sheen of perspiration on her face. Not surprising, since it was muggy as hell in the city, and even in the air-conditioned interior of the coffee shop, it was warm.

Blue eyes framed by dark lashes looked at him, assessing, questioning, curious. But he didn't let that deter him from scrutinizing her, because it wasn't the ex-CIA agent in him inspecting her, it was the man in him, the one whose blood was rushing to his groin with a speed he couldn't quite comprehend. All he knew was that this woman intrigued him on so many levels, the least of which was a professional one.

In dark blond waves, her hair fell to her shoulders, drawing attention to her spaghetti-strap top with the built-in bra that accentuated her firm breasts— which were the perfect size for her lean five-foot-seven frame. Her cleavage was of the same olive skin as her face, a skin that tanned easily. And perhaps without tan lines. Not that his mind should go in that direction. After all, he wasn't here to pick her up. Not for any romantic reasons anyway. Though, of course, to further his mission, he needed to get close to her. Just how close he didn't know yet.

For an instant, he wished that this woman wasn't the hacker he was after, but simply a regular customer of the quaint coffee shop. But the pendant and the computer bag that was slung bike-messenger-bag-like across her torso suggested otherwise.

"Uh… sorry… uh…" he stammered, both to convey the hapless man, but also because for a second he did feel just a little bit tongue-tied at so much physical perfection. "Uh, Michelle, is it?"

She tilted her head to the side, suspicious now. "How—?"

He jerked his thumb over his shoulder. "The barista called out your latte; the one I spilled. Sorry about that again."

Michelle seemed to relax. "No worries." She motioned to his torso. "At least you spilled your drink on yourself and not on me."

Nick flashed a warm grin, knowing that it was one of his special assets, one that made women feel comfortable with him. "Yeah, bit clumsy of me, wasn't it?" He reached for a napkin from the counter and patted the stain on his shirt, but there was no way of removing it. All he could do was pat it as dry as possible. "Well, guess that one's ruined."

Michelle chuckled. "Brown looks good on you."

Nick winked and used her light-hearted response to draw her in further. "Yeah, sure, have your fun. Laugh at the guy who's just made a fool of himself in front of a pretty woman."

The resulting blush on her cheeks looked good on her and confirmed that his charm was working. This would be the angle he could use to get to her and find out what she knew. With a bit of luck, he'd know in a few days—maximum a week—whether she could help him get what he needed.

4

He'd called her pretty, and that made her smile. After the day Michelle had had so far, the stranger's compliment felt like soothing lotion on a sunburn. Her meeting with her blackmailer—yes, *blackmailer*, because that's what he really was, no matter what government agency he was working for—had left her rattled. The pressure was on. Either she produced, or she would land in jail, and that was a place she didn't want to go to.

She'd much rather be in the company of a cute stranger, even if said stranger was a bit clumsy. At least the guy was no threat to her. The only danger she faced from the brown-haired hunk who was smiling at her, was being doused with coffee. And that was something she could easily survive.

Michelle watched as he dumped the soiled paper napkins in the trash bin and grabbed a new lid for his half-spilled coffee, securing it on the cup.

"I don't mean to be pushy or anything," he suddenly said, "but can I buy you a biscotti or a muffin to go with your latte?"

Michelle shook her head. "That's really not necessary. Besides, it's not like I need the extra calories." Keeping a trim figure was hard enough since she spent most of her days and nights in front of her computer.

She needed no sugar to jeopardize her health and weight.

A charming smirk, accompanied by a long look up and down her person, was his answer. "I'm sure you'll burn them off in no time."

She opened her mouth, not really knowing how to reply to that, when the barista interrupted.

"Michelle, your drink is ready."

Michelle nodded to the stranger and reached past him. "Thanks, Elise."

"Let me pay for that," the hunk insisted once more, pulling his wallet from his pocket.

"Not necessary," the barista replied. "Spills happen all the time. Besides, Michelle's a regular."

"Well then," he said, "thanks, and sorry again." He took a step away from the counter to let her pass.

Michelle took her drink and brought it to her lips, taking a first sip.

"Uh, Michelle."

She lifted her eyes above the coffee cup and looked at him, curious what else he wanted. "Yes?"

"I'm Nick, by the way. I'm new to the neighborhood." He offered his hand.

Hesitantly, Michelle shook it. "Hi, Nick. I'm Michelle, but then you already know that."

A broad grin made his face look younger than he seemed at first sight. She allowed herself to look at him more thoroughly now. He had a stubble beard, the kind a man who didn't have time to shave for two or three days would sport. It made him look rugged. His hair was medium-brown, but not dull. There was a healthy sheen to it. His eyes were green-brown, his skin on the light side as if he spent lots of time indoors. He wore a short-sleeved light-blue polo shirt and black cargo pants.

Despite their loose fit, it was evident that his legs were muscular, just like his arms, though he didn't look like a bodybuilder. He was lean.

"Listen, I get it if you don't want to be seen with me." Nick motioned to his shirt. "Stains and all, you know." He grinned disarmingly. "But considering you made me spill my drink, maybe you could make it up to me by keeping me company while I finish what's left of my mocha?"

"Now *I* made you spill your drink?" She had to laugh at that.

"Yep. The moment I saw you, I lost all control over my body."

Michelle rolled her eyes and walked toward her favorite spot, a large armchair in one corner. Was Nick coming on to her, or was he just being overly friendly? "The way I remember it is that you didn't even see me. That's why you spilled your coffee."

He winked. "Darn, you got me." Then he suddenly leaned in, lowering his voice. "Normally that line works, you know, but I guess you're too smart for that."

Michelle laughed. She had no defenses to his boy-next-door charm. It was disarming. And non-threatening, and that's what she needed right now. Some normalcy in her life.

She motioned to the second armchair, while she slunk down in her favorite spot and set her computer bag down. "Guess I'm not getting rid of you that easily."

Nick sat opposite her and lowered his backpack to his feet. "I'm kind of like caramel, sticky but sweet."

She chuckled. "So that pick-up line… Has it actually ever worked for you?"

He shrugged. "I'm still refining it. Rome wasn't built

in a day either."

"So that's a *no* then."

"Wow, do you always jump to conclusions this fast?"

"Only when the evidence is pretty clear."

Both sides of his mouth tilted up. "What are you, Michelle, some kind of detective?" He leaned across the small table between them and set his drink down. "Should I be afraid of you?"

"Should you?" She ran her eyes over him once more. Maybe he should be afraid of her. After all, he looked rather innocent, and she was anything but.

By all accounts, she was a criminal, though she'd never really seen herself that way. She'd been a hacker since she'd first surfed the internet. Exposing things the government wanted to hide from its people had been her mission in life. Anonymous had been her family, anarchy her religion. But all that was gone now, because she had to serve the very enemy she'd fought against for so long: the US government. She couldn't even run to her old friends, the other hackers, because doing so would only endanger them, expose them. She had to get out of this by herself.

Which begged the question why she was wasting time flirting with Nick. Because, yes, she was actually flirting with him. She would be better off getting back to work and trying to deliver the person *Deep Throat* was looking for.

However, everybody deserved a break once in a while. And what was the harm in talking to a nice guy for a few minutes? It was relaxing, and maybe this was the way to recharge her batteries and get a second wind for today.

"So you're a local," Nick said, just as she opened her

mouth, talking over him, "You're new to the neighborhood?"

Embarrassed she chuckled. "Go ahead."

"No, no, you first," he insisted.

"Did you move here recently?"

"Yes, this week. I'm from a small town in Indiana."

Just as she'd thought: an innocent in the big city. "What brings you here?"

"Work. I needed a change of scenery."

She nodded. "Yeah, I get that." She wanted a change of scenery, too. Preferably a sandy beach in a country that didn't extradite to the US.

"You work here in D.C.? At the university?" he asked.

"At the university?" Her eyebrows snapped together.

He motioned to her computer bag. "You look like you could be a lecturer or something."

She smiled. If only she had a harmless job like that. "I think you need to work on your detective skills a little more," she joked. "I could be a student."

Flashing his white teeth, he said, "But you're not. Not that you look old, but you look a lot more serious than any student I've ever met."

"I could be a graduate student or a resident."

"Yes, but they are generally too tired to stay awake." He pointed at the young female doctor napping in a chair across from them. "Or too focused on their thesis." Nick pointed to a young man typing away on his laptop so furiously that she was wondering if either he or his computer would start smoking soon.

"Point taken," Michelle admitted, enjoying the little game they were playing more than she should.

"You're gonna keep me guessing, aren't you?"

"You seem to have fun. Don't most men like a challenge?"

"Guess so. But I'm just a country bumpkin from Indiana. And you're a sophisticated woman from the Capital. I've got the feeling you'd just be playing with me." He winked.

The country bumpkin routine she didn't buy at all, though it was cute, she had to admit. "You're quite the charmer, aren't you? Is that why you moved to D.C.? To try out your country charm with city women?"

"Something like that." He reached for his mocha and took a sip.

"So what do you do then?"

"For a living you mean?"

"Yeah, for a living. Unless, of course, you're independently wealthy and are just mingling with the working masses for kicks."

"I wish." He grinned. "But I'm a working stiff."

"And you're not gonna tell me what you do, right?"

"You strike me as the kind of woman who'd rather find out for herself. Am I right?"

"Are you trying to make yourself more interesting than you are?"

He leaned over the table, lowering his voice. "Is it working?"

She met him halfway. "I'll tell you once it is."

"Well, I'd better leave then, before we become too familiar and all my mysteriousness is going out the window." He rose quickly and grabbed his backpack. "It was nice meeting you, Michelle. Maybe I'll see you again sometime."

"Yeah, maybe."

She watched him as he marched toward the entrance

door, his gait determined. His butt muscles flexed with each step, and she wondered what other moves he had. Moves she didn't mind him using on her. Moves of a more intimate nature. She licked her lips at the thought. It had been a while since she'd been with a man. Maybe that's what she needed to unwind: a passionate fling. It didn't have to mean anything. In fact, it was better if it didn't. Her life was too much of a mess already anyway. She didn't need a relationship to add to it.

At the door, Nick stopped, but before he pushed it open, he looked over his shoulder, grinning straight at her.

Embarrassed that he'd caught her staring, she took a sip of her lukewarm latte, pretending she hadn't watched him. But they both knew she had and with undeniable desire. Because, despite the brief interaction, there'd been a spark.

And maybe that spark could ignite something.

A quick fire.

A flame that would burn brightly before it fizzled out again just as quickly.

5

Nick had waited for the right moment for several days. It was time.

He'd done his homework and had found out where Michelle lived, what her routine was, who she met, where she shopped, and what she ate. Most of the information he'd gathered simply by following and watching her without her noticing him. The rest he'd gleaned from internet searches. There wasn't much online about her, almost as if somebody had taken great pains to wipe out her digital footprint. Either she'd done it herself or somebody in a high enough place had done it for her.

In either case, Michelle was on the path to becoming a ghost. Here today, gone tomorrow. Instinctively Nick knew he didn't have much time to make a move. Today he'd go to the coffee shop and ask her out. He'd use all his charm to get her into bed, and then he'd look at that precious computer of hers, the one she never left home without, the one she never let out of her sight, not even when she used the restroom at the coffee shop, when he'd seen plenty of other customers leaving their laptops unattended while using the facilities.

Freshly showered and shaved, Nick waited at the next pedestrian crossing for the light to change. Beside him several people waited while a woman jogged in place, her eyes pinned to the lights across the street.

The premonition came out of nowhere like it always did, though he didn't always know immediately what he was looking at. This time he did. He recognized her immediately: Michelle. She was leaving the coffee shop, bumping into a customer on the way out. The man was cursing at her, but Michelle didn't even turn her head as if she didn't notice him. She appeared distracted, with a worried look on her face. Something was bothering her.

Nick felt himself reach out his hand, wanting to wipe the worry from her face, but in his vision Michelle kept walking, approaching the intersection where the light turned at that moment. She only briefly looked to her right, before stepping into the crosswalk. She didn't even see the taxi coming from the left. It hit her and flung her into the air. Behind the cab, her body slammed onto the hard asphalt like a rag doll. He knew immediately that she was dead. Knew it with a certainty that sent a chill to his bones and froze the blood in his veins.

"No!" he cried out and pushed the vision aside.

Tossing a quick look to either side of him, he dashed through the intersection, darting between the cars, drawing vile curses of the motorists onto himself. But he didn't care. He had no time to lose or Michelle would die.

Why he had the visions and when, or how they appeared, Nick didn't know. It was his special gift—and the reason he lived in hiding. But today, he would use his gift to save a human life. If he wasn't too late already.

The light backpack he always carried slung over one shoulder, Nick ran through the busy early afternoon crowd that clogged up the sidewalks, pushing people out of his way if they didn't let him pass quickly enough. Curses and angry shouts followed him, but he barely took any notice. He was close, so close. Just another two blocks to the coffee shop.

He raced down the sidewalk, briefly stepping onto the street when a wheelchair user blocked his way. A car honked at him, but he kept running, darting between two vehicles to make a right turn into the street where the coffee shop was located at the end of the block.

A man he recognized from the premonition approached the door of the coffee shop. The door almost hit him in the face as it was opened. The woman exiting was Michelle.

Shit!

From the corner of his eye, Nick saw something flash yellow. He snapped his head to the side. The cab was passing him.

"Michelle!" he called out at the top of his lungs, waving at her.

She neither heard nor saw him and kept walking, approaching that fateful crosswalk.

Nick launched into an even faster sprint, pushing off the hot asphalt with all his strength. His heart raced as his lungs worked overtime.

Gotta get to her! Run! Damn it, run!

"Michelle!" he cried out again, but a car honking drowned out his voice.

A few more yards, just a few more. You can do it!

He darted past a woman with a small child, catching up with the taxi. Ahead of him, Michelle stood at the crosswalk, looking to her right, away from him and the approaching cab. Everything seemed to happen in slow motion now. The cab approaching the intersection...

Michelle lifting her foot to take a step into the street…

"Michelle!" Nick barreled toward her.

Michelle ripped her head in his direction, eyes wide, mouth open, freezing in her current position, one foot on the street, one on the sidewalk. Nick lunged for her, turning her sideways in a split second, away from the traffic, inserting himself between her and the taxi, which had just reached them.

He pushed her away from him, toward the middle of the sidewalk. He tried to pivot with her, but the mirror of the cab caught in the strap of his backpack, ripping it from him and swiping his arm. The impact knocked him sideways. Nick was slammed against a metal newspaper rack, his left arm and side taking the brunt of it. But he didn't have time to worry about that now, nor about the screeching tires or the excited shouts around him.

Instead he searched for Michelle. When he finally found her, she was in the middle of the sidewalk, upright, but visibly shaken. He ran his eyes over her, but saw no obvious injuries.

Relieved, he slumped to the ground and rested his back against the newspaper rack. "Thank God," Nick murmured to himself, air rushing from his lungs now.

"Jesus Christ!" Michelle ran toward him, staggering a little and looking shaken. "Oh my God!"

"You all right, Michelle?" He looked up at her.

She breathed heavily as she crouched down to him. "That cab would have hit me!" Her lips trembled. "If you hadn't been there…" She closed her eyes for a moment, swallowing hard.

He reached for her hand, but winced at the pain in his arm and side. He breathed through it, willing the sensation to subside.

Michelle's eyes flew open and she shot a look at his arm. "You're hurt. Don't move. I'll call an ambulance."

Instantly, Nick shook his head. "I don't need an ambulance. I'm fine."

He didn't want an ambulance. Nor did he want a police report about the incident. While he had built a fake identity for himself, he wasn't about to test how well he'd covered his tracks.

Several bystanders crowded around. A man pushed through them: the taxi driver.

"You all right, buddy?" he asked, his voice shaking.

Nick quickly nodded.

"Shit!" The cabbie ran his hand over his head. "You stepped right in my path. Wasn't my fault."

A few pedestrians grunted angrily.

"Typical cab driver!" one of them cursed.

Nick used his good arm to push himself off the ground and, using the newspaper rack for leverage, pulled himself up. "I'm fine. Nothing happened." He pasted a thin smile on his face, nodding to the cab driver once more. "I'm all right. No need to hang around."

"You need a doctor to look at you. You could have a concussion," Michelle insisted.

Nick put his hand on her forearm and squeezed it. "I'm fine. Trust me."

The cab driver tossed him an unsure look, scratching his neck. "You sure? You not gonna sue me afterward?"

"I'm not gonna sue you. It was entirely my fault."

Finally, the cab driver marched back to his taxi. Nick turned to the other pedestrians who continued to hover, making sure they didn't miss anything.

"Honestly, nothing more to see here," he insisted and made a shooing motion.

"Is that your bag, ma'am?" A kid pointed to a computer bag on the sidewalk.

Michelle nodded and the boy handed it to her. "Thank you."

Slowly, the people disbursed. Nick glanced around. It was possible that somebody had already called 9-1-1 and the police were on their way. It was best not to risk hanging around here any longer. He reached for his backpack, glad to see that it was still intact from landing on the curb.

"Somebody has to look at you," Michelle said beside him.

He smiled at her, her concern touching him. "It's just a little bruise. I'll survive."

"Please, let's get you to a hospital."

"I can't. I don't have health insurance right now." It was true, although that wasn't the reason he didn't want to see a doctor. "I just need to ice down the area."

Michelle let out an annoyed huff. "Damn it, do you have to be so stubborn?"

He grinned. "You think I'm stubborn?"

She rolled her eyes. "Well, then let's go to my place. I'll look at your injuries and I swear if I think it looks bad, I *will* deliver you to the hospital myself."

At her bossy statement, Nick felt like saluting as if she were a drill sergeant in the army. But he suppressed the urge. "Yes, ma'am."

6

At least Nick wasn't objecting to her helping him.

"Can you walk?" Michelle asked, looking him up and down.

"I can. Where do you live?"

She motioned toward the path she'd originally been heading down. "It's not far. Just a few blocks."

Michelle hoisted her computer bag over one shoulder and waited for the light to change to green, letting out another breath. She was still shaking, but the reality of what had just happened was settling in. She'd been about to cross the street without looking. And had Nick not been there, she would have walked right into the path of the taxi. Everything could have been over in seconds. She shuddered at the thought.

"You okay?"

At Nick's concerned voice, she lifted her face to him. "I guess it's only just now sinking in. I can't believe I was so careless. It was so lucky that you were there. How did you realize—"

Nick took her hand in his and squeezed it. "Don't think about it any longer. It'll just drive you crazy. I'm happy that I caught you in time."

At the odd phrasing of his words, she snapped her eyebrows together. "Were you looking for me?"

"Actually, I was on my way to the coffee shop, hoping that I might see you, when I saw you at the intersection."

"Oh." It was odd since they hadn't seen each other since their first encounter a few days earlier.

"Yeah, when I saw you there, I realized you'd already left the coffee shop, so I called out to you." Nick grinned, shrugging. Then he motioned to the changed light, and together they crossed the street. "Took me a few days to scrape together all my courage to ask you out for coffee. I didn't wanna waste that opportunity. So I ran to try to catch up with you."

Her heart started beating faster, and this time it wasn't out of panic or shock. "You wanted to ask me out for coffee?" And instead he'd saved her from getting hurt.

Nick cast her a sideways glance. "Figured I'd try my country bumpkin charm on you once more; see if it works better this time."

In disbelief, she shook her head. Was this man for real? Not only was he a hero, saving her without regard for his own safety, but he was also self-deprecating, sweet, and absolutely charming. Not to mention handsome and sexy as hell. She quickly glanced at his hands. And apparently still single. Jesus, why could she not have met a guy like him earlier, when her life hadn't started to careen out of its tracks?

"I don't know what to say." She reached for his arm.

Wincing, he said, "No need to say anything. But a bag of ice would be great right about now."

"So sorry," she apologized when she realized that she'd just squeezed his injured arm. "Let's get you inside, and then I'll take care of your arm."

She pointed to a three-story brownstone. "I'm afraid it's a walk-up."

"Nothing wrong with my legs."

Michelle turned to the door and unlocked it. She entered, Nick on her heels, and walked ahead of him, climbing the old creaking staircase.

"You live alone?"

She looked over her shoulder. "Yes, it's just a small one-bedroom, cheap enough so I don't need a roommate."

"Good."

For an instant, her heart stopped. Was it wise to bring a man she'd only met for the second time today to her apartment? Was she inviting trouble by letting him into her place, where they would be alone? After all, she knew nothing about him.

Nothing apart from the fact that he was charming— which apparently serial killer Ted Bundy had been, too—and that he'd saved her life. That latter part helped her make up her mind. Nick had risked his own life to save hers and gotten injured as a result. She owed him to at least make sure he was all right. And she couldn't blame him for not wanting to go to a hospital. Without insurance, they would charge him an arm and a leg just for getting an x-ray and an icepack.

"Here we are," she announced as she reached the top floor and stepped onto the landing. There were two apartments on this floor. She pulled her key ring from her computer bag and inserted the key in the lock.

When she pushed the door open, she turned and saw Nick hesitating in the hallway. She waved him in. "Come in, I won't bite."

He smirked. "Promise?"

Michelle dropped her keys onto the side table in the short hallway from which one door led to the bathroom and the other to the bedroom. Ahead of her, an arch led into the living room with an adjacent tiny kitchen. It wasn't much, but at least she had privacy here.

"Nice place," Nick commented and followed her into the living room.

"Take a seat. And take off your shirt," she demanded and marched into the kitchen.

The door between living room and kitchen had long been removed because of lack of space. She opened the freezer and rummaged through it, finally finding a bag of frozen peas. It would have to do. She snatched a clean dish towel from a drawer and turned back to the living room only to slam to a halt.

Nick stood in the door frame, his chest bare and glistening. He was even better built than she'd suspected the day she'd first met him. In fact, he was positively ripped. Her mouth started watering at the sight of his six-pack-abs and the well-defined pectorals that seemed to twitch.

The only sound she managed to produce from her dry throat was *"Uh."* Great, she was turning into a drooling teenager. How pathetic.

"Sorry, didn't mean to startle you." The deep timbre of his voice bounced off the walls of the tiny kitchen.

In the small room he looked even more imposing, even more attractive, more tempting.

"Is that the ice?"

He motioned to the bag of peas, prompting her to spring back into action.

"Yes, yes. Sorry, I don't have real ice cubes, but this'll do the trick." She turned sideways. "Why don't you sit down here then, and I'll look at you." Not that she wasn't already *looking* at him. Or better yet, *ogling* him.

He squeezed past her to the single barstool next to the miniscule breakfast counter that was just big enough for one person. Awkwardly, she turned to try to avoid brushing against him, but it happened nevertheless.

A bolt of adrenaline shot through her at the unexpected contact. The accompanying heat wave scorched her from the inside, adding to the stifling temperature in her top-floor apartment. Right now, she wished for air conditioning, though she wasn't sure it would help cool her body down.

Nick took a seat on the barstool and turned toward her. She placed the bag of frozen peas on the counter and reached for his arm.

"I'm just gonna touch your arm lightly to see if it's broken, okay?"

He only nodded, but remained silent. Michelle felt his eyes on her and tried to remain calm. It was only natural that he was watching what she was doing, she told herself. In his situation, she would do the same. It didn't mean that he was checking her out. Besides, he was probably in pain, and not even men had romantic feelings when in pain, right?

Slowly, she ran her hands over his arm. His forearm felt fine, and when she squeezed hesitantly, he didn't protest. When she reached his elbow, she tested his range of motion, and again, nothing struck her as odd.

"All good," he commented.

She brushed her hand over his upper arm and applied a little bit of pressure. Instantly, Nick jerked back and groaned.

"Sorry." She caught his gaze. "I need to check a little

more."

"Mmm-hmm." His eyes were unreadable. Had they turned darker?

The warmth of Nick's skin made her fingers tingle. She took a steadying breath, hoping he didn't notice how touching him affected her. Hell, she was no blushing virgin! He wasn't the first man she'd touched. He wouldn't be the last either. Though it had been a while since she'd been with somebody. Maybe too long. Perhaps that was the reason why touching him got her all flustered.

Pulling herself together, she continued examining his arm. Even though he hissed when she squeezed his bicep, she didn't think his arm was broken.

"I think it's just bruised. It'll probably turn blue in a day or two." She exchanged a look with him.

"Just as I thought. Thanks."

"Hold on," she said. "How about your ribs?" She pointed to his side. "You crashed against the newspaper rack quite hard. Lift your arm."

Nick followed her command and she placed her hand over his side, pressing lightly.

He shrank back. "Okay, that's enough playing doctor for one day," he said lightly, though his facial expression told her that he'd gotten bruised there, too.

Michelle tilted her head. "And there I was having so much fun," she said sarcastically. She sighed. "Honestly, men."

She grabbed the bag of peas and placed it over his upper arm. "Hold this."

While he pressed the makeshift icepack to his bicep, she wrapped the dish towel around it then knotted it. "That should do."

She opened the freezer again and snatched a bag of sweet corn from it. "This is for your ribs. You're gonna have to press it against your side for a while."

"Aye, aye, ma'am."

She braced her hands at her hips. "And don't make fun of me. I'm just trying to help you, you stubborn idiot." She sniffed in a short breath.

"So I'm an idiot now?" he asked way too softly— almost as if he knew what was going on inside her.

Tears sprang to her eyes. Nick could have gotten killed today. *For her.* For saving her miserable life, when she knew her life was practically forfeit anyway. Because if she couldn't produce the results Mr. Smith wanted, he'd have her thrown in prison. And right now, she was at a dead end. As if somebody had put a wall up right in front of her. One she couldn't penetrate. She was running out of options and out of time.

"Why did you do that?" A sob tore from her chest. "That cab could have killed you! You don't even know me. You don't even know whether I'm worth risking your life for. You idiot." The last word barely made it over her lips, tears choking off her voice.

She felt his hand wrap around her wrist a moment later, pulling her to him. His arm came around her back, dragging her closer until she was captured between his spread legs, chest-to-chest with him.

He used his forefinger to tip her face up so she had to look at him. "Every life is worth saving." He paused, smirking. "As for calling me an idiot: I'd like an apology for that." His gaze dropped to her mouth.

Her breath instantly hitched, awareness permeating every cell of her body. Her pulse began to race, and perspiration slicked her skin.

"A really nice, long apology." He dipped his head until his lips were floating just an inch above hers. "How about that apology now?"

His voice was drugging, his strong arm imprisoning her. His breath blew against her face, tempting her further.

"Just one kiss," she murmured.

"Two. You called me an idiot twice."

"Two then."

The moment the last word left her mouth, she felt Nick's lips on hers. At first the touch was soft and gentle, a mere brushing of skin on skin, of warmth sliding against warmth. Instinctively her lips parted as she took in his masculine scent, inhaling his aroma, taking it deep into her lungs. A pleasant shiver ran down her spine, making her tremble in his arms.

An appreciative hum came from his lips, reverberating against hers, the vibrations spreading a tingling sensation over her mouth and face.

She knew then that two kisses wouldn't be enough to satisfy the sudden hunger that was growing inside her.

7

Nick tilted his head and captured Michelle's lips fully, tasting her drying tears and her sweet breath. Her sudden emotional outburst had taken him by surprise, yet at the same time given him the chance to do what he knew he had to: get close to her so he could find out what she knew. He pushed the twinge of guilt that surfaced to the back of his mind. Deep down he knew this was wrong, but he couldn't stop himself.

Seeing her die in his vision had been too real, and knowing that had he arrived only two seconds later, the vision would have come true, still sent chills down his spine. That was a feeling he couldn't ignore. What he needed now—what they both needed—was a few moments of sheer and utter abandon. A brief celebration of life, of lust and passion, of tenderness and ecstasy. For a short while, he would forget what his real mission was and concentrate on only one thing: making the woman in his arms forget the fact that she'd narrowly escaped death today.

He wanted to shower her with passion, make her body hum with pleasure, and lose himself in her. Just for a short time. That part wouldn't be a lie. It would be real and honest.

Nick ignored the pain in his side and focused only

on Michelle, on the softness of her lips, the delicious taste of her mouth, the insistent strokes of her tongue as she dueled with him in a match that neither could win. *Hunger* was the word that came to mind when her hands dug into his shoulders, holding on to him for dear life as if she was afraid he'd toss her to the side.

He slid his hands down below her waist, feeling her firm ass through the thin fabric of her summer skirt. Goddamn it, was she wearing anything underneath that thin scrap of cotton? It felt like she was naked.

Nick growled involuntarily, intensifying his kiss, while he pressed her against his groin, where his cock was already as hard as a crow bar.

Michelle moaned into his mouth, her body stiffening for an instant. Yes, she could feel his erection, knew what was coming, because a kiss wouldn't suffice now. He needed more from her. He needed to be inside her to make the horrors of the last hour vanish. To make him forget.

Impatiently, he slid his hands underneath the fabric of her skirt. He nearly jumped out of his pants when he felt bare skin beneath his fingers. He palmed her ass, exploring her, and realized she was wearing a thong. He should have known that a hot woman like Michelle wore sexy underwear like that. Not that at this moment he needed any additional turn-on in the form of sexy lingerie.

Michelle kissing him with such unrestrained passion was turn-on enough. And Michelle rubbing herself against his cock was almost too much. But she was doing it, and he wasn't going to stop her. Just as she wasn't stopping him when he pulled her thong down to her thighs until it finally dropped to her feet.

Now he had full access to her sex and made use of it. He slid his hand down her ass to the juncture of her thighs, reaching between them. She complied immediately and widened her stance so he could bring his hand between her legs.

She was warm and wet there. A drop of her juices coated his finger and he rubbed it along her moist cleft. She jolted under his intimate touch, but didn't pull back. Instead, she rocked her pelvis against his cock as if asking for more.

Nick ripped his lips from hers. "You want that, yeah? You want my cock?"

Passion-clouded eyes stared at him. Her face was flushed, and she dropped her lids, but he wouldn't allow her to evade him. "Look at me."

Her eyes flew open and she pinned him.

"Do you want that?" He rocked his cock against her and rubbed two fingers along her wet sex, gently probing at the entrance to her body. "Do you want me inside you?"

"Yes." She put her hand on his nape and pulled him back to her so there was only a sliver of space between them. "I want you. Now. Here."

Just as well that he was prepared for this. He'd shoved a couple of condoms into his pants pocket before leaving his place. Those would come in handy now.

"Good, 'cause that's what I've wanted to do from the moment you made me spill my mocha."

"I didn't make you spill your mocha."

"Did, too."

He captured her lips again, stopping her from voicing any further protest. Kissing her, Nick lifted her off her feet and spread her legs, wrapping them around his waist. He marched into the living room, his cock sliding against her center with every step. The thrilling sensation even made the pain in his arm fade into the background.

When he reached the sofa, he laid her onto it and lowered himself between her thighs. He didn't lose any time and lifted her skirt to expose her now naked sex. The sight robbed him of his breath. She was entirely bare. Nothing was hidden from his view.

"Baby," he groaned.

How was he going to survive this? Another few seconds and he'd come right in his pants. *Fuck!* He had to get himself under control.

Nick lifted his gaze and met Michelle's eyes. "You're absolutely gorgeous." Then he lowered his head, but continued to keep eye contact. "I hope you don't mind, but I skipped lunch. And I love buffets." And the kind of feast that was spread out in front of him was impossible to resist. "All you can eat, you know."

Her breath hitched before he lowered his mouth to her smooth folds and took his first taste. Slowly he licked over her bare skin and gathered up the dew that was trickling from her. With his hands on her thighs, he spread her wider.

"Open up for me," he coaxed and suckled along her delicious folds.

Michelle spread her legs wider, lifting one over the back of the sofa.

"There you go. Just like that." He scooped his hands under her ass and tilted her pelvis toward him. Then he dove back to her sex and sucked her like a man who hadn't eaten in days.

Michelle was so easy to read. Every moan and sigh, every move she made told him what she liked and what she craved more of. He adjusted to her wishes, licking her more gently now, with longer strokes. She was getting wetter with every second, her moans becoming louder and more frequent. Her hands tugged at her spaghetti top, and he realized that she was perspiring.

Nick lifted his head from her and helped her rid herself of her top and the skirt. When she finally lay naked before him, he swept his eyes over her. She was as sexy as sin itself. And the fact that he was still wearing his pants made the whole situation even more exciting.

Nick took her hand and pulled it to the front of his pants, pressing it against the erection that pulsed there. "Feel what you do to me."

Michelle pulling her lower lip between her teeth nearly made him spill, or was it the fact that she squeezed his cock right at that moment? It didn't matter. What mattered was getting rid of his clothes, or there would indeed be a disaster on the horizon.

He lifted himself off the couch and shucked his shoes, then unzipped and pulled his pants off. When he hooked his thumbs into the waistband of his boxer briefs, he met her eyes. She stared at him with open desire.

"Yes, look at my cock. Look at what you'll feel inside you in a moment." Slowly he pulled his boxer briefs down and revealed his erection.

When he saw the look of admiration and eager anticipation on her face, pride swelled inside him. He would make sure that look turned into one of satisfaction and ecstasy shortly.

Reaching for his pants, he pulled a condom from the

pocket and ripped open the packaging.

"You came prepared."

At her words, he snapped his gaze to her. Michelle was propping herself up on her elbows, her nipples pointing at him.

"Can't blame a guy for hoping he'd get lucky."

She smiled softly. "Is that what you call it?"

He slowly rolled the condom over his hard-on. "What would you call it then?"

Michelle gave his cock a pointed look. "Maybe *I'm* the one who's getting lucky."

Nick threw his head back and laughed. "A woman after my own heart." Then he lowered one knee onto the sofa. "So, tell me, what would you like? I'm open to suggestions, because frankly, as long as I get to be inside you, I don't care which way."

"Stop talking." She dropped back into the cushions and crooked her finger, inviting him to come closer. "Just let me feel you."

"Yes, ma'am."

With a grin that was surely going to become permanent, Nick lowered himself between her legs, bringing his cock to her center. Guiding himself along her moist sex, he allowed her warm juices to coat the condom.

When she moaned and arched her back off the sofa, he slid his cock over her clit, teasing the tiny organ. If he had any self control left, he'd finish her off by licking her clit until she came, but that was something that would have to wait for another time, because right now he couldn't wait another second to be inside her.

"Tell me you want my cock," he demanded.

Her hand came up and wrapped around his nape,

pulling him down to her. "I want to feel your cock inside me. And if you don't do it right now, I'm going to scream!"

"Michelle, let's get one thing straight: you're going to scream either way," Nick promised and plunged inside her, seating himself until his balls slapped against her flesh.

He watched with male satisfaction how her eyes closed and all the air rushed from her lungs, how she pulled her lower lip between her teeth and how her hand tightened around his nape, her fingernails clawing into him. Even the little bit of pain it caused him he welcomed.

When he withdrew to thrust again, he felt his injured side, felt the pain in his arm and ribs, noticed how the icepack was sliding down his arm and tossed it aside. There was time later to ice his wounds. Right now, he needed to make love to the gorgeous woman beneath him. That was his only focus.

Shifting most of his weight to his uninjured side, and bracing himself on his knees and one elbow, he began to move inside her. God, she felt good. Smooth, warm, welcoming. She enveloped him like a glove, like a tight bandage that caressed and soothed at the same time. Her interior muscles were tight and strong, holding him like a vise.

Nick brushed a strand of her dark blond hair from her face and gazed into her eyes. "So beautiful." And yet she was his enemy, though she didn't know it, had no inkling of who he was or why he was here. In a way, it made her an innocent. He was the predator. A predator who wanted nothing more than to please the beautiful creature in his arms. Who wanted nothing more than to make her feel pleasure and satisfaction. Who wanted nothing more than to feel her submit and give herself to him if only for a few moments.

He threw his head back. Goddamn it, he didn't want her to be the enemy. He didn't want to have to use her. And, at that moment, he wished for nothing more than to be wrong about his suspicion that Michelle was the person who'd been chasing him online. But all evidence pointed to her. The Guy Fawkes pendant that even now dangled around her neck mocked him, even though its bearer knew nothing of the turmoil she was causing him.

"Oh God, Michelle!" he cried out and took her harder. Almost as if to punish her, when in reality he wanted to punish himself.

"Nick! Oh yes!" She rocked against him, her tempo increasing, her breathing erratic.

He tore his eyes from the pendant, trying not to think about it, and looked at Michelle's glowing face instead. Beads of sweat formed on her forehead, giving her skin an enticing sheen. Her lips were parted, tempting him to capture them for another kiss.

"I haven't had my second kiss yet," he murmured.

A soft laugh burst from her lips then. "But you did." She lowered her gaze, and he immediately realized what she was referring to.

"Oh that." He winked. "That was just a quick taste. Maybe later I'll get a longer one?"

Her hand came up, and she stroked her index finger over his lower lip. "Are you for real?"

"As real as it gets."

Before his conscience could intervene, he took her lips for a hard kiss, trying to prove to himself that he was making love to Michelle because he was attracted to her, not because he needed to find out what she knew. And why shouldn't he be attracted to her? She was beautiful, sexy, and full of life. And she felt good in his arms. It had been a while since he'd felt like this, since he'd felt he could let himself go and indulge in this very physical pleasure without having to look over his shoulder to see who was after him.

The way Michelle responded to him made everything male in him come to life. In her arms he was only a man, not the ex-CIA agent who could see future events, not the man who would kill to protect his life and that of his fellow agents, the ones who'd gone underground to survive. No, in Michelle's arms, he was only a man who wanted to feel the love of a woman, even if it was only physical and fleeting. But he needed this, needed to feel the connection of his body to hers. To feel alive again and not like the ghost he'd become.

Michelle was giving him this, was showing him what life could be like again if only he defeated his enemies. With her tantalizing body, Michelle gave him what he craved most: a place where he was safe and welcome.

Harder and harder he took her, his quest for release more urgent now. He shifted his angle, watching for signs from Michelle to make sure she would climax with him.

Severing the kiss, he lifted his head and gazed into her eyes. Heavy-lidded she looked back at him.

"Baby, you feel so good. So amazing." He clenched his jaw, realizing how imminent his orgasm was. "I'm close. Tell me what you need."

She bucked toward him. "Harder."

He complied with her wish, pulling back his hips and slamming into her. His neck muscles strained as he tried to hold on to his control while repeating the action again and again.

"Yes!" she cried out and arched off the cushions, offering her breasts to him.

He took the offering and dipped his face and sucked one hard nipple into his mouth, closing his lips around it. Beneath him, Michelle trembled, and her interior muscles clamped down on him, imprisoning his cock in her warm channel.

A shudder raced through his entire body, and a bolt of energy shot into his balls, sending hot semen through his cock. He exploded, joining her in her climax, rocking with her as they both came down from their high. Floating blissfully, without thought, without worries…

Breathing hard, he sank down onto her, his knees shaking from the intensity of his orgasm, his heart racing like a bullet train, his side and arm aching now.

Michelle blew out a breath. "Wow."

"Yeah, wow," Nick replied.

8

Nick pressed a kiss into Michelle's hair. He'd pulled her on top of him on the couch, not wanting to crush her with his weight. He liked the feel of her warm body as she lay there, relaxed and breathing evenly.

"Are you falling asleep?" he asked, chuckling.

"Mmm."

"Guess I must have bored you."

She lifted her head and smiled at him. "You've worn me out, that's what you did, and you know it." She pressed her cheek back onto his chest.

He liked how easy she was to talk to. If he weren't on the run, he wouldn't mind having a girlfriend like Michelle, maybe even a serious relationship.

"I think you've got it the wrong way 'round. *You* wore *me* out."

She laughed softly, and her breath ghosted over his nipple, to his own surprise hardening it in an instant. Fuck, he still wanted more. Taking her just once hadn't been quite enough.

"Are you complaining?" she asked.

He gave her a good-natured slap on her ass. "No complaints. Just an observation."

She wiggled on top of him, and he palmed her ass with both hands, stopping her from rubbing herself against his cock.

"Go ahead, keep doing that, and I'm gonna have to bend you over that armchair and teach you some manners," he warned and pressed another kiss on the top of her head.

She lifted her head and laughed. "Who says I have no manners? Didn't I take care of your injuries like a good little nurse?"

Nick lifted one side of his mouth into a smirk. "More like a naughty little vixen luring me into her lair so she can devour me. Remember, I'm just an innocent boy from Indiana. I have no defenses against experienced women from the city."

"Not even you believe that. You don't strike me as innocent. And I wasn't the one doing the seducing. I remember distinctly that you were the one asking for a kiss."

"True, but I had no idea you'd rub your hot little body all over me, making me lose all control. And there I'd planned on taking you out for a coffee, trying to get to know you better." He looked at his watch. "Guess it's too late for that now. It's more like dinner time."

"So you really wanted to ask me out on a date?"

"Sure did." He lifted his hand, making an all encompassing sweeping motion. "Guess I've got it backwards. Normally, sex comes after dinner." He combed a hand through her hair, enjoying the silky feel of it. "Though, if you don't object, I'd like to take you out for dinner now."

Her eyes widened. "You mean, even though you've already gotten what you wanted?"

"Who says I have?" He winked.

"Normally, guys make themselves scarce once

they've gotten a girl into bed."

"Way I see it, we're not in bed." He patted the sofa cushion. "I believe this is a couch. And who says all I want is sex? I think you'd be selling yourself short if you thought that."

He looked deep into her blue eyes and felt how his heart started beating out of control. He wasn't lying to her. She did have a lot to offer—to the right guy. Unfortunately, he wasn't that guy, although if circumstances were different, he wondered if he could be.

"You really know how to turn on the charm," Michelle said.

"I do my best." Then he gave her another slap on her backside. "Now, how about that dinner date, or were you just gonna use me for sex and then toss me out on my ass?"

For far too long she looked at him, contemplating her answer. He shifted, his pulse kicking up. What was going through that pretty little mind right now? Best to grab the bull by the horns and turn things around.

"Oh my God, you actually have to think about that!? Way to boost a guy's self-confidence." He pulled himself up to sit, laughing, when Michelle started snickering.

"Sorry, couldn't help myself. I love it when a guy gets all flustered and insecure."

Nick planted a kiss on her nose. "You're a strange woman, Michelle."

She opened her mouth for a protest, but he put his finger over her lips, stopping her.

"Just as well that I have very peculiar tastes."

When her eyes softened and her lips curved up, he knew he'd won.

"Do I have time for a shower before dinner?" she asked.

"Take all the time you need."

She lifted herself up and stood. He couldn't help running his eyes over her body, admiring her firm breasts, her slim waist and soft hips, her long legs, and everything in between. When she turned to give him a view of her shapely ass, he groaned, wishing he could shower with her, but he had something more important to do.

"Do you mind if I switch on the TV while you shower?" he asked.

Michelle looked over her shoulder and pointed to the coffee table. "If you can figure out the remote, help yourself."

Nick reached for the black device and gave her a mock-chiding look. "I'm a guy. We invented remotes."

Shaking her head, Michelle disappeared down the hallway. Moments later, he heard the water running in the shower.

Nick jumped up, pressed the TV power button and turned up the volume, not even looking what channel was on. He gathered his clothes and dressed in fifteen seconds. Now he was ready.

He quickly scanned the living room, knowing instinctively he'd find nothing of importance here. Nevertheless he did a cursory search of the few drawers and surfaces anyway. It turned up nothing. His next stop was Michelle's bedroom. The door was opposite the bathroom door, which thankfully Michelle had shut. Nick now eased the door to the bedroom open and entered.

There wasn't much: a queen-sized bed, a dresser,

night tables, a few boxes along one wall. The built-in closet was small and jam-packed with clothes, no files, no electronic equipment. Continuously listening to the sounds from the bathroom, Nick continued his search, opening the drawer of one nightstand. It was full of underwear. He rummaged through it, but only lingerie turned up.

He rounded the bed and searched the other nightstand. Several loose condom packages greeted him, together with tissues and lubricant. Nick grinned involuntarily. Good to know that Michelle had some extra supplies, just in case they burned through the few condoms he'd brought.

A quick perusal of the boxes turned up nothing but books and old photos. He checked his watch: Michelle had entered the bathroom three minutes earlier. He should have plenty of time to go through the rest of the apartment. He left the bedroom and stepped into the hallway. There, below the side table, lay her computer bag. He crouched down and opened it, tossing a quick glance to the bathroom door, listening intently. The water was still running.

The bag held a laptop, several cables, as well as notepads, pens, and the product tag for the bag itself. He pulled the laptop from its compartment and opened it. Though he was almost certain that Michelle wouldn't leave her computer unprotected, he had to find out if she'd, by some lucky chance, not password-protected it.

He booted up the machine, drumming his fingers on his thigh while he waited impatiently for the wheel to stop spinning. When the screen filled with color and presented him with the request to enter a password, he wasn't surprised. It would have been too easy. He quickly initiated the shut down and set the computer aside, looking through the bag once more. There had to be something.

He flipped through the notepad, but apart from some scribbles that looked like a shopping list, he didn't find anything. The moment the computer powered down, he slid it back into the bag. It didn't want to go in all the way, so he pulled it out again and checked. He found a piece of paper on the bottom of the compartment and looked at it. It was a manufacturer's warranty for a flash drive.

But where was it?

Shoving the computer back into the bag and closing it, Nick stood up. His eyes fell on the side table, where Michelle had tossed her keys when they'd entered her apartment. He picked the key ring up. Not only did it hold several keys, but a USB flash drive dangled from it.

"Gotcha," he murmured.

The sudden echo of his voice startled him. That's when he realized that the water wasn't running anymore. Michelle was done with her shower. He'd never met a woman who was that quick.

Shit!

9

Michelle wrapped the large bath towel around her still damp body and tucked in one end to hold it in place. Her hair was still wet, but she'd combed it. Considering the heat in D.C., it would dry in no time. With a last glance in the mirror, she turned the doorknob and opened the door.

She found Nick sitting on the couch—fully dressed now—staring into the TV. He turned his head.

"Hey," he greeted her with an easy smile.

"I'll be just a minute more," she told him. Her gaze fell on the TV and she had to do a double-take. "You're watching the Hallmark Channel?" What guy did that? Was Nick a true romantic at heart with whom she could actually watch sappy romances on TV? This was too good to be true.

Nick hastily reached for the remote. "Uh, no, ah, actually, I was just channel-surfing, trying to find ESPN." He pressed a button, and the channel changed. Then he moved to the next one in the lineup as if to prove that he told the truth.

Michelle chuckled. "Sure you were." She turned toward the bedroom.

"I was!" he called after her. "I was looking for a sportscast."

She didn't reply and walked into her bedroom, closing the door behind her. As she dropped her towel onto the bed and rummaged through her closet to find something appropriate to wear, she smiled to herself. Nick was unusual, she had to give him that. When they'd made love, he'd been intense and demanding, while simultaneously proving to be a very considerate lover, one who not only took care of her needs, but seemed to actually have a need to satisfy her. And he had. Satisfied her. Immensely.

But outside of bed, Nick was different: gentler, sweeter, almost shy. And he seemed embarrassed, almost flushed, when she'd caught him watching a made-for-TV romance, as if he didn't want to reveal that softer side of himself. A side she really liked.

Michelle slipped into a thin summer dress and took a matching cardigan from the hanger. She opted for high heels, wanting to feel sexy tonight. She inspected herself in the full-length mirror inside the closet door and twirled in front of it. She definitely looked presentable.

Taking a deep breath, she left the bedroom and walked back into the living room. The TV was off, and Nick wasn't sitting on the couch anymore. She turned on her own axis. Had he left without her?

"Nick?"

Footsteps coming from the kitchen made her turn. He came walking back into the living room, jerking his thumb over his shoulder.

"Hope you don't mind. I helped myself to some water."

Relieved, she exhaled. "Of course not. I'm sorry, I should have offered you something to drink earlier. I'm such a bad hostess."

He walked up to her, his eyes fairly drinking her in. "Oh, I wouldn't say that. You were very welcoming." He graced her with a smoldering look, one that made her knees tremble.

She wiped her suddenly damp hands on her dress, fidgeting.

"You look very nice," Nick murmured, taking another step closer that brought them chest-to-chest. With his index finger, he tipped her face up. "Absolutely stunning, in fact." He brushed his lips over hers in a feather-light kiss. "Now you're making me really hungry."

She swallowed hard, knowing he wasn't talking about food. And suddenly she didn't care about dinner anymore.

Nick took her by surprise when he stepped back and reached for her hand. "Let's go and have that first date, shall we?"

Almost disappointed that he hadn't thrown her down on the nearest flat surface, she followed him to the door. He took the small backpack that he'd tossed there upon entering her place and opened the door. Turning to the side table, Michelle grabbed her keys and shoved them into her handbag, then slung it diagonally across her torso, following Nick out and letting the door slide shut behind her.

Muggy air greeted her when she stepped outside and walked along the sidewalk next to Nick. Though it was still light, and would remain so for another few hours, dark clouds hung in the sky and she could almost smell the coming thunderstorm.

"Where are you taking me?" she asked, giving him a sideways glance.

Nick pointed in the distance. "It's only three blocks. Are you okay walking in those shoes or would you rather take a cab?"

She was touched by his concern. "I can walk, no worries."

"Good." He paused. "Tell me a little about yourself, Michelle. I'm curious about your life. Are you from D.C.?"

Hesitant to reveal anything about herself, she asked, "Are we doing twenty questions?"

"No, but we *are* on our first date, and from what I recall about first dates, people tell each other stuff like where they're from, what their favorite color is, things like that."

"From what you recall?"

"It's been a while since I've been on a date," he admitted, sounding almost embarrassed about it.

"How long?"

"Too long I guess, since it appears that the rules have changed since I last had one."

"The rules haven't changed," she admitted. "I just don't go on many dates."

"Well, we're a pair, aren't we?" He squeezed her hand and pulled it to his mouth, pressing a quick kiss on her knuckles. "So how about I start with something to break the ice?"

"I think we already broke the ice earlier."

Nick let out a belly laugh. "You're something, Michelle. I'm surprised no guy has snatched you up yet. Girls like you don't stay unattached for long."

She shrugged. "I'm not really the kind of girl who's looking for something permanent." It was a lie, of course, one she'd had to tell herself for a while now. Her life was way too chaotic to be thinking of settling down anytime soon.

"Mmm." Nick looked at her from the side.

To bridge the awkward pause that was building between them, Michelle asked casually, "So, what were you gonna tell me about yourself to break the ice?"

"What I do for a living. But if you're not interested, we can talk about something else."

"No, no, please. Tell me what you do."

"It'll probably sound boring. Maybe I should just make something up instead."

She stopped walking and turned to face him. "No, please don't. It can't possibly be all that boring. Besides, you don't have to impress me. You already got me into bed, remember?"

"How could I forget?" He winked and took her hand again to continue walking. "I work with computers."

"Doing what?"

"I make websites for people. You know, small businesses mostly. It's not a bad job, and I'm pretty good at it."

"That's great. You work for yourself, then?"

He nodded. "Independent contractor. I prefer that to being shackled to some company and having to be accountable to a boss."

"Yeah." Like she had to be accountable to Mr. Smith. And she hated that, hated that he was blackmailing her.

"How about you? What do you do?"

"Consulting," she shot back. "But I'm looking to make a change."

Like flee the country and disappear just as soon as she could set everything up and make sure Mr. Smith couldn't track her down. Until then, she had to play by his rules and execute his orders.

10

Nick felt the flash drive burn a hole in his pants pocket during the entire dinner at the cozy Italian neighborhood restaurant he'd taken Michelle to. Somehow he had to find a way to look at the contents of the flash drive, copy them, and put the memory stick back onto Michelle's key ring before she noticed it missing. Which meant that he had to continue being his charming self so Michelle would invite him back to her place after dinner.

It wasn't a hardship at all. Michelle was fun to be around. She had a quick wit and a sharp tongue, a wicked sense of humor, and an infectious laugh. Yet with every laugh they shared, with every eye contact they made, his guilty conscience grew. However, he had no choice but to continue his deception. Michelle could be the key to the information he needed, information that might save not only him and his fellow Phoenix agents, but maybe thousands—if not millions—of people. He couldn't let his own feelings get in the way of the greater good.

If Michelle was the person who was trying to prevent him from accessing the CIA's secret servers, then she knew something and would be able to lead him to the person who'd destroyed the Phoenix program and killed Henry Sheppard.

"Dessert?" Nick now asked, looking across the table at Michelle.

She shook her dark blond locks. "I'm too full."

"You sure?"

"Absolutely. How about we get out of here?"

He leaned over the table, lowering his voice to a seductive murmur. "I don't want the evening to end yet."

Her eyelashes fluttered. "It doesn't have to."

Her words sent a thrill through his core, and he snapped his head to the side, catching the waiter's eye. "Check, please."

When the waiter placed the tab in front of him, Nick pulled several bills from his wallet and placed them on the little tray.

"Do you always pay cash?" Michelle asked.

"My credit card got stolen last week. I'm waiting for the bank to send me a replacement," he lied.

In reality, he didn't use credit cards when he could avoid it. Cash was much harder to trace and safer if one wanted to stay off the grid.

"Ready?" he prompted Michelle and stood, offering her his hand to help her up.

"Ready."

As they walked to the exit, Nick eyed the signs to the restrooms. Now was the time, or things could get dicey for him later. He stopped.

"Sorry, do you mind if I stop at the restroom?"

"No, go ahead. Actually, I'll go, too."

Nick headed for the men's room and dove into the first stall. He sat down on the toilet, pulled his laptop from the bag and booted it up, while he pulled the flash drive from his pocket. The moment his computer started up, he unlocked it with his password, shoved the memory stick into the port, and copied the entire contents onto his hard drive. He had no time to look at what he'd copied, didn't even bother to shut down the computer properly or eject the stick safely, just slapped the lid shut and pulled the flash drive from the port.

A few seconds later, he left the stall and walked out of the restroom.

Michelle was already waiting for him. She smiled. "Beat you to it."

Nick shook his head in disbelief. "You can give a guy complexes, you know that?" He put his arm around her waist and guided her to the door of the restaurant.

The hostess opened it for them. "Thank you for your visit."

"Good night," Nick responded and walked out the moment a lightning bolt split the sky. Only a second later, thunder sounded above him, and the clouds opened up, unloading raindrops as thick as peas.

"Damn!" Michelle cursed, stopping under the awning in front of the restaurant.

Nick looked at her thin summer dress, which would most likely become transparent once soaked. And while he wouldn't mind that particular kind of view, he was sure she wouldn't appreciate it.

"I think we'd better try to get a cab."

"You've obviously never tried to get a cab during a D.C. downpour." She shook her head. "We'll be standing here all night. I say we make a run for it."

He looked at her with a newfound appreciation for her no-frills attitude. "You sure?"

"You chicken?"

"No, just a gentleman." He grinned and took her

hand. "But since you clearly don't care about gentlemanly manners, I'll submit to your wishes."

Michelle winked at him. "Submit, huh?"

He rolled his eyes. "Don't get any ideas!"

He tugged at her hand, and they dashed out from underneath the protective canopy, running along the sidewalk. Instantly they were doused from above as if they'd stepped into a shower stall, while passing cars splashed them from the side. There was no escaping the water.

Luckily, Nick knew that his computer was well protected in its water- and shockproof cover inside his backpack.

It didn't take them more than four minutes to bridge the distance from the restaurant to Michelle's apartment. When Michelle opened her handbag to dig for her keys upon reaching the main entrance of her apartment building, Nick stretched out his hand and took them from her.

"Allow me, milady!" he said gallantly and bowed in an effort to distract her.

"Playing knight now, are you?"

He turned toward the door, hiding what he needed to do by showing Michelle his back. "Knight in shining armor actually," he said jokingly, buying himself more time to hook the flash drive back onto the key ring. He turned the key in the lock an instant later and opened the door.

Michelle rushed inside and he followed, shaking off the excess water from his hair and body while the door fell shut behind him. Michelle was already climbing the stairs, eager to get to her apartment, and he hurried after her. Her wet dress showed every curve of her body, clinging to her like a second skin. Through it, he could see that all she wore beneath was a thong, no bra. The sight made him hard in an instant.

Arrived at the door to her apartment, Nick pulled Michelle into his arms, unable to hold back his desire for her a moment longer.

"Do you know how sexy you look just now?"

"I look like a drowned rat," she claimed, laughing.

"A very sexy drowned rat," he conceded and pressed her against the door, sinking his lips onto her hot mouth. Her lips parted immediately, allowing him to kiss her without restraint. Lust boiled up in him. Collecting all his remaining self control, he severed the kiss, breathing hard.

"We'd better get inside before we give your neighbors a show they'll never forget." He reached past her and inserted the key into the lock.

"You're a bad influence," Michelle said, but the sparkle in her eyes confirmed that she didn't consider this to be a bad thing.

Nick pushed the door open and nudged her inside. He tossed the keys onto the side table and kicked the door shut, before setting his backpack down. Then he pressed her against the wall beside the bathroom door.

"Yeah, a really bad influence," he mumbled and crushed her lips with his.

11

Her clothes were clinging to her, and Michelle knew she looked terrible, but it didn't matter, because Nick made her feel beautiful. His mouth was hungry on hers, his hands eager to free her of her wet clothes, his pelvis rocking against her with an urgency and rhythm that left nothing to her imagination.

With trembling hands she tugged on his shirt, pushed it up, so she could slide her hands along his naked skin and caress him. He shuddered under her touch, sending a thrill through her at the knowledge that she could bring this man to his knees.

For a brief instant, Nick released her lips and pulled his shirt over his head, revealing his muscled torso. Lust surged inside her, making liquid heat pool at her sex. Nick's hands were on her dress then, unzipping it in the back and pushing the fabric down to her waist. Another shove and the dress slid past her hips and pooled around her feet.

Her nipples were hard peaks, exposed to his view now because she didn't wear a bra. His eyes turned molten when he stared at her, his hands already reaching for her breasts, touching them, his knuckles sliding over her damp skin, making her shiver all over.

"Fuck, baby!"

Then his mouth was back on hers, his hands kneading her breasts, teasing her nipples, while farther below, he rubbed his erection against her center. But there was still too much fabric between them. She wanted all those barriers gone. She needed a skin-on-skin contact, needed to feel him as close as was humanly possible.

She pushed against him, made him step back a little so she could reach the button of his pants. She flipped it open then went for the zipper.

"Damn it, Michelle," he cursed when she pushed his pants and boxer briefs down to his thighs and freed his eager shaft. "I'm not gonna last."

"I don't care."

She pushed his pants down to his ankles and followed in the same direction, until her head was level with his cock. God, he was beautiful. Pumped full with blood, thick veins snaking up its sides, his hard-on demanded all her attention. Eagerly, she wrapped her hand around the root, gripping him firmly so he couldn't escape.

Nick groaned. She looked up and saw him bracing himself against the wall behind her with both hands, his eyes pinning her.

"If you're gonna do that," he said hoarsely, "then do it quickly while I still have an ounce of control left."

By the looks of his straining neck muscles, it wouldn't be long until he lost that self control. Already now Nick seemed like putty in her hands—rock-hard putty. And she rather liked that feeling. In fact, loved the power it gave her. The power to make a man surrender.

"Mmm." Michelle licked her tongue over the purple head of his glorious shaft and gathered up the moisture that had collected there. The salty taste spread in her mouth, making her hungry for more.

Nick let out a shuddering breath, while his hips jerked toward her. "I need... I need to..."

She knew what he needed and gave it to him. Her lips wrapped around the tip of his erection. Slowly, with her tongue along the underside of his cock, she descended on him, taking him as deep into her mouth as she could.

A loud moan bounced off the walls of her small hallway.

Gently, Michelle let his cock withdraw from her, before sliding down on him again. Her hand remained at his root, guiding him in and out. With every descent and every withdrawal she increased the speed and pressure. Nick's hips flexed in the opposite direction to hers, his cock thrusting into her mouth as she sucked him deeper.

"Fuck! Michelle!" he cried out, throwing his head back. "You've gotta stop."

But despite his impassioned plea, Nick continued moving his hips back and forth, fucking her mouth frantically. Eagerly, she licked and sucked him, moved her hand up and down the long stalk, ready to take what he was willing to give her, when he suddenly pulled back.

Her gaze shot up to him and she saw him breathe heavily. "I need a condom. Now!" He reached for her, pulled her up. "Do you have any?"

She motioned to the bathroom door. Before he could move—impeded by the pants around his ankles—she was already in the bathroom, rummaging through a drawer. When she turned around, condom in hand, he was behind her, fully naked now, stalking toward her.

He took the condom from her hand, ripped the

package open with his teeth and rolled the latex over his cock, closing his eyes briefly and clenching his jaw as he did so. Then he pinned her with his eyes.

"Turn around," he ordered gruffly, motioning to the sink.

Without protesting, she pivoted. His hands were on her an instant later, bending her over the bathroom countertop.

Michelle lifted her head and watched in the mirror, how his passion-clouded eyes roamed over her backside. With a harsh exhale, he hooked his thumbs into the waistband of her thong and pulled it down to her thighs.

Then their eyes met in the mirror.

She felt the tip of his cock at her wet entrance, nudging her nether lips apart. His jaw tightened a moment before he plunged into her, seating himself balls-deep.

Michelle shuddered under the impact, but Nick's hands on her hips were holding her so tightly that she wouldn't slam into the counter despite his forceful move.

"See what you do to me?" he murmured and withdrew, only to thrust back into her with even more force.

"I thought you liked it," she teased, loving the knowledge that she was driving him wild. She liked this side of him, just as much as she liked his quiet, boy-next-door side.

"I love it," he confessed, meeting her eyes in the mirror. "Too much, in fact. Now you're gonna pay the price, baby."

It was a price she had no trouble paying. She loved the way he took her, like a man who knew what he

SEEK

wanted and didn't take no for an answer. Like a man who was used to his orders being followed. His gruff command to turn around hadn't turned her off in the least. On the contrary, it aroused her. To be dominated like this turned her on, made her wild, and awakened something primal in her, something entirely female.

"Yes, take me!" she cried out, not caring if that made her sound desperate or submissive. All she wanted was to be taken by him, to feel him pound into her with his cock until neither of them could move any longer.

"Yeah, I'll take you," he promised, bringing one hand around her hip to slide it to her front.

A wet finger on her clit made her gasp with pleasure. His hot breath at her ear, whispering to her made her close her eyes in anticipation.

"I'll fuck you until you come, and then I'll do it again, and again, and again. Is that what you want, Michelle, me taking you like this?"

"Yes," she choked out on a shallow breath. "Oh God, yes!"

She lost her ability to form a coherent thought after that. All she felt was Nick's cock sliding into her from behind, while his fingers strummed her clit as if it were a string instrument he wanted to tease a sound from.

When that sound finally came, it was a relieved outcry bursting from her lips, while her body shuddered under the power of her orgasm. Just before she collapsed, she felt Nick's cock spasm inside her, a loud moan accompanying his climax.

~ ~ ~

It always started with somebody handing him a tall

231

glass of iced tea. It was no different this time. The hand, wrapped around the inviting beverage, came into view, though the person it belonged to never did.

Nick tried to force his head to turn this time, but his body didn't obey him. He only saw the cool liquid he so desperately needed and reached for it.

Don't drink it! he tried to scream to himself. But no sound came over his lips.

Instead, he lifted the glass to his lips and gulped down the ice-cold tea until only ice cubes were left. For a moment he closed his eyes, enjoying the cooling effect the drink had, but it was only temporary.

He knew where he was, and yet he didn't. The terrace of a large house. A garden beyond. Then the shore. Waves splashing against the narrow strip of sandy beach. An ocean maybe? Or a lake? A large one.

He gazed out onto it, following the ripples on its surface.

Only five sailboats were on the water despite the sunshine and the ample wind that filled their sails and propelled them forward. Why only five when the entire lake should be brimming with activity? When the houses to the left and right all had boat docks, and yachts waiting to be taken out onto the water. To be played with.

Did they know like Nick knew? Did they too sense the impending doom? Had they fled already, knowing it was too late to change the outcome?

"Please don't do this," Nick begged.

From behind him, a voice replied, "It's done."

But he couldn't accept that. He had to do what needed to be done.

His laptop sat on the wooden table, several windows

open. Green computer code scrolled in one black window so fast, it looked as if it were raining numbers and letters.

His eyes blurred, and he tried to focus them, tried to make sense of it all. But his gaze drifted to the other window, the one that showed a video feed of a large concrete building. The angle was so narrow that he couldn't make out where the building was located. It could have been in the middle of a city or right in a desert, and Nick wouldn't have known.

In a third window, a clock was counting backward.

Abort. His lips formed the word automatically. He had to stop it. Save what was there to be saved.

From the corner of his eye, he noticed the white sails whizz by him. He spun his head in their direction and saw them fight against the increasing wind. But he knew if he didn't stop the countdown, they would have to fight against something even stronger than the wind. And they would lose.

"Abort," he whispered and lifted his hands to the keyboard, noticing all of a sudden how heavy they were, as if filled with lead. Like bricks, they landed on the keys, creating a row of gibberish among the scrolling code.

He willed his pinky to press the *escape* button to clear his typing, but his finger didn't move, didn't execute his brain's order.

Do it, damn it! Nick wanted to scream, but his tongue felt thick and sluggish.

He stared at his hands, barely able to focus on them now. They looked frozen in place, paralyzed.

His heart began to race. Again and again he tried to move his fingers but failed. Failed not only himself, but his fellow Phoenix, and his country.

Nick held his breath like he always did. But no matter how often he'd seen this vision play out, he never looked away, always hoping against all hope that this time the outcome would be different. It wasn't.

The explosion on the screen was of massive proportions. The shockwave reached the water moments later, blasting the boats off their course and into the air, crushing them as if they were made of matchsticks. Bits of sail cloth flew like tiny birds in the churning air.

But by that time the shockwave had reached Nick, too, and he was flung in the air and catapulted toward the wall. For a split second before he hit it, he saw the house he'd been in: a mansion, though it wasn't his.

"Nooooo!"

His own scream pulled him from the vision. Bathed in sweat, he reared up. There was darkness all around him. He was in bed. Next to him, somebody moved.

"Nick?" It was the panicked voice of a woman.

Breathing hard, he tried to concentrate, tried to remember where he was. It took him three seconds to find his bearings.

"I'm fine," he said, already dragging his legs out of bed to sit up at the edge. "Just a bad dream. Go back to sleep, Michelle."

He felt her hand on his back and instinctively jerked away.

"But, you're—"

"I'm fine." He jumped up. "I'll take a shower if you don't mind, then I'll go."

Before Michelle could voice a protest, he left her bedroom and closed the door behind him. Outside in the hallway, he ran a shaky hand through his damp hair and tried to calm his pounding heart.

The vision, unlike all his other premonitions, came only during sleep and was becoming more frequent, as if to show him that the event he was seeing was coming closer. Yet he was no closer to averting it than he'd been three years ago when he'd first had this premonition after the murder of the founder of the top secret Phoenix program.

He was running out of time.

12

Michelle stared at the closed bedroom door Nick had just disappeared through. She leaned over to her bedside table and switched on the lamp. Soft light illuminated the otherwise dark room. She glanced at the alarm clock. It was just after five in the morning.

Her heart still raced. She'd been sound asleep when Nick's scream had woken her. It had sounded as if he'd been in mortal danger and for an instant she'd wondered if somebody had broken into her apartment. But it was clear now that Nick had had a nightmare.

But why? What grown man had nightmares? It was the stuff kids dealt with, when they dreamed about monsters. Or maybe people who'd gone through some recent trauma. But Nick struck her as thoroughly balanced. But what if he wasn't? Had she made an error in judgment? What was wrong with the stranger she'd invited into her bed?

Heart beating in her throat, Michelle jumped out of bed and slipped on a T-shirt and a pair of yoga pants. When she entered the hallway, she heard the shower running. She flipped the light switch in the hallway. Careful not to make a sound, she looked around and quickly found what she was looking for.

Nick had dumped his backpack underneath the side

table. Darting a look back to the closed bathroom door, Michelle crouched down and opened the zipper. She peered inside. One compartment held his laptop. She didn't pull it out, but instead looked through the rest.

There wasn't much: a set of keys, a cell phone with a charger, and a power cable for the laptop. She was about to close the bag again, when she felt a bulge. She opened the zipper as wide as she could, but there was nothing to see. However, there was clearly something there. She let her fingers do the searching, until she finally found a hidden zipper.

Glancing back at the bathroom door to assure herself that Nick was still in there, she took a deep breath and unzipped the hidden compartment. Holding her breath, she reached her hand inside.

Her fingers connected with something cold. She ran them along the metal item and felt its outline. Her heart stopped as her hand wrapped around the handle of a weapon. Slowly, carefully, she pulled it out. A handgun. She wasn't an expert, but she could tell it was a pistol with a magazine.

Her hand shook. The trembling spread to her entire body.

Fuck! What was Nick doing with a gun?

Fear suddenly gripping her, she shoved it back into the compartment and zipped it up again, then closed the backpack and placed it back where she'd found it.

Looking around, she tried to think what to do. Was Nick dangerous? Was he a criminal? Who the hell was he? Her eyes darted around and she looked back into her bedroom. There, over the back of a chair hung Nick's pants. He hadn't taken them into the bathroom with him.

She dashed into the bedroom and took the pants off the chair, searching the pockets. She pulled out his wallet. Casting a nervous look over her shoulder, she opened his wallet and examined the contents. Cash. A drivers license. She pulled it out, read it. The name was Nicholas Young, the address was in Washington D.C. It had been issued two years earlier. Hadn't he said that he'd only just moved to Washington? How could he have a drivers license that was already two years old?

She looked through the remaining compartments of the wallet and felt something rigid. She dug her fingers into it and pulled out the item: a credit card. Her breath caught in her throat. Last night, he'd paid cash, claiming that his credit card had been stolen and he hadn't received a replacement card yet. Why would he say that, when clearly he had one? Was it an old one that had expired? She looked at the expiration date. No, it was still valid. Then her eyes darted to the left of it, where his name was embossed.

She slapped her hand over her mouth so she wouldn't scream. The name didn't match his drivers license. Marcus Tremont it said there.

Shit!

Shaking now, she shoved the wallet back into his pants pocket and ran into the living room. She pulled her computer from her bag and switched it on. While it booted up, she drummed her fingers on her thighs, continuously darting nervous looks back to the hallway. But the water in the shower kept running.

The moment her computer was on, she unlocked the screen with her password and pulled up a browser. She first searched for Nicholas Young. There were too many hits. The name was too common. Even an actor and a baseball star were among the search result. She would need time to go through them all.

Damn!

She typed in Marcus Tremont instead. There was only one Marcus Tremont. She clicked on the Facebook link. The profile picture was blank and there were no posts in his timeline, none she could see without being his friend anyway.

Who was Nick? And why was he here?

The answer hit her in the face like a closing door. Smith! Her *Deep-Throat-like* handler had to be behind it. Had he sensed that she was getting desperate to make a run for it? Did he already realize that she was preparing for her escape and wanted to make sure she didn't get away before she'd delivered what he wanted?

Why hadn't she thought of this earlier? He must have had tabs on her all along, having her watched every moment just in case she didn't comply with his demands. How stupid had she been! Nick running into her at the coffee shop and then, later, when she'd nearly stepped in the path of the taxi couldn't be a coincidence. Smith had set it up. And for all she knew, he'd even orchestrated it so that the taxi would almost hit her so Nick could save her and thus gain her confidence.

And she'd fallen for that cheap trick. Hadn't she seen this kind of thing happening countless times in movies and TV shows? She should have recognized it for what it was: a ploy. A trick for Nick to get close so he could watch her, maybe even gain her trust so she would tell him what she was planning.

She wanted to curse, to scream, but she couldn't. She had to play along now, not let him know that she knew, that she'd discovered his deception and was onto him.

239

She had to remain calm and behave as if nothing had happened.

The door of the bathroom opening nearly made her jump out of her skin.

Way to go, Michelle, she chastised herself silently. *That'll look normal.*

Nick didn't come into the living room, but headed straight for the bedroom. She heard him get dressed. She used the little time it bought her to take deep breaths and calm herself. When she heard his footsteps again, she quickly slammed the lid of her laptop shut and stood up.

"Michelle." His voice was hesitant.

Slowly, she turned, facing him. She tried a smile but failed.

"Sorry, I, uh… didn't mean to frighten you earlier." He ran a hand through his damp hair, looking utterly crushed. "The nightmares, they've become less frequent."

"Nightmares?" she echoed.

"Yeah. I was in Iraq. It was hell." He dropped his gaze to his feet.

"Iraq? You were in the war?" Did that explain at least his nightmares? It could. And oddly enough it could also explain other things. If he was ex-military, then it made even more sense that Smith had hired him to keep tabs on her.

"Yeah. One tour, but it was enough." He paused. "Listen, I'd better go. I've got work to do. I'll call you tonight?"

She nodded quickly, eager for him to leave her apartment. When he walked up to her instead, she tensed. He froze a foot away from her, clearly having noticed her apprehension.

"I'm sorry again, I know it must have scared you." He leaned in and pressed a kiss to her cheek.

"It's okay." Michelle forced a smile.

"Talk later, okay?"

Nick turned and walked to the door, grabbing his backpack on the way out. Only when the door snapped shut behind him was she able to breathe again.

"Oh God," she murmured to herself. "I've slept with the enemy."

13

Nick pulled his laptop from its compartment and placed it on his desk, before he tossed the backpack in the corner, angry at himself.

He was used to lying to cover his ass, but by God, he'd hated lying to Michelle, telling her he was an Iraq vet suffering from post traumatic stress. What a cheap shot that had been. There were lots of real Iraq vets out there dealing with PTSD and worse. And there he was, using them to cover up his real issues.

He'd never served in the military, though he'd served his country as a CIA agent for many years. He'd sacrificed his life to keep the people of this country safe, and how had they repaid him? By chasing him down like a dog. It was time to fight back.

But first things first.

Nick navigated to the folder where he'd saved the information from Michelle's flash drive and looked at the files. One was a picture file. He clicked it open. It was a portrait of Michelle. He recognized immediately what it was for, the lack of a smile and the way her head was turned, giving away its purpose. It was a passport picture. Only, why would she have a digital version of it? Passport pictures were normally submitted in printed form when applying through the post office.

Curious, Nick perused the other files.

One was a resume. He scanned it quickly. There wasn't much. A few jobs as a software consultant and a degree from an online university, as well as a list of computer programs Michelle was proficient in: C, Fortran, JavaScript, Lisp, Python. She clearly knew her stuff.

Nick closed the document and continued. A small text file drew his attention. He opened it and read the two lines of information: Jennifer Miller, birth date: May 5, 1984, hair: dark blond, eyes: blue, height: 5'7". All information needed for a passport, though the name didn't match. Was Michelle Andrews trying to become Jennifer Miller? To what purpose? He opened the next text file. It only contained one item: an email address.

Nick logged into one of his bogus email accounts and drafted a message, leaving the text blank and only putting one word into the subject line: *Inquiry*. He pressed *Send* and waited. Sixty seconds later, his email account pinged. The message landing in his inbox was from *System Administrator*, and the subject line said *Undeliverable*. The text stated that the email address didn't exist. Just as he'd suspected. Whoever had used this email address had already deactivated it.

"What are you up to, Michelle?" he murmured.

He opened document after document. Job applications and documents with hyperlinks. He followed the links and reviewed them in his browser: research on different countries, one leading directly to a PDF document. He flew over the text, wondering what she was looking for, when one word stuck out: *Extradition*. He read the sentence. *There is no extradition treaty in place with the U.S.*

It was clear now: Michelle was running from the law.

He tried to piece together what he knew about her so far: a past with Anonymous that could have gotten her into trouble with the authorities; electronic files that could be used to get a fake passport; a bogus email address that most likely put her in touch with a person who could procure such a passport; research on countries that didn't extradite criminals back to the US; and Michelle being the prime suspect for trying to keep him out of the CIA's servers. It all fit. Somebody who knew about her past had to have hired her. Had that person offered her a large sum of money, maybe even provided the contact to get a fake passport so she could start a life far away from here?

Or was somebody using her past against her, forcing her to flush him out, and she was doing this against her will? Either scenario was possible. In any case, it meant he couldn't trust Michelle, though he'd already known that from the start. The information he'd uncovered from her flash drive only cemented what he'd already suspected: that she was trying to get the drop on him. But he was smarter.

Just as he was opening the next document from Michelle's drive, an alert pinged in his inbox. He switched screens and read it.

Finally.

The notification was from an advertisement he'd placed on the Dark Web. He logged off his current internet connection. From his desk drawer he retrieved a pre-paid jetpack and jammed it into one of the slots in his laptop, then connected to the web from there. He would dispose of the jetpack to ensure his ISP address remained secret after he was done so nobody would be able to trace him to his current location.

It took only moments until he was in the right place on the Dark Web to retrieve the message that had been sent to him. There was no sender's name. But the message itself was compelling. Somebody had seen his meeting request and wanted to set up a time and place. All keywords the person used were the right ones. Keywords the Phoenix used. While some of them could of course be used by anybody, the fact that all of them were in the message pointed to the conclusion that the person who was contacting him was a fellow Phoenix.

Still, Nick knew to be careful. There was always a chance that an enemy was coercing a Phoenix to reveal his secrets by whatever means necessary. Not even a Phoenix was immune to torture. Therefore, he'd take all necessary precautions before he set the meet. He wouldn't go in unarmed.

But he had to go. He couldn't let this opportunity go by. For too long he'd been searching for his fellow agents so he could finally unravel the mystery in his darkest premonition. He needed to stop whatever was going to happen. It was big. He knew that instinctively, bigger than what he could handle himself.

He needed help.

Help only another trusted Phoenix could provide. It was worth the risk.

14

The message had been clear. Michelle was to go to a specific spot in Constitution Gardens tonight and record what she saw. There would be a clandestine meeting. If she performed well, Smith had texted her, maybe she'd even be rewarded for it. Michelle scoffed at that. What kind of reward was Smith thinking of? To kill her quickly should the people who were meeting clandestinely in some deserted corner of Washington discover her and try to torture her to tell them what she knew—which was nothing—so she wouldn't have to suffer?

Great. It was bad enough that she had to spy on some hacker online, now Smith actively put her in harm's way by sending her out on a nightly mission. Hell, she wasn't trained for this. Why didn't he use one of his covert agents—which he surely had, Nick being one of them!—or do the dirty job himself? No, he had to use a weak woman for that, one who didn't even know karate or any other form of self-defense. A fat chance in hell—that's all she'd have when it came to survival.

Damn it.

In her hiding place, behind a bush, she kept quiet though she wanted to scream at the injustice of it all. Wasn't it enough that Smith had assigned her a watcher?

Michelle had arrived under cover of darkness only

moments after the sun had gone down and it was dark enough so nobody would notice her creeping around and get suspicious. Hours before the presumed meeting was to take place, she was already waiting, poised to record whatever she saw.

Meanwhile, the mosquitoes swirled around her, eating her alive. It hadn't cooled down despite the thunderstorm the night before. In her black, long-sleeved T-shirt and her dark pants, she felt too hot and woefully overdressed, though it meant that the mosquitoes only caught her hands, neck, and face, although she could swear that some were trying to work their way up her pant leg. She slapped at her lower leg, where she felt the sting, and cursed under her breath.

Bloodsuckers!

There were still tourists around, taking pictures of the various monuments in the park, which were lit up by strong spotlights. Lincoln Memorial, of which she had a good view across the Reflecting Pool, was one of them. People were taking pictures on the stairs, selfies with the sitting statue of President Lincoln behind them, or group photos, asking other tourists for help. But the longer she waited, the less people she saw. The tourists finally withdrew, returning to their hotels or other, more interesting sights by night.

Michelle crouched between the bushes, looking around herself. She didn't want to miss the arrival of the mysterious strangers or be spotted by them.

The silence in the large park was eerie. There was the sound of birds fluttering in the dark, and the annoying buzzing of some overeager flies and mosquitoes, but all human-made sounds were in the distance. Cars driving on Constitution and Independence Avenues, others crossing Arlington Memorial Bridge. In the dark, the sounds carried far. But they were also soothing, almost comforting, because they confirmed that normal life continued—while her life was taking a turn for the worse. She knew it. She could sense it in her bones, feel it by the way the hairs at her nape stood up as if to protest.

She shouldn't be here. She should be on a plane to South America, fake passport in hand. But she was still waiting for that fake passport. Her contact—recommended by an old friend from Anonymous—had urged her to be patient. If the passport needed to pass federal inspection at a US airport, it needed to be perfect. He couldn't rush it, but he'd promised to deliver it in two days, just before her ultimatum with the mysterious Mr. Smith ran out. She would be out of here before he could throw her into prison. And he would, given half a chance, because the hacker she'd been so close to nailing, had gone dark. The entire week, she'd not seen his digital signature anywhere. As if he knew she was onto him.

The sound of a twig breaking shattered the silence and made her snap her head in the other direction. She tried to adjust her eyes, searching in the dark for the person who'd created that sound, but saw nothing. The area it had come from was too dark—not lit up like the monuments around her. She would need night-vision goggles. Smith should have thought of that. Clearly, her blackmailer wasn't quite as smart as he pretended to be. How was she going to see anything, and know what to record? Hell, her cell phone wouldn't be able to pick up anything if she didn't even know which direction to point it in.

There, another sound! This time, it was clearly footsteps. Their echo was difficult to pinpoint. Was the sound coming from the right or the left? She shifted, and her T-shirt got snagged on a branch. She jerked back. The ripping sound resonated in the silence.

Shit!

~ ~ ~

The person hiding in the bushes was no Phoenix, Nick assessed immediately. He was close enough that he would have been able to sense the special aura a Phoenix gave off. It was something he'd discovered early on after he'd been recruited by Henry Sheppard. He'd instantly felt a kindred spirit with the older man, as if he'd known him a long time.

Sheppard had told him that it was like recognizing like. One Phoenix recognizing another. It was a survival instinct. Nature had made sure that some of its special children knew each other and could come to each other's aid should it be necessary.

Nick had no illusions that the person hiding in the darkness meant him harm and wasn't just a lost tourist. He recognized that the stranger was holding his breath, trying not to be heard. But he couldn't see his would-be assailant, because the area was pitch-black, while only a few yards away there was sufficient light from the monuments and the city itself to see outlines and shapes.

Not knowing what training the person lying in wait had, Nick took no chances. One wrong move and he could have a bullet in his brain or a knife in his heart. And he was rather fond of his life and not ready to trade it in for an eternal sojourn in a wooden box six feet under.

Nick had undergone basic CIA training at The Farm, training that encompassed self-defense, hand-to-hand combat, and weaponry, even before he'd been recruited into the Phoenix program by Sheppard. He'd been selected by a CIA recruiter for his computer skills right out of college and assigned to data security at Langley a full two years before Henry Sheppard had taken notice of him. Even after being drafted in the Phoenix program, he'd continued to work at Langley in his less secret capacity as a data security analyst.

Nick had become particularly fond of his Glock, a handgun that handled well and was currently holstered under his left arm, ready to be deployed at a moment's notice.

Setting one foot in front of the other, treading lightly so as not to make any sounds, Nick stalked toward the copse of trees and bushes. He circled to the left, slowly approaching. His breathing was even and silent, his eyes trained on the target in front of him. While night-vision goggles would have come in handy and given him a definite advantage, he knew he could make up for this lack of equipment with his other senses—including his impeccable sharpshooting skills.

Calmly, he reached into his jacket and pulled the Glock from its holster. A few more steps. He was close.

A rustle in the bushes as if the assailant was moving, shifting, sensing that he'd been discovered.

But it was too late. Nick was already onto him. Behind him. Only a few feet now. Nick lifted his leg, set it down a foot ahead of him. He felt the twig beneath his sole too late and cracked it. The sound echoed in the night.

A sharp intake of air was the response, then a sudden movement right in front of him: the stranger spinning around to face him. He wasn't tall for a man, average in fact, and lightly built.

Nick lunged forward, slamming the man into the tree. A split second later, he pressed the Glock's cold barrel to the would-be assailant's forehead, cocking it.

"One wrong move, and this bullet will make mush out of your brain."

A loud gasp, the sound too high-pitched to come from a man, startled him for a second. Just as the uncontrollable trembling did.

"Nick! Don't!"

Shock charged through his bones, paralyzing him for an instant. But then his training kicked in.

"Michelle!" he ground out. He hadn't expected her, though he should have.

"Oh God, thank you," she let out, seemingly relieved. "Please, take that gun away. You're scaring me."

"Am I?" It could all be a ploy to get him to lower his gun so she could take him out. He moved closer. "Are you armed?"

"Armed? No!"

He used his free hand to frisk her, first her front, then he reached behind her to check if she'd tucked a gun into the back of her jeans. She hadn't.

"What are you doing?" Panic laced her voice. "Nick, tell me what's going on!"

"I was gonna ask you the same question." He moved closer now, close enough so he could make out her facial features.

Yeah, it was definitely Michelle, dressed all in black

like a ninja, her dark blond hair hidden under a scarf she'd tied at her nape. At least she hadn't blackened her cheeks with shoe polish.

"I was just, uh, you know, going for a walk," she mumbled.

He pressed her harder against the tree trunk. "Try again, *honey*!"

She pulled her shoulders down, puffing up her chest. "I swear! I was just minding my own business, and then I heard something, so I figured, I'd hide. You know, there are muggers in the park at night."

He scoffed. "Yeah, right. Then why the fuck would you take a walk in a dark park at night when it's so dangerous, huh? Care to explain that?"

"Well, then what are you doing here? Spying on me?"

"Don't try to turn the tables on me. We both know what's going on here. You set me up to come to the park."

"To do what?" she spat, defiance spewing from those lips he'd devoured the night before.

"To kill me," he ground out, shoving his face practically into hers. Her blue eyes sparkled now, picking up light from somewhere in the vicinity as she glared at him.

Michelle gnashed her teeth. "With what, you idiot? Maybe with the gun you're still pointing at my head?"

He had to give her that: she wasn't caving easily, more proof that she was smart and out to trick him.

"Now get off me!" She tried to push him, but he was heavier and stronger, and had no intention of relinquishing his superior position just because she was a woman.

"Not until you tell me what you're doing here. Were

you the one setting up the meet?"

"What meet?"

The way her eyes shifted at her words, he knew she was covering, buying herself some time to get out of her predicament.

"You know what meet." He looked her up and down. "Of course it was you, wasn't it? Who else would know how to navigate the Deep Web but a former member of Anonymous?"

Her chin dropped and air rushed from her lungs. She tried to catch herself, but it was too late; she'd already given herself away.

"I don't know what you're talking about."

"Don't you?" With his free hand, he reached for her necklace and pulled on it, until the pendant emerged from underneath her black long-sleeved T-shirt. "Odd choice for a piece of jewelry, don't you think?"

Her eyes narrowed. "I can wear what I like."

"Sure you can. And I can draw whatever conclusions from it that I like. And that, *my sweet*, is a Guy Fawkes mask, the symbol of Anonymous. Which you were a member of. What happened? The authorities catch you when you were a hacker?"

"I was never a hacker! And you have no right to question me. You're the one who's got something to hide, not I." She motioned to the gun he was still pointing at her head. "You're the one with the gun, remember?"

"And that is exactly the reason why you should be answering my questions truthfully and not dishing up any more lies. I'm growing impatient, Michelle, and you know what happens when I get impatient?"

She stared at him quizzically.

"My hand starts to tremble. It's a little tick, you know."

"You wouldn't."

He shook his head. Michelle had courage, the kind of courage that could get her killed one day. "Don't test me. Tell me the truth, Michelle, or would you rather I guessed what you're up to?"

"Be my guest!"

"Well, then." He loosened his hold on her by a bit while he lowered the barrel to her neck. "You were a hacker associated with Anonymous. You got caught at some point, hacking into some government agency or another. You're talented. So talented in fact that they made you an offer: to work for them. How am I doing so far?"

She pressed her lips together.

"Good. I'm on the right track then. Shall I continue, or would you rather take over and tell me the rest?"

"There's nothing to tell."

He slammed his fist into the tree trunk next to her head. She flinched.

"Goddamn it, Michelle, I swear I'm going to strangle you if don't drop your stubbornness and tell me what I want to know. Don't you get it? This is not a game. Lives are at stake here." He moved in, bringing his face to hover only inches from hers. "Were you the one to set up the meet?"

She shook her head, trembling now. "I was told to record whoever was showing up here." Tears brimmed at her eyes. "I didn't know it was going to be you."

He breathed a sigh of relief. Finally, Michelle was talking. Softening his voice, he asked, "The person you work for, who is he with? CIA? NSA?"

She gave a helpless shrug. "I don't know."

Nick growled. "Michelle."

"I swear I don't know." She sucked in a breath. "I don't know who he is. He contacts me and tells me what to do. I have no choice."

He studied her face for a moment, wheels clicking into place now. "His offer to work for him wasn't really an offer, was it?"

Silently, she shook her head and dropped her lids.

"Is that why you're getting a fake passport made?"

Her head shot up and she pinned him with her eyes. "How do you know that?"

"The flash drive on your key ring. You had image files and information on it that pointed to it."

She braced her hands at her hips, suddenly furious. "You took my memory stick? That's private property. You had no right!"

He shrugged. Private property rights weren't really his concern right now. He had bigger fish to fry. "Should have encrypted it."

"There's no need to encrypt it! It never leaves my sight."

He pasted a grin on his face. "It did when you took a shower."

"You, you…" Her hands came up as if she wanted to hit him, but he stopped her by pressing the gun harder against her neck.

Her eyes darted to it. "Don't you think that's a little overkill right now? You've assured yourself already that I'm not armed. Or do you use that gun as an extension of your dick?"

He chuckled involuntarily. He couldn't really blame her for being angry; neither could he take that kind of insult lying down. "My dick needs no extension, as you well know."

She huffed indignantly.

But she'd made her point, and knowing what he knew of her so far, Michelle posed no physical threat to him. He put the safety back on the gun and holstered it, but didn't step back, keeping her trapped between his body and the tree trunk.

"Now that we've established the size of my dick, let's continue. What else did your mysterious handler want you to do?"

"Just record the people who were going to meet here and then text him the file."

"I don't mean tonight. I mean in general. You were stalking me online, trying to prevent me from hacking into a server."

Her mouth gaped open for a second, before she spoke. "So that was you."

"Yeah, that was me. You're pretty good, but you made a mistake."

"How?"

"Doesn't matter. I traced your IP address to the coffee shop."

She nodded. "So it wasn't a coincidence then. Too good to be true. You played me all this time. Got into my pants just so you could figure me out, that it?" She tossed him an angry glare.

"And trust me, I enjoyed it, and so did you."

"Jerk! I would have never slept with you had I known—"

He pressed his body to hers, grinding his hips into her pelvis, snatching her wrists with both his hands, and pinning her against the tree.

"You don't know anything, Michelle. Or do you know how I fought with my conscience whether to seduce you or not? Whether to take you to bed or not? How I agonized over it, knowing that it was wrong to touch you when I knew I was doing it to get information from you?"

He lowered his lids, only looking at her parted lips now.

"While all this time, I wanted you, wanted to be with you and make love to you as if we were normal people who are attracted to each other. Do you know that I wished that my suspicions were wrong? That you weren't the hacker they'd sent to catch me?"

He released her wrists and shoved a hand through his hair, realizing something for the first time.

"Damn it, I slept with you because I wanted you. I could have gotten the information I needed by other means, too. By breaking into your place, or by mugging you. I didn't need to get this close. But I wanted to."

Just like he wanted her now beyond all reason.

Unable to stop himself, he sank his lips onto hers, taking her mouth in a fierce kiss.

15

Nick's unexpected kiss robbed her of her breath. All Michelle could do now was cling to him. Her knees were too weak to support her weight, and only the tree at her back and Nick's body pressing into her were holding her up. She had no strength left, no fight left in her. Nick holding the gun to her head and having looked like he was actually going to use it had squashed any kind of resistance she'd tried to mount. She'd been surprised at herself that she'd held out as long as she had. But no longer. Because resisting Nick's kiss was impossible.

His words continued to swarm in her head, bouncing around like ricochets, urging her to believe what he'd said. That he hadn't wanted to use her. That he could have done it without sleeping with her. That he'd only slept with her because he'd wanted her.

She shouldn't believe it. No. She *couldn't*. He was only saying this to gain her trust so she would tell him everything. He knew too much already. But the way he acted made no sense. If he worked for Smith, why was he asking her all these things? He would already know that she was beholden to Smith. Or was she wrong? Was he in fact *not* one of Smith's pawns? Was he truly who he said he was, the hacker she'd been charged to find?

She pushed him away, making him release her lips.

Resisting the urge to rub her fingers over her mouth to verify that he'd truly kissed her with such passion, she glared at him instead. She needed answers.

"Are you saying you're not working for Smith? That he didn't send you to check up on me? To keep me in line?"

"Smith?"

"The guy who's making me do all this."

"Why would you think that?"

"Because it's just a little too convenient that you showed up just after he gave me an ultimatum."

Nick grabbed her shoulders. "What ultimatum?"

"If I don't deliver the hacker to him in ten days, he'll throw my ass in jail, though I think he didn't mean it. I think he plans to kill me because he's afraid I know too much."

"When did he give you the ultimatum?"

"A week ago yesterday."

"That leaves you two days."

Michelle swallowed hard. She could count, too. She knew her time was nearly up. "He said if I did well tonight, then, maybe, he'd let me off the hook." She snorted. "Like that's ever gonna happen now." She pushed back the tears of desperation that threatened to turn her into a pitiful mess and looked at him. "You've gotta let me go. I don't care what you're involved in. I don't even want to know. But I need to get out of here."

"You really think he's not gonna find out what you're planning? Don't you think he already knows that you're trying to procure a fake passport and are planning your getaway to South America?"

For a moment, she froze. How did he know about South America? Then it clicked. "The flash drive. It was on there, my research."

Nick nodded, his face a mask of seriousness now. "I think we can help each other."

She shook her head and her torso, trying to shake off his hands, but he held firm. "Yeah, that's how he put it, too. And look what happened. I'm in a deeper mess than I ever was before. Why would I trade in one blackmailer for another? How's that gonna help me?"

"I'll make sure you stay alive. I can protect you against Smith. If you help me."

"Do what? Don't you get it, Nick? You're the better hacker. You traced my digital signature. *You* found *me*. That wasn't supposed to happen. So how could I possibly help you when you're so much better than me?"

"It's not about that. It's about who you know. Smith. I need to get to him. If he knew that I was trying to get into the CIA's servers, then he also knows why. And that means he knows what I am."

Confused, Michelle shook her head. "Then why would he need me to find out? That makes no sense."

"It makes perfect sense," Nick shot back. "Because he knows *what* I am, but not *who* I am."

"I don't understand."

"You don't need to. All you need to know is that, if you tell me where I can find Smith, I'll help you disappear."

She shook her head in disbelief. "And how would you know anything about how to disappear?"

His head came closer, until all she could see were his penetrating eyes. "I disappeared three years ago. None of my enemies has been able to find me. And I'm right under their noses."

"Enemies? Like Smith? Is he your enemy?"

"If he's looking for me, most likely."

Curiosity got the better of her, even though she'd told herself and Nick only moments earlier that she didn't want to know what he was involved in. "What did you do?"

"It doesn't matter."

But she couldn't let it go. "Smith is government, I know that much, though I'm not sure what agency. Probably CIA. That means you did something the government didn't like. Espionage? Treason?"

Nick chuckled unexpectedly. "Those are mighty words for an anarchist like yourself."

"I'm not an anarchist. I believe in democracy. All I ever did was expose corruption and wrongdoing in the government."

"By hacking into classified information together with your friends at Anonymous, I suppose?"

"Look who's calling the kettle black. Besides, Anonymous is doing good things, too. They've pledged to shut down Al-Qaeda's online presence."

A smile formed on Nick's lips. "I'm not defending the government, Michelle, so you can stop your tirade. We're on the same side, or at least I hope I'm able to convince you to come to my side. You need me."

She contemplated his words, falling silent for a good long moment. Could he really deliver what he was promising? A new start, somewhere nobody could find her? Where she was safe from Smith and whatever government agency he worked for?

"You know you want to say yes. Let me make the decision easier for you."

She raised an eyebrow, wondering what he was planning, when his hand came up to caress her cheek.

"I won't hurt you, Michelle. I'll protect you. Trust me."

"Trust isn't a thing you can force."

"But it's something that can grow. You trusted me with your body, now trust me with your heart and your mind."

Slowly his lips approached her mouth. His breath whispered over her skin, tempting her to surrender, to give herself over to this man, this stranger who'd taken her body to unknown heights. At the same time, he'd lied to her. How could she trust him now?

"Nick, please…" She didn't know what she wanted to tell or ask him, didn't know why her fingers suddenly clawed into his shirt, holding him close.

"Baby, just let me help you. Let me keep you safe."

His lips brushed against hers so gently that she wasn't even sure he was touching her. Only when the pressure against her mouth intensified and a hot tongue swept over her trembling lips, did her resistance crumble.

"I'm not your enemy," he murmured against her lips and dipped his tongue between them.

The clicking of a gun paralyzed her and made Nick spin around in her arms.

"Wow, you sure are a smooth operator," a male voice drawled. "Guess even I can learn something from you."

16

Hand on his gun, Nick froze. The man standing only a few feet away, pointing a gun at him, caused the small hairs on his skin to stand to attention. A familiar tingling spread over his body, and he recognized it instantly. He was facing another Phoenix. This wasn't the mysterious Mr. Smith Michelle had told him about, or at least he hoped not. Only Michelle could confirm.

"Leave that gun right where it is," the man ordered.

Nick turned his head sideways, without taking his eyes off the stranger. Tall and athletic-looking, the man appeared to be in his early thirties, his dark blond hair buzzed short like a military cut. "Michelle, is this him? Is this Smith?"

She peered past him. "It's not his voice."

"What?" Did that mean what he thought it meant?

"I've never seen him. I only know his voice."

The stranger clicked his tongue. "You shouldn't have let me get the drop on you. Getting sloppy, my man."

The fact that the man addressed him as if they knew each other unnerved Nick, but he pretended that he didn't mind. "You're late," Nick said instead.

"Actually, I was early." He motioned to Michelle, who was now trying to squeeze past him. Nick pushed her behind his back. "Just like this one here showed up early. I was wondering what she was planning."

"We need to talk," Nick said firmly. Preferably without the other Phoenix pointing a gun at his head. Clearly the man had trust issues, and while Nick had been close to wiping out Michelle's reluctance to trust him with seduction, the same method wasn't going to work on his fellow Phoenix.

Not that he could blame the guy. Nick himself wasn't sure whether he could trust him either. Sheppard had warned them that should the program ever be compromised they'd have to assume the worst: that one of their own was a traitor. That one of their own could come to hunt them down, using the very skill that had made them brothers against them.

"Yeah. Alone," the stranger responded. "Lock her up."

"No!" Michelle protested, her head darting past Nick's shoulder.

The stranger's gun veered toward her. "You don't have a say in this."

"But I do," Nick countered, glaring at the man.

"Unarmed, you don't."

"You know I'm not unarmed."

The man cocked his head to the side. "And just how fast a draw are you?" He made a small movement with this gun. "It takes way less time to pull the trigger with the finger already on it. So don't be stupid." He motioned to a path beyond the copse of trees. "There's a shed down there, a couple hundred yards away. She'll be fine in there while we talk."

Nick glanced at Michelle, seeking eye contact. She stared back at him, frightened. "I won't let anything happen to you."

Why he felt he had to make her that promise, a promise he was determined to keep, he wasn't entirely sure, particularly since at this moment he wasn't in the position to make promises—not with a gun pointed at his head.

Michelle pressed her lips together and swallowed. "Walk."

Nick reached for Michelle's hand and followed the stranger's order. The time it took to reach the storage shed tucked away between some trees seemed to take forever. During the entire time, Nick went through various scenarios of how to turn the tables on the guy following them. But every scenario meant putting Michelle's life in danger. It was better to take a wait-and-see approach, until he could figure out whether the guy was friend or foe. At least, Nick would be alone with him at that point, which would mean he'd only have to worry about his own life.

The lock on the shed was perfunctory at best and gave way easily.

Nick urged Michelle into the dark interior, noticing her shiver at the prospect of being locked up.

"Take her phone," the stranger ordered.

Nick stretched his hand out, nodding to Michelle to follow the barked command. She dug into her pocket and pulled it out, placing it in his palm.

"I'll be back soon. Trust me."

She lifted her eyes to his then, staring long and hard at him. "I hope I won't regret this."

So did he. With a last look at her, he closed the shed door, when his fellow Phoenix handed him a chain.

"Loop it through the handle and that hook, then tie it."

Nick did as he was told. When it was done, he turned back to the man.

"This way."

They walked to a small hedge, where the guy stopped. "This'll do. She won't be able to hear us here."

Nick stopped and pivoted, watching to his surprise how the man holstered his gun and adopted a more relaxed stance.

"Name's Stingray."

"Fox." Suspiciously, Nick glanced at the gun now on Stingray's hip. "What changed your mind about me?"

"Overheard you talking to that woman for quite a while. Told me enough to know you're clean." He motioned to the shed. "Doesn't mean I was gonna reveal who I am in front of her. Neither should you. Can't trust anybody. Nice attempt though with her. She might play ball if we're lucky."

He ignored Stingray's last comments and asked instead, "And how am I gonna know whether you haven't turned against the Phoenix?"

"'Cause I'm telling you."

"Not good enough."

"You're still alive. Could have shot you a hundred times over and you wouldn't have known what hit you."

Nick couldn't argue with that, though that didn't mean he liked the guy's modus operandi. "Enjoy that macho stuff much?"

Stingray grinned from one ear to the other, looking overly smug. "It gets the job done."

"Don't think Michelle appreciated it much," Nick said dryly.

"I'm not really concerned with what a civilian is thinking. I've got more important things on my mind."

SEEK

"Which would be?"

"The Phoenix are under attack."

"No shit. You're only catching onto that now? Where were you three years ago?"

"In the same situation as you: running for my life. I'm sick of running and hiding. It's time to act."

"Why now?"

"Because the shit just hit the fan." Stingray glanced around, listening, looking, before turning his face back to Nick. "Talon is dead."

Though he didn't know the person Stingray was referring to, Nick assumed the name was a codename. "A Phoenix?"

Stingray nodded, a sad expression on his face. "He'd gone bad. Worked for our enemies. By the time he changed his mind and wanted to make good, it was already too late. But what's done is done. Can't wallow in the past. We know something big is coming. Something real bad."

"What is it?" Nick asked, drawing in closer, curious now.

"You have the dream, too? The dream about the inferno, the destruction?"

Shocked, Nick stumbled back a few paces, his mouth gaping. How could Stingray know about the horrific premonition that haunted his sleep?

Stingray nodded to himself. "So you do. Ranger has it, too. That's why I figured all of us have that same dream."

"Ranger? You're in contact with another Phoenix?"

"Yeah, he's in D.C. with me now. Along with Talon's sister, Lisa. Doesn't leave her side." He shoved a hand through his hair. "Anyway, Ranger and I realized that we see slightly different parts of that premonition, and it made us think that maybe others do, too. If we have all of the parts, maybe if we piece them together something might start making sense. That's why we started looking for others from the program."

"How do you know Ranger? You sure he's not bad like Talon?"

"We go way back. Military service," Stingray said, then stopped himself.

"I was never in the army," Nick interjected.

"Well, for all that was worth. Talon served with us, too. And he went bad. No guarantees, right?" He lifted his shoulders to a shrug. "I just know I can trust Ranger."

"What do you want from me?"

"Same you want from us. Resurrect the Phoenix, let them rise once more. That's why you put your feelers out there on the Dark Web for us to find you, isn't it? We're here, and we're ready to fight." Stingray put his hand on his holster to underscore his words.

"It's not that easy. This isn't gonna be a shootout at the OK Corral, buddy. I'm working a different angle." Nick looked his fellow Phoenix up and down, still unsure whether to trust him fully, though the fact that he was still alive—as was Michelle—was one point in Stingray's favor.

"As long as it'll take us to the same goal, I don't care much which way we're gonna play it." Stingray motioned toward the Lincoln Memorial. "Then let's go. I'll introduce you to Ranger and we'll come up with a plan of action." He already turned and took a few steps.

"I'm not leaving Michelle here."

Stingray stopped and looked over his shoulder.

"You'll have to. She can't come with us. She's a civilian, and she knows too much already. She's gonna lead our enemy right to us."

Nick squared his stance and fisted his hands at his sides. "I won't leave her. And that's final. We need her. She has information that's critical to what I'm planning."

"She's got pretty tits and a hot ass, that's all."

"Fucking asshole!" Nick growled and marched toward him.

"She's got no information. She admitted it herself. She's never seen that guy, that Smith. She won't be able to help us identify him, so put your dick back in your pants. Just because you've got the hots for her doesn't mean I'm gonna let her come."

Nick lunged at the guy and landed a blow in his face. His fellow Phoenix lost no time in punching back, knocking Nick's head sideways.

When Nick pulled his fist back for another hook, Stingray growled, "Damn it, Fox, why didn't you say she was your girl?"

Nick froze in mid-movement.

"She is your girl, isn't she? It's just… from the things I overheard earlier, I couldn't really tell. Apologies."

Slowly, Nick relaxed and dropped his fist. Apparently he'd just given away something to his fellow Phoenix that he hadn't realized himself yet: he didn't just have the hots for Michelle. He cared about her wellbeing, cared about *her*.

Without a word, Nick turned and walked toward the shed.

17

"Ouch!"

Michelle cursed as her hand slipped from the shovel's handle and another fingernail broke at her attempt to pry the door off the rickety shed. If she continued like this, she soon wouldn't have any fingernails left.

But she couldn't stop. She had to get out of here. What if that stranger was going to kill Nick? And once Nick was dead, the guy would take care of her. She shivered despite the muggy night air, and not only because she was in fear of her own life. To her surprise, she also worried about Nick, even though she shouldn't. He really didn't deserve it.

He'd insinuated himself in her life with lies. She didn't know what to believe anymore. Unfortunately that didn't stop her from caring about what happened to him. She'd spent a wonderful night with him and experienced a closeness to him that she hadn't felt with any other man before.

It's only sex, a voice in her head cautioned her. Was that true? Maybe. Then why was her heart contracting in pain when she imagined Nick lying on the ground, a bullet in his head? She tried to shake off the image. She couldn't let that happen. Somehow she had to help him.

She wanted to believe that he would do the same for her in the same situation, though she had no idea if he would really risk his life for her.

However, there had been that brief moment when the gunman had shown up, when Nick had shielded her with his broad back, almost as if it had been an automatic reaction. A protector instinct that had kicked in. Because she was a woman? Or because she was the woman he'd slept with the night before? If only she knew.

His words still echoed in her mind.

I didn't need to get this close. But I wanted to.

Was it the truth? She was inclined to believe it, not because she was a hopeless romantic—which she was— but because Nick clearly had the skills to get to the information he wanted without sleeping with her. Hell, he'd managed to steal her flash drive *and* return it without her noticing, because, yes, she'd checked her key ring the moment they'd thrown her into the shed. And the flash drive dangled from it as if it had never been gone.

Nick could have easily broken into her apartment while she slept and taken what he needed. There'd been no need to even make her acquaintance. Had that been his plan at the beginning?

"Doesn't matter," she muttered to herself.

Being in Nick's arms had felt right. And now he'd offered her a way out of her current predicament, and— goddamn it—she wanted to accept his offer and believe that he could deliver what he promised. But for that to happen Nick had to stay alive. She could always kick his lying ass later and tell him what she thought of him.

The sound of a rattling chain tore her from her musings.

Shit! Shit! Shit!

Panic rose from her stomach to her throat, sending her heart racing and making her breath stutter to a halt. She gripped the shovel's wooden handle more tightly, holding onto it with both hands now, raising it for leverage.

Somebody pulled on the chain. The door moved back and forth on its hinges for a moment, before opening outward.

"There we go."

It was the voice of the stranger.

Without another thought, Michelle took two steps forward, clearing the door frame, before she swung at the dark figure waiting there for her.

"Shit, no, Michelle!"

Nick's outcry came in mid-swing, too late to pull back the shovel and divert its path. The dark figure—the stranger—lunged to the side, avoiding a hit to his head, but a second person—Nick—stood beside him. As the shovel completed its arc it landed right on Nick's ass, sending him flying into the dirt.

Nick grunted.

She dropped the shovel and was already running to him, crouching down next to him.

"Fuck, Michelle, what did you do that for?"

"Oh my God, did I hurt you?"

A belly laugh from the stranger made her whirl around.

"I think you guys have some real relationship issues you've gotta work on," the stranger said.

"I was aiming at you," she ground out.

"Maybe you wanna teach her some target practice, Fox."

Groaning, Nick pushed himself up to stand and reached for her, pulling her up, looking past her to the other man. "I blame you for that hit, not her. If you hadn't insisted on locking her into a shed full of gardening tools, that wouldn't have happened." Then he looked at her. "Michelle, meet Stingray." He paused for a moment. "An old colleague of sorts."

She turned slowly, looking the stranger up and down. His gun was holstered at his side now, and he looked somewhat less scary than earlier. But only just somewhat. "Mr. Stingray."

The guy chuckled. "Not mister, just Stingray. You know, like Bono."

Michelle nodded, then glanced over her shoulder at Nick. "You gonna tell me what all this was about?"

"Later. We've gotta get out of here first." He motioned to Stingray. "Lead the way."

Nick made a motion to follow the guy, but Michelle grabbed his arm. "You're forgetting something."

"I told you, I'll fill you in later."

"That's not what I'm talking about." She sighed. "But if I don't text Smith a recording soon, he'll know something went down, and he'll be looking for me. I've gotta disappear right now, or he'll get me."

Nick froze.

"She's right," Stingray said, turning back to them.

The two men exchanged a look, then they both started grinning.

"Well, then let's give this Smith dude something to keep him busy," Nick said.

"Always wanted to do a little acting," Stingray replied. "You want me to do an accent? I can do Colombian real well."

Nick rolled his eyes, while Stingray pulled Michelle's cell phone from his pocket and navigated through the menu.

Michelle leaned into Nick, bringing her mouth to his ear. "Can you trust him? He was pointing a gun at your head earlier."

"Just as I was pointing a gun at yours. Yet you trust me."

"I didn't say that."

He moved his head back to lock eyes with her. "But you do." He tipped his chin in Stingray's direction. "I trust him about as much as you trust me right now. That'll have to do."

"Hey, if you lovebirds would stop doing whatever you're doing, we could get this show on the road."

Michelle stepped away from Nick abruptly, feeling herself blush in the dark. They weren't lovebirds, far from it. They were... Well, she didn't really know what they were. No word came to mind.

"I'm ready," Nick announced and walked up to Stingray.

18

Stingray opened the back of a dark van. "Hop on in."

Nick got inside and offered his hand to Michelle to help her up. The interior was dark, but not empty.

"Who's she?" a big, dark-haired man sitting on one of the benches asked, suspicion rolling of him in waves.

"Fox's girl," Stingray explained from behind them and hopped in, pulling the door shut behind him.

"Fox? So your name isn't Nick Young?" Michelle murmured next to him.

"I'll explain later." Right now there were more important things to discuss. He offered his hand. "You must be Ranger."

The other Phoenix nodded and motioned to his shoulder. "I'd shake your hand, but I had a bit of run-in with a bullet the other day, and it hurts like a bitch when I move my arm."

"No worries." Nick lowered himself on the bench and pulled Michelle to sit next to him.

"So you're Fox." Ranger looked past him at Stingray. "Did you explain to him why we're here?"

"Yep."

"Did you tell him about the premonition?"

"He did," Nick interrupted, sensing Michelle's inquisitive look. He squeezed her hand in reassurance, but this wasn't the time to go into long explanations about his special gift.

"You have 'em, too? The premonition about the inferno? The destruction? Your skin melting from the intense heat?" Ranger pressed.

"Yeah. Though I'm not actually there when it happens."

"What?" Stingray asked.

Nick turned his head and looked at him. "I'm somewhere at a lake, on a porch of some fancy mansion."

"Tell us more," Ranger insisted.

"I'm in front of my computer. Somebody I can't see gives me iced tea to drink. I think it's poisoned, because as soon as I drink it and try to type something into the computer, my hands are paralyzed. I can't do it. I can't stop it. I'm helpless. On the screen, I can see the explosion. Then the shockwave hits the lake and catapults five sailboats right out of the water, turns them into matchsticks. It's all I see before I get slammed against the side of the house."

"Sailboats on a lake?" Stingray mused, rubbing his chin. "Wonder whether that means anything."

"Could be a location," Ranger said. "And the person who gives you that iced tea that paralyzes you? Can you remember anything about him? Or her?"

Nick shook his head. "I only see a hand. It's a man, I can tell that much."

"Any rings, scars?" Ranger asked.

"I don't remember any."

"Next time you have the premonition, focus in on that. We need to find out who's behind this. In Stingray's and my visions we don't see any man. You might be the first one who's gotten a glimpse of our enemy."

"Next time?" Michelle interrupted, her gaze bouncing back and forth between the three of them. "You guys have visions? You're psychic?"

Ranger growled, tossing an angry look at Nick. "I thought she's your girl. You could have mentioned that she doesn't know what you are. Damn it."

Nick put a protective arm around Michelle, pulling her against his side. "She won't talk. We have the same enemies."

Michelle nodded quickly, tossing a scared look at Ranger. "I'm no threat to you."

"That remains to be seen," Ranger ground out. He glared at Nick. "Involving civilians. You should know better."

The pinging of a cell phone saved Nick from having to respond immediately.

Ranger pulled his cell from his shirt pocket and looked at the display. "That's Lisa at the safe house. She's worried that we're not back yet." He punched in a short message, then put the phone back in his breast pocket.

"Apparently Michelle's not the only civilian involved," Nick said with a motion to Ranger's cell phone.

Ranger's eyes narrowed.

Stingray cleared his throat. "Let's not get sidetracked here. Since it's pretty clear that we're all seeing the same thing, it's important that we get the Phoenix back together. Not only are our enemies trying to pick us off one-by-one, they're also planning something major. We have to prevent it. Problem is we don't know the others or where they're hiding." He motioned to Nick. "We were lucky to find you."

"I've been working on a solution for that for a while."

Both Ranger and Stingray slid forward on the bench opposite Nick's.

"What solution?" Stingray asked.

"Sheppard kept a private file on all his Phoenix. Names, pictures, backgrounds. Separate from the CIA's classified personnel file—which I have the feeling has been destroyed by our enemy already."

"And Sheppard's file? You think it still exists? Wouldn't whoever killed him have destroyed that one, too?" Ranger asked.

"I don't think so. I was able to figure out that Sheppard used a second login at the CIA. The only thing is, I can't find it."

"I don't get it," Stingray said.

"It's not easy to explain, but I've found digital fingerprints of somebody accessing certain files, but I can't trace who. In the end it always loops back to Sheppard's old login, and that's been disabled long ago."

"A ghost login," Michelle said.

Nick whirled his head to her. "You know what I mean?"

She nodded eagerly. "I've heard of something like it." She looked at Ranger and Stingray. "I was a hacker. Anyway, I've heard of ghost logins being set up by members of Anonymous to mirror a real login. But when somebody comes across it and tries to trace it, it always leads back to the real login, the one the person was shadowing or mirroring. It's impossible to trace or find. It's not hackable." She locked eyes with Nick. "Was that what you were looking for when you hacked into

SEEK

those servers?"

He nodded. "I was trying to get into the system administrator's logs to search for the login."

"If it's a ghost login, that wouldn't have helped you. It's not in the logs."

"Shit!" Nick shoved a hand through his hair and tossed a regretful look at his fellow Phoenix. "Then I have no way of getting at Sheppard's files either. Sorry, guys. That's a dead end."

Ranger lifted a hand and winced involuntarily. "Crap. Wrong side." He forced a smile. "You say it's a login, right?"

Nick nodded. "Yeah."

Ranger exchanged a look with Stingray. "You're thinking what I'm thinking?"

Stingray nodded, grinning. "Lisa's bracelet from her brother."

Nick felt his forehead furrow. "What's a piece of jewelry got to do with Sheppard's files?"

"It's not the bracelet. It's what we found inside. Talon gave the bracelet to his sister for safekeeping. Inside it, we found two strings of names and numbers, all jumbled up. We couldn't figure out what it was, but before Talon died he told Lisa to find you and give it to you. That you would know what to do with it." Ranger reached into his back pocket, pulled out his wallet and removed a strip of paper from it. He handed it to Nick. "That's it."

Nick looked at it. Michelle reached for his hand and pulled the piece of paper closer to her face. Nick exchanged a look with her. "What do you think?"

"It's got the right length. All logins have a minimum of ten digits. Same with the passwords."

"Can we give it a try?" Ranger asked, sounding hopeful now.

"We sure can," Nick said, bracing one hand on his thigh. "Only thing is, if this is the ghost login, then the only place it will work from is from inside CIA headquarters." He'd known all along that once he found Sheppard's second login, he would have to get into Langley to execute the rest of his plan behind the CIA's firewalls.

"Are you telling us that we need to break into Langley?"

"I wouldn't call it breaking in…"

Stingray tilted his head, giving him a doubtful look. "What would you call it then? A suicide mission?"

"It won't be a suicide mission," Nick assured him. "I have a way in. I've got Sheppard's access card."

"What?" Stingray's eyes widened.

"Well, not his actual card, but all the data that I can imprint onto a blank card to get me into Langley."

"That's genius," Stingray said.

"That's stupid," Ranger interrupted. "And I'll tell you why: the CIA would have deactivated Sheppard's access after his death."

Nick grinned. "Yeah, they would have, but they couldn't, because miraculously, right after Sheppard's murder, somebody moved his access credentials to a hidden archive."

Ranger's chin dropped. "You?"

"Yours truly. Without the system administrators knowing where the data was stored, they couldn't deactivate it. Sheppard's access card is still there. And only I know where the credentials are hidden. All I need to do is hack in, pull down the data, alter it, and transfer it to a new card. Simple as that."

"When you say alter it, what exactly do you mean by that?" Ranger asked curiously.

Nick motioned to his face. "I'm gonna have to replace Sheppard's photo on file with mine."

Stingray scratched his neck. "And you're sure you can hack into their servers?"

Nick looked at Michelle who sat next to him in stunned silence. "Considering the one person who would have been able to stop me is now on our side, I don't see a problem." He squeezed her hand. "Right?"

"Piece of cake," Michelle confirmed and looked at the other two Phoenix. "Besides, I'll give him a hand."

"Well, then, I guess we only have to discuss what you'll do once you're inside Langley. What do you need us to do?" Stingray asked pointing to himself and Ranger. "I'm afraid neither of us is a computer expert, but we can have your back." He put his hand on his gun, stroking it.

"I'm afraid your little friend there will have to stay home for this mission," Nick said, grinning. "But you can do something else for me. You can be my eyes and ears while I'm inside."

Nick exchanged a look with Michelle, who nodded instantly, understanding what he meant.

"I can tap into the infrared security system so they can watch any movements," Michelle confirmed.

Nick nodded. "Let's set it up."

19

Nick's new friends made sure that they weren't being followed. Finally, after what seemed like an eternity, Stingray stopped the van and looked over his shoulder.

"Get some rest. It's going to be a tough day tomorrow."

Nick nodded and reached for Michelle's hand. She rose from her seat and allowed him to help her out of the van, before slamming the door shut and heading for an apartment building.

Michelle was silent when he unlocked the building door, then led her up to his apartment and ushered her in. She watched him as he flipped the deadbolt and set the chain.

She waited for him in the middle of the living room, arms crossed over her chest. She wanted answers, and truth be told, she was surprised that she'd waited so long. Well, maybe the fact that those two guys, Stingray and Ranger, had looked a little menacing had contributed to her artificial patience. Or maybe it had taken her a little longer to get over the shock of having had a gun pointed at her head and being locked up in a shed, before she could wrap her brain around what was going on.

Nick glanced at her from under his dark lashes, casting her an assessing look. "How are you doing?"

"Well, let's see. Considering you threatened to kill me tonight and your new friends are a little overeager with their weapons, and the fact that you all seem to be in some deep shit with the CIA, not to mention that whole weird stuff about being psychic, I'm doing rather splendidly, I think."

Nick took a few steps toward her, sighing. "I'm sorry, Michelle, but what happened tonight wasn't something I was planning."

"I can see that. What you were planning was to use me."

He nodded, didn't even refute her claim. "I did. But like I told you already tonight, sleeping with you wasn't part of that plan." He stretched his hand out and brushed his knuckles over her cheek.

She let it happen, the touch having an oddly calming effect on her. "I know you explained. It's just a little hard to believe, particularly since it looks like there's so much at stake for you and your friends." Too much to really be concerned about the feelings of a woman. "So you were CIA? I'm sure they taught you not to let your feelings get in the way of a mission."

"They tried. But there are times in the life of a man when he has to make his own decisions. And making love to you wasn't part of my mission." He looked down at his feet. "But I understand if you don't want to believe that. You don't know me."

Surprised by his quiet demeanor, she sighed. "No, I don't know you. I don't know what's going on. You said you'd explain everything. So explain. What is this? Your talk about visions, is that all just a smokescreen?"

He lifted his head. "I wish. But it's very real. For all of us. For all the Phoenix. It changed our lives. It connects us. But it also makes us a target."

"I want to understand," she said softly. "I *need* to understand."

"I promised to tell you, so I will." He took her hand and motioned to the sectional that filled half the room.

She followed him to it and sat down next to him.

"What I'm telling you, you can never tell anybody else. Anybody with knowledge about this is a threat to our enemies as well as to us."

Michelle nodded quickly. "I wouldn't know who to tell. I'm on my own." And she certainly wouldn't want to draw any attention to herself by telling fantastic stories. Who would believe her anyway?

"My special skill… I think of it as a genetic defect. To my knowledge nobody from my family has it. At least nobody ever told me about it. Not that I'm close to any of them these days. My parents are divorced, and I guess neither my father nor my mother wanted to be reminded of the mistake their marriage had been. I think they were both relieved when my visits became less frequent, and they were able to concentrate on their new families."

"That's a shame," Michelle threw in.

Nick shrugged as if he didn't care. "It is what it is. I already had a new family, one that understood me better. I was already with the CIA when Henry Sheppard recruited me. At first I thought it was for my IT abilities, which was the field I was in at Langley, but then I realized he knew that I had ESP. He'd already started a top secret program within the CIA, hiring others like me, training them. We were unique. But Sheppard understood us. He knew what it was like to be born with a special ability that you couldn't switch off. That would sometimes haunt you."

SEEK

"The visions?"

"They would come out of the blue. Like a movie playing in front of your mental eye. So real that you thought it was happening right in front of you." He met her gaze then. "I saw you. The day you took me back to your apartment."

"You saw me?"

"You crossed the street without looking to the left. The taxi hit you. It flung you over its roof and tossed you on the asphalt behind it. You didn't move." He sought her eyes. "You didn't make it, Michelle."

Her breath caught in her throat, panic rising with it. "No!" She slapped her hand over her mouth.

Nick reached for her hands, pulled them into his lap, his thumbs stroking the back of them. "That's why I ran to catch you before you could cross the street. That's why I was there."

"You saw me die?" Her voice was a whisper.

He released her hands and cupped her face. "I couldn't let it happen. And when you invited me to your place to take care of my bruises, I knew I couldn't leave without making love to you. I know I should have just thanked you for the icepack and left, but knowing what had nearly happened made it impossible for me to keep my cool. I needed to feel you."

Tears stung in her eyes. "You really saved my life…" She sniffled. "But then why did you almost kill me tonight?"

He closed his eyes for a short moment. "I thought you'd been sent to kill me. Michelle, the Phoenix are hunted. Somebody killed our leader three years ago, and the rest of us have been on the run ever since. Somebody is after us and will kill us first chance he gets. Whoever it is wants to wipe us out. We're a threat to him. And I think I know now why: he's planning something big."

"That premonition, the one with the inferno," Michelle murmured.

"Yes. It's an event in the future. And only the Phoenix know it'll happen. If we can figure out what it is, we might be able to prevent it. And I think the person who killed Sheppard knows that. That's why he needs us all dead." He brushed a hand through her hair. "When you showed up at the meet tonight, I thought you were one of his hired assassins. I'd guessed already you were working for him. I just wasn't sure whether your expertise went beyond computing."

"So you think Smith is the man who killed Sheppard?"

"Absent of any other leads, I have to assume it. At the very least, he's connected to whoever wants us dead. He got you to try to keep me out of the CIA's servers. He knows I'm trying to get at files so I can resurrect the Phoenix. That's why he used you to deny me access. But I have to get at those files. With them we have a better chance of finding the others."

"Don't you think he's using those same files to find all of you?"

"He probably is. We have to be faster, or he'll pick us off one-by-one."

Michelle shivered. "We can't let that happen."

He smiled suddenly. "We?"

"Well, we're a team now, aren't we? Or are you planning on pointing your gun at me again?"

He chuckled softly. "Not that kind of gun."

Michelle sucked in a breath of air, releasing it on an outraged huff. "Oh my God, I can't believe you just said that. What is it with men? Is there ever a time when you're not thinking of sex?"

Nick winked at her. "I'll let you know as soon as that happens."

20

Before Michelle could throw something at him, Nick pulled her into his arms and immobilized her.

"I can't help myself with you," he confessed. "I'm not normally so aggressive when it comes to women. I'm more the shy kind of guy from—"

"Yeah, yeah, from Indiana," she interrupted, rolling her eyes. "How about you drop the act and show me who you really are? Don't I deserve that after you nearly shot me tonight?"

"I didn't nearly shoot you."

"Pointing a gun at my forehead says otherwise."

"I'm never gonna live that one down, am I?"

"Not as long as I can use it as a bargaining chip," she admitted.

"I give in. What do you want?"

She lifted her chin. "You. The real you. Just for tonight. I want you to show me what's behind that façade."

"You might be disappointed. The man behind the secret agent isn't all that interesting. Just a normal guy with a not-so-normal gift. That's all."

Michelle smiled a knowing smile. "Maybe that's what I find interesting: a normal guy. My life is crazy enough. I just want to pretend for one night that I have a normal life with a normal guy and forget that the government is after both of us."

"Just for one night?"

"That's all I need."

He looked deep into her eyes, searching their blue depths for more. Was it really only one night she wanted? And what did he want? Would he be satisfied with just one, knowing that hoping for more was foolish?

"And after that?" he found himself asking.

She looked to the side, avoiding his gaze. He didn't force her head back, didn't make her tell him what she really wanted, because he knew instinctively that he couldn't give her more. "Let's not think of tomorrow."

"All right, then." He lifted her into his arms and stood. "Let's go to bed."

She laced her hands behind his neck as he carried her to his bedroom. Nick flipped the light switch on his way in, and the bedside lamps went on, bathing the room in a soft glow.

"Sorry about the mess. I don't generally have visitors."

He set her on her feet.

"I don't care. I just hope you have condoms here."

He motioned to the bedside table. "Plenty. You won't have to worry about that." He caught a curl of her hair and wrapped it around his index finger. "You should worry about how sore you'll be in the morning."

Michelle pulled his head to her face. "Don't make promises you can't keep."

"Is that a challenge?"

"What if it is?"

"Then I'm afraid *Normal Guy* here will have to draw

upon his secret agent skills and show you that making fun of him is only gonna get you in trouble."

She pouted. "But I already *am* in trouble."

"Oh, this is a very different kind of trouble." He reached for her long-sleeved T-shirt and pulled it over her head. "It's the kind of trouble that is best enjoyed naked."

Her jeans landed on the floor a moment later, together with her shoes and socks. She looked utterly sexy in her black bra and matching thong.

"Does the rule about nudity apply to you, too?" she murmured.

Nick already tore at his shirt, ridding himself of it. The rest of his clothing joined his shirt only seconds later, until he stood in front of her in the nude. He'd never been shy about his body, but the way Michelle ran her eyes over him now made him more aware of it than he'd ever been before. Her gaze traveled over him until it stopped at his groin.

He took his fully erect cock into the palm of his hand and squeezed it, before stroking from tip to root. When she licked her lips, Nick involuntarily groaned, his eyes focused on those lush lips.

Her gaze shot to his face.

"Strip for me," he demanded, his voice hoarse from the arousal taking over his body. When Michelle reached behind her back, he stopped her. "Take your time with it. I like watching."

She smiled sinfully. "So that's the real Nick. Not the shy boy from Indiana, but the insatiable voyeur."

"Nothing wrong with a little voyeurism in the right place." He tilted his chin in her direction. "I loved watching you in the mirror when I took you last night.

Call that voyeurism if you like. Either way—" He pointed to her bra. "—strip, baby, or I might just have to bend you over that sink again to get my kicks."

Nick noticed the visible shiver that raced over her body and the goose bumps it left in its wake. He couldn't help but smile. Yes, Michelle had thoroughly enjoyed their little interlude in the bathroom. Just thinking of it now ratcheted his own arousal higher, adding more girth to his already hard cock.

Finally, Michelle complied with his demand and slid both hands up her torso, slowly stroking her breasts. She looped her fingers under the straps of her bra and nudged them off her shoulders. The silky fabric covering her peaks started to slide, but caught on her hard nipples and prevented a further disrobing. With a coquettish look Michelle ran her fingers to her breasts and underneath the thin cups, pushing them down farther. Now her nipples were covered by her hands.

Nick gave his cock a hard tug. "Squeeze them."

Like a good girl, she did. Then she took her nipples between thumb and forefinger and rolled them.

At the erotic sight, a groan burst from him, and a drop of moisture leaked from his shaft. "Take it off," he growled.

Slowly she moved her hands behind her back to work the clasp. The action thrust her breasts toward him as if she was offering them to him. He was unable to resist and crossed the distance between them with one step.

His hands were on her breasts the moment the bra fell to the floor. They felt warm and firm in his hands. He squeezed them, gently at first, but the feel of her delectable flesh in his palms was too much to bear. He dipped his head and licked first over one then the other peak.

"How about my panties?" she asked, an air of innocence in her voice.

"I'll take care of those."

His lips around one hard peak, sucking as much of her breast into his mouth as he could, he slid his right hand down the front of her torso, until his fingers bumped against the lace waistband of her thong. Without stopping, he dipped below it, reacquainting himself with her bare sex.

With his left hand, he grabbed her leg and lifted it up to hold against his outer thigh. Michelle's arms came around him to hold on for balance, while his fingers were already busy diving deeper.

Her cleft was moist and warm. Juices slicked his fingers and the scent started to permeate his bedroom. He lifted his head from her breasts.

"Aren't you a naughty girl? Look how wet you're already, and I haven't even started yet."

With heavy-lidded eyes she looked at him "Then you'd better start."

"Yeah, I'd better." He set her leg down again, then used both his hands to strip her of her panties. "Lay on the bed."

Not taking her eyes off him, she stepped back and lowered herself onto the duvet with catlike grace. She angled one leg to give him a view of her most intimate place, as if he needed that obvious an invitation.

Nick followed her onto the bed, pushing her legs farther apart to make a space for himself. "Did you enjoy when I licked you the other day?"

Her eyes widened and a blush rose to her cheeks.

"You know I did."

"Then maybe we should start with that," he proposed, dipped his head to her sex and pressed his lips to her warm and moist flesh. With his tongue, he parted her folds and lapped up her arousal.

Beneath him, Michelle trembled, making pride swell in his chest to know that he could give her this kind of pleasure. He wanted her to forget the fear of the last few hours and show her that he didn't only bring danger and menace into her life, but that he could deliver passion and pleasure as well.

When she put a hand on the back of his head and caressed his scalp, a shudder traveled through his body, sending a flame of hot desire into his groin. He moaned into her flesh, letting her know how she affected him, how her touch aroused him and her taste made him want more.

"Oh Nick," she murmured on a breathy exhale, her hips undulating.

Her words and actions spurred him on, made him lick her with even more purpose. Every moan she released, every movement of her body added to his excitement of pleasuring the beautiful woman in his arms, in his bed. Because she trusted him now, trusted him with her body, and maybe, some day, she could trust him with her heart, too. But he knew he had to earn this trust.

A change in Michelle's breathing told him that she was on the verge of her climax. A fierce sensation of possessiveness charged through him at the knowledge that he was the one to drive her to such heights. And the thought that there might be other men after him made him growl, even though he had no right to think that way. There was nothing he could offer Michelle; nothing but a life on the run.

Michelle twisted in the sheets, her moans now more pronounced, her hands fisting the duvet, knuckles white as if holding on for dear life.

He wrapped his lips around her clit and sucked the little nub into his mouth, pressing down on it, while he teased her folds with his wet finger.

Her body exploded on a moan, and he drove his finger into her spasming channel, feeling her muscles clamp down on him, imprisoning him in her warmth. Wave after wave wracked her body, her orgasm taking her, while he continued to lick over her clit, wringing more pleasure from her body.

When she collapsed with a contented sigh, Nick lifted his head.

Michelle was a sight to behold. Her face was flushed, her body glistening, nipples hard and tempting as hell. Her eyes were half-closed, but she looked at him, a soft smile playing at her plump lips.

Without a word, he leaned toward the bedside table and retrieved a condom from there. He rolled it over his aching cock and positioned himself between her spread thighs once more.

Locking eyes with her, he guided his erection to her wet sex, nudging her nether lips apart gently. In slow motion, he slid into her, feeling how the walls of her channel enveloped him in a loving caress.

Michelle's legs lifted and she wrapped them around the back of his thighs, pulling him to her. "That's good," she murmured.

"Yes." And he could make it even better, not by taking her hard and fast, but by taking his time tonight.

By loving her slowly and tenderly. As if they had all the time in the world.

He braced himself on his elbows and knees, making sure not to crush her under his weight, and brushed a strand of her hair from her face. Slowly he pulled his hips back, allowing his cock to slip from her until only the tip was still inside, before descending again on a measured exhale.

"I want to make love to you all night." He brushed his lips on hers, letting her taste herself, and caressed her face with the pads of his fingers. "I want you to know that I would never hurt you."

Her lashes fluttered and she looked into his eyes. "I know that now."

"No matter what happens tomorrow, I want you to remember tonight. I want you to know that if I could, I'd give you so much more than just one night."

She opened her mouth to protest, but he put a finger across her lips.

"You deserve so much more."

He took her lips and kissed her, putting all those things he couldn't say into it, while his hips moved in an easy rhythm, his cock sliding in and out of her, unrushed, unhurried. Because tonight wasn't about the race to release, it was about the journey, about the pleasure of getting there. It was about Michelle.

His body heated and sweat built on his skin. It made the contact of skin-on-skin even smoother, even more natural and sensual.

The warmth in Michelle's eyes as she gazed at him filled his heart with hope. Her hands were on him, touching him, exploring him, caressing him. His entire body hummed with awareness, pleasure building inside him, making his heart beat faster and blood race through his veins as fast as a locomotive.

Though he didn't want to climax yet, his body didn't give him a choice in the matter. Being connected to Michelle in such an intimate way, he hurtled toward the inevitable. He couldn't have stopped it any more than he could stop a tsunami.

When the first bolt of pleasure charged into his cock, he tried to hold it back, but the wave was already cresting, already hitting him broadside. Hot semen exploded from the tip of his cock, and spasms rocked his body, making his hips jerk and his cock slam into Michelle's soft center with such force that he feared he was going to hurt her.

But when their eyes locked, all he saw was pleasure in those blue orbs. Then her body stilled for a split second, before a visible shiver overtook her and her interior muscles gripped him tightly.

Her cry of release went through him, reigniting him, sending another intense wave of pleasure over him.

Breathing hard, he collapsed on top of her, managing only in the last second to brace himself on his elbows. His knees were shaking. Noticing Michelle's heaving chest, he rolled onto his back, releasing her.

He turned his head to the side, looking at her, unable to say a word. She shifted, facing him. He reached for her, intertwining his fingers with hers.

Wordlessly, she stared at their joined hands. He knew then that letting her go would be the hardest thing he'd ever done.

21

"You clean up pretty nice," Michelle said, pointing to Nick's navy business suit.

They were sitting in the back of the van that Stingray was driving toward the CIA's headquarters in Langley, Virginia. Ranger was following them in a second car, an inconspicuous Toyota Corolla, his girlfriend, Lisa, driving a gray Buick. At first Michelle hadn't understood the need for so many cars, but Stingray had explained that Nick needed to drive himself to the parking lot, since he was the only one who could get a car through the gate with his CIA identification. The rest of them would have to wait at a safe distance. Once Nick was back, he'd have to ditch the car he'd used to get into the CIA, and they needed to be able to switch cars, in case they were being followed. Hence the need for the Buick.

Nick tugged on his tie. "Dress code is pretty formal inside Langley. I don't wanna stick out like a sore thumb."

"Don't worry, you'll fit right in," Stingray said from the driver's seat as he pulled over by the side of the road.

Behind them Ranger came to a stop too, as did the Buick.

Michelle glanced out the windshield. She could barely make out the little hut with the armed guards in the distance, the entrance to the CIA campus everybody had to pass through to get to the headquarters building.

She must have looked worried, because Nick took her hand, and squeezed it reassuringly. "I've been in there many times. I know my way around."

"What if you're recognized?" she asked.

"Even if I am, there are so many covert agents swarming around that place that nobody will ask me any questions. That's just how it is in there. Isn't that right, Stingray?"

The other Phoenix nodded with a grunt. "Sure is. Though it's not without risk." He motioned to the ID Nick had pinned to his breast pocket. "That'll get you in, sure, but you know as well as I do that the code embedded in Sheppard's ID will throw up all kinds of red flags. And once those work their way to the right person, your gig is up."

Michelle felt as if somebody had just choked the air out of her. "What?" She glared at Nick. "Why didn't you tell me about that? I thought nobody knew about the ID."

Nick shifted in his seat, seemingly uncomfortable. "That was the case while it was hidden in the secret archive, but the moment I activated it for myself, it became visible to anybody who cares to look." He shrugged. "Don't worry, this is a bureaucracy like any other. The system security administrators working for the CIA are just as overworked and underpaid as anybody else. They don't have time to chase every single abnormality."

She didn't believe him. The way he avoided her gaze now told her that he was aware of it, too.

"I've got at least an hour before they figure out the

ID is bogus," Nick tried to placate her.

"At most," Stingray threw in.

Nick tossed him a sideways glance. "You're not helping."

"If you're talking about backing you up when you're lying to your girlfriend about the risk you're taking, then, no, I'm not helping. I wasn't aware that was part of my job."

Michelle leaned closer to Nick. "I thought after last night…" She hesitated, searching Nick's gaze. "I thought we were gonna be honest with each other."

He brushed his knuckles over her cheek. "We are. But I didn't want to worry you. Trust me, I can do this. I worked as an IT analyst in Langley for many years. I know how things work there."

"You didn't mention that before," Stingray interrupted.

Nick shrugged. "How do you think I was able to hide Sheppard's ID in the first place? The moment I got his distress call, I did what I could to leave a back door open for myself. I knew that one day I would need to be able to get back in. But I had to run, just like the rest of you. It was all I could do in the few minutes I had." He looked back at Michelle. "I'll be in and out in no time. They won't even blink."

Despite his reassuring explanation, the doubt inside her didn't subside. "Are you sure?"

"Positive. Now—"

The pinging of Michelle's burner phone interrupted him.

She pulled it from her pocket, her heart beating in her throat. Only one person knew this number and would contact her on it: Mr. Smith.

Before she could read the text message, Nick took the cell from her and looked at it. When he looked up again, concern spread over his face, making worry lines appear on his forehead and around his eyes and mouth.

"Fucking bad timing," Nick ground out and exchanged a look with Stingray.

Michelle took the phone from him and read the message. *Now* Smith wanted a meeting? Damn it. "In two hours? That won't give us any time to set a trap for him." She looked at Nick. "We have to leave now. You have to go into Langley another day."

Nick shook his head. "I can't. The ID is already active. Tomorrow, hell, this afternoon, it will already have been flagged as bogus and they'll arrest me the moment I set foot in the building. It has to be now or never."

"Crap, crap, crap!" Michelle cursed. There was only one solution then. And as much as she hated it, she knew it was their only chance. "We have to split up."

"Out of the fucking question!" Nick bellowed.

"Just hear me out."

"Michelle, you're not meeting him alone. That's suicide."

"I have no intention of meeting him alone. But somebody has to go there to set up surveillance." She pointed to the text message. "He wants to meet on the island that houses Lady Bird Johnson Park. I know it. It's across from the Pentagon, separated by Boundary Channel."

"Boundary Channel?" Stingray asked.

"A waterway that connects to the Potomac," she explained and looked back at Nick. "There are two ways to get on and off the island: via George Washington

Memorial Parkway or with a boat. There's a marina on the southern tip of the island, Columbia Island Marina."

"What are you saying?" Nick asked.

"Somebody has to set up electronic surveillance there in case he slips through our fingers. We have to be able to track whether he leaves the island by car or by boat. And I'm the only one who has the technical knowledge to do that."

"So do Ranger and Stingray," Nick protested, looking at Stingray for support.

"That's right. I know my stuff." Stingray looked insulted.

Michelle tossed him a glare. "I know my stuff better, no offense. Besides, Nick needs you here. If something goes wrong, you'll have to get him out."

She could see Nick battling with the decision before him. "Then take Ranger with you."

She shook her head. "He's injured. He won't be much help. I can work much faster on my own. I'll be done long before Smith shows up. By that time, you'll have left Langley and can meet me outside Arlington and then we can surprise Smith together. It's the best solution."

Nick glanced at Stingray. His friend nodded after a few seconds.

"She's right, man. We're running out of time."

Nick took both of Michelle's hands in his. "You go there, set up the cameras and you get out. You hear me? No hanging around there. Just in and out. If you're not at the Arlington Metro in exactly one hour, I'm going to whip your butt when I catch you. Is that clear?"

She nodded, her heart racing at his impassioned statement.

"Make sure Stingray can get a hold of you while I'm in there. Do you have a cell on you?"

Michelle shook her head. "Only the burner from Smith."

Nick glanced at Stingray, who already nodded and said, "I've got some spares."

Nodding in agreement, Nick addressed her again, "Take the van. It's got all the equipment you'll need." He turned to Stingray. "I'll take the Toyota. Wait in the Buick with Ranger and Lisa, and take the communication system with you so you and I can communicate when I'm inside and you can watch my back."

When Nick turned back to her, his gaze was heated. He pulled her into his arms, kissed her fiercely, then released her just as abruptly, and exited the van.

22

Nick exhaled a sigh of relief when the guard at the gate returned his identification and lifted the gate to let him pass. He pressed his foot on the gas and accelerated the Toyota, driving down the long driveway flanked by trees and bushes.

The entire Langley campus was surrounded by a thick forest, sitting there like an island. Several massive parking lots—all above ground—surrounded the large building, or rather buildings, since CIA headquarters was really made up of three separate but interconnected buildings. Once inside any of them, a person could get to any part of it—given the right access credentials of course.

An inner courtyard was partially covered with a massive tent-like canopy, other areas were open and provided some greenery to relax within the concrete-and-glass structure.

Nick drove to the parking lot closest to the main entrance. In case something went wrong, he would need to get to his car quickly to leave the CIA campus before they locked the place down. It was still early. Many employees were only just arriving. He'd timed it that way, knowing that during busy times he had a better chance of slipping through unnoticed. In the morning, everybody was too concerned with getting their first cup of coffee and not fully awake yet.

Nick exited the car and locked it, then walked calmly toward the entrance. From the corner of his eye, he observed other men and women doing the same. Some held paper coffee cups, others carried briefcases. Most were dressed in suits or other business casual clothing.

For three years, Nick had waited for this opportunity, and now it had finally come. As if he still belonged here, he walked through the glass doors, entering the white-and-gray marble-and-granite entrance hall. Nothing had changed. A row of turnstiles awaited him. Beyond them the well-known CIA seal made of white-and-gray granite tiles was laid into the floor.

He lined up at one of the turnstiles, waiting his turn to swipe his identification card. The person ahead of him marched through it quickly, and he followed, swiping his card.

A high-pitched beep sounded, and a red light flashed at his turnstile.

Adrenaline shot through him.

Shit!

A security guard walked up to him, glancing at his ID. "Sorry, sir, we've been having some problems with this one this morning when people come through too quickly. Please try again now."

Nick plastered a fake smile on his face and nodded. "No problem."

Heart beating in his throat, he swiped his card again. A green light flashed at once.

"Go ahead, sir," the security guard said, waving him through. "It's all good now. Have a nice day."

"You, too."

Relieved, Nick marched through the turnstile and walked to the end of the hall. Sweat trickled from his neck and disappeared beneath the collar of his starched dress shirt. Another incident like that, and he'd have a heart attack at thirty-three.

Focusing on the task ahead, Nick let his gaze roam. He still knew his way around, though it had been over three years since he'd last been at Langley. The maze of corridors had never seemed daunting to him before. He'd loved the challenge, loved to figure out the fastest way from point A to point B.

Acting as if he belonged there, Nick walked confidently. He never hesitated, always planned ahead, his mind constantly mapping out the path in front of him, so he would never have to stop to orient himself. He wouldn't give anybody a reason to look at him with suspicion.

He didn't take the elevator, but used the stairs instead, not wanting to be in a confined space from which it would be difficult to escape should anybody recognize him. Though it was unlikely, there was always a chance of running into somebody who knew Sheppard and therefore knew the badge that hung on Nick's pocket wasn't his, even though the picture was of his face.

It felt like an eternity until he reached the right corridor. He approached the door that said *Restricted Area* and stopped. Outside of it were a card reader and a camera.

Nick swiped his card, then lifted his face toward the camera, knowing that a facial recognition software was about to scan his face and compare it to the picture on file—the picture he'd uploaded to the CIA's systems himself.

Several seconds passed, then he heard a click. Nick pushed against the door. It opened inward. He stepped through it and let the door close behind him. It was quieter here, though he knew he wasn't alone. Along the corridor were several rooms with their doors closed.

"I'm in," he whispered into the tiny mic hidden beneath the lapel of his jacket.

"Good, we've got you."

He heard Stingray's reply in his ear and sighed with relief. The GPS in the heel of Nick's shoe was sending back a signal to his fellow Phoenix. The infrared system Michelle had tapped into and showed Stingray how to use, was doing the rest.

"Walk straight ahead," came the first instruction through his earpiece.

With an outward calmness, Nick passed the closed doors until he reached a bend in the corridor.

"Now left."

He turned left.

"Third door."

Nick counted. At the third door, he stopped. There was only a number on it, no other indication of what lay behind it.

"Is it empty?" Nick asked, keeping his voice low.

"Yes. Infrared indicates no human inside. It's a go."

Nick pushed the door open and slipped in, easing it shut behind him. The humming noise in the room was created by the many computers lining one wall.

"I'm going silent," he advised Stingray.

"Understood."

Nick walked up to the first computer and touched the mouse. The login screen came on as expected. He pulled the paper Ranger had given him from his pocket and placed it next to the keyboard, then typed in the string of numbers and letters into the login and password area on the screen. Praying he was correct that this was Sheppard's ghost login, he pressed the *Enter* key.

It only took a second for a blue desktop to appear. *Welcome, Henry,* it said in large letters before the writing faded into the background, and made way for several icons.

It wasn't hard to navigate the area. Sheppard had been an organized man, keeping everything in its proper place.

Under a folder named *Stargate*, the CIA program Sheppard had once been part of and from which he'd created the Phoenix program, Nick found a folder simply named *My Boys*.

For a brief instant, Nick's heart clenched. Sheppard had truly been a father to him, and most likely to the other Phoenix, too. To know that he had seen them as his sons, brought back the pain of losing him. But he had no time to wallow in that pain now.

Nick clicked on the folder.

Shock made him jerk back. The folder was empty.

"Shit!" he cursed.

"What's wrong?" Stingray asked.

"Not now!"

Frantically, Nick searched the remainder of the folders. Empty, all of them!

"Fuck!" he cursed. "Somebody got here ahead of us! The files are all gone!"

"Shit!" Stingray ground out.

"Wait!" He'd just had an idea. "The recycle bin." Maybe it hadn't been emptied and the deleted files were still sitting in there.

Nick clicked on the icon. Empty, too.

"Fuck!" All this for nothing. He kicked against the desk, frustrated. "Somebody knew we'd be coming."

"Get out of there!" Stingray ordered. "Now!"

"There must be another way," Nick mumbled to himself. There had to be. He scanned all icons on the desktop once more.

"Damn it, Fox, you've gotta leave!"

Nick shook his head, when his eyes suddenly fell on an icon he'd ignored. "The backup system."

"What?"

"All computers are backed up regularly. The backup files are kept for quite some time." He only had to figure out where the backup files were kept.

Quickly, Nick opened the control panel and searched for the right area then scanned the information and found the file path he was looking for.

Moments later, he'd navigated to it. There were hundreds of backup files pertaining to Sheppard's files. They were listed chronologically. The last one had been made about a month after Sheppard's death. Since then, the files in his cloud hadn't been backed up, most likely because the system hadn't detected any activity.

Nick opened the last backup file, the one made after Sheppard's death, but no folder with the name *My Boys* was among it. This meant that somebody had erased it within a month after the Phoenix program's leader had been murdered.

Remembering Sheppard's date of death all too well, Nick clicked on the file with a date only two days prior.

"Shit, Fox!" Stingray's voice came through his earpiece. "Somebody's coming. You've gotta hightail it outta there."

"I only need a minute," he said, already perusing the contents of the backup file. "There! Got it!"

The folder named *My Boys* was right there. Nick clicked on it, and a long list of individual files appeared, all carrying only initials.

Nick pulled a flash drive from his pocket, jammed it in the computer's USB port. Immediately, an alert flashed on the screen: *Copying disabled*. He'd expected this, but thanks to his years in the CIA's Data Security department, he knew a way around it. He typed in the appropriate command and seconds later, copied the entire folder. A window popped up, indicating the number of megabytes it was copying and the time left.

"Damn it, Fox! Get your ass out of there now!"

"Almost there, just twenty more seconds!"

Drumming his fingers on the desk, he watched the time on the window decrease. "Ten seconds."

"Now, Fox, now!"

The window closed, indicating that the copying process was complete. Nick pulled the flash drive from the USB port and shut the computer down.

He headed for the door.

"Fuck!" he cursed and whirled back around. "The login credentials."

"Leave 'em!" Stingray ordered.

"Can't!" He rushed back to the computer, snatched the piece of paper from the desk and ran back to the door. He eased it open.

"Turn right! Into the office next to you."

Nick followed Stingray's command without hesitation and dove into the room next to the one he'd just exited. Just in time, as it turned out. Footsteps passed by his door. Then the door to the other room was opened and closed.

"Now, out!" Stingray ordered.

Breathing heavily, Nick exited the room and walked back the same way he'd come. At the door, he stopped for a brief moment, then he pushed it open and left the restricted area.

As he walked through the maze of corridors, back toward the main entrance, he glanced at one of the clocks on the wall. It was high time that he left. His hour was almost up. Shortly, a vigilant system administrator would realize that the ID Nick was using belonged to a dead man. But before that happened, Nick had to get back to the computer Stingray and Ranger were using to keep tabs on him, and replace his photo on Sheppard's ID with Sheppard's original one.

He increased his speed, but didn't run. It would only draw suspicion onto him. At the next turn, he reached the entrance hall. Ahead of him was the oversized seal of the CIA, and beyond it were the turnstiles.

Nick let his eyes roam. The security guard who'd assisted him earlier was gone, probably on a break. Somebody else had taken his place. Good. It meant the guy wouldn't get suspicious seeing him leave again so quickly.

Trying to appear as relaxed and calm as he could under the circumstances, Nick walked past the turnstiles and through the glass doors into the open air. He didn't look back, and continued in the same tempo until he reached the Toyota.

"I'm outside."

"Good. We'll be right there."

Nick unlocked the car and got inside. When the

engine started, he felt a little better already, but only once he'd passed through the gate, leaving the CIA campus, did his heart beat normally again.

The Buick with Ranger, Stingray, and Lisa was waiting for him in a side street about two miles from the CIA's security gate.

Nick pulled over, killed the engine, and took out a special antiseptic wipe, ripped open the package and proceeded to wipe down the steering wheel, gear stick, and anything else he'd touched. Not only would it make sure he didn't leave any fingerprints behind, it would also get rid of any DNA. He finished by wiping the outside door handle, before he stuffed the used wipe and packaging into his pocket then got into the waiting Buick.

Stingray was driving, pulling into the street the moment Nick was inside the car.

"You got it?" Ranger asked eagerly.

He sat in the back with Lisa, his girlfriend, a pretty woman with a kind smile.

Nick patted his jacket pocket. "I've got it." Then he looked at his watch. "Step on the gas, Stingray. Michelle is waiting for us."

Ranger handed him his computer, jetpack already attached, and Nick didn't lose any time wiping out any trace of his picture on Sheppard's old CIA access card.

It took them less than ten minutes on the George Washington Memorial Parkway to reach the Arlington Metro station.

Nick searched for the van. "Do you see her?"

"Nothing," Ranger said.

"Shit!" Nick cursed and looked at his watch again. Then his nape began to prickle uncomfortably.

"Something isn't right. Shit, something happened to Michelle."

23

Michelle cursed. She'd wanted to place only one more camera, but had remembered too late that the northbound lane on George Washington Memorial Parkway didn't have an exit on Columbia Island. So she'd had to double-back after installing a camera right off the highway where the Pentagon Lagoon Yacht Basin was flowing back into the Potomac River. The bridge was a strategic point from which any boat leaving the lagoon could be watched.

Unfortunately the detour had cost her precious minutes. Minutes, it now turned out, she didn't have. Because she wasn't the only early bird.

"Well, look who couldn't wait to meet," the stranger said in a menacing voice, as he gripped her elbow.

She knew immediately that this wasn't Smith. His voice sounded different, and he let her see his face. Smith had always made sure she never got a glimpse of him so she couldn't identify him.

One thing was immediately crystal clear: this man had been sent by Smith to get rid of her.

"Let's go somewhere more private," he suggested, jamming something hard—and concealed beneath the jacket that he'd slung over his forearm—into her side.

She didn't need to see the item to know it was a gun.

She also knew immediately why he wanted to head away from the path that led back to where she'd parked the van. A group of three-to-five year olds was playing in the open meadow only a few yards away, supervised by three young kindergarten teachers. He couldn't kill her here, or he would have several witnesses and a panicked group of kids on his hands.

Just as Michelle knew she couldn't call out to the three teachers for help either. It would only endanger the children. For all she knew, the man currently holding a gun to her ribs had no scruples killing innocent children in order to save his own ass.

She was on her own.

"Move!" he ordered between clenched teeth.

She cast him a sideways glance. He looked so normal. Not like a villain, but more like a boring accountant on his way to work. That's why she hadn't even noticed him, though clearly he'd noticed her.

Michelle had no choice but to put one foot in front of the other. But she had to somehow buy herself time. "Smith sent you? What does he want?"

A little chuckle came from the man. "What do you think?" He pressed the barrel of the gun harder into her side to make his point.

"Why? I've done everything he wanted."

The assassin nudged her in the direction of a public restroom, which was partially surrounded by bushes and trees.

"Apparently your employer wasn't quite satisfied with your job performance."

"I can improve," she hastened to say, realizing that once they reached the restrooms there was nothing to prevent him from killing her out of sight of any witnesses.

"I believe your probationary period is over. And guess what?" He leaned in. "You didn't make the cut."

Her heart beat frantically, and her palms were sweaty. "Whatever he's paying you, I can pay you more."

A snort was his answer. He didn't believe her. Well, she wouldn't believe herself either.

Michelle eyed the one-story brick building that housed the restrooms and saw a man exit from one side. He walked toward them.

The assassin pasted a smile on his face and said for the benefit of the man passing them, "Honey, your stomach will feel better in a second, I promise you."

The fake sweet tone of his voice made her want to puke and make his lie about her stomach trouble true.

The moment the other man was out of earshot, her assailant hurried her along. "Let's move."

She pretended to stumble over her own feet, letting out a gasp. He gripped her elbow even harder, his gun slipping for a moment, but then he pulled her along again. The distraction had worked, however: she'd managed to pull the cell phone Stingray had given her from her pocket, press what she hoped was the redial button, and drop it into the grass. Stingray had programmed in his number, and they'd tested it before she'd left with the van. She could only hope now that he would get the message that she was in trouble. It was a long shot, but what else could she do?

"Stop, please," she begged loudly, praying that the call had already connected and would pick up her voice from this distance. "My ankle. I think I sprained it. Please don't take me into those public restrooms. Please don't kill me."

"Shut up, you bitch!" he growled, looking around. He seemed satisfied that nobody was close enough to have heard her or seen her struggle.

Her gaze darted past the structure ahead of them, where sailboats and motorboats were docked at the small marina. But it was quiet there, too.

With every step they got closer to the public restrooms, hope that the cavalry would arrive in time faded a little bit more. A hand clamped around her heart and squeezed it tighter with every second. Soon, it would all be over. This wasn't how she'd imagined her end: shot in a public restroom, her body lying on the urine-stained concrete floor. A cold shiver raced down her back, and her hands trembled.

Tears welled in her eyes, and she didn't even try to blink them back. Nobody would see them, nobody but her killer.

"Please," she murmured, but he'd already opened the door to the women's restroom and shoved her inside.

A single neon light flickered on the ceiling. Except for the dripping faucet it was quiet. There were three stalls, their doors open. The smell of human waste hit her immediately, making her nose twitch uncomfortably. A morbid thought came: at least she wouldn't have to bear the stench for long.

For the first time since the assassin had caught her, he released her elbow and pushed her from him, toward one of the stalls. She whirled around, needing to watch him. As if seeing the gun would somehow help her stop him.

With a serenity only a professional killer could exhibit, he pulled a silencer from his jacket pocket. He placed the jacket over the waste bin, then slowly screwed the silencer onto the barrel of his pistol.

"It won't hurt," he promised.

"Please, just let me go. I promise I'll disappear today. Nobody has to find out that you didn't kill me. I'll leave the country."

The assassin shook his head. "Sorry, lady, but I always fulfill my duty."

Instinctively, she shrank back, stepping deeper into the stall until her legs backed up against the toilet bowl.

The cocking of the gun echoed off the walls. The sound thundered in her ears and made her heart stop. This was it then. The end.

Another sound, that of creaking door hinges, reached her ears a split second later.

Her head veered in the direction of the door as it opened. Oh, no, another innocent woman would have to die because she was about to witness a murder.

"No! Run!" Michelle screamed at the person she couldn't even see, because the assassin was blocking her view of the door.

He spun around, his back to her now, his gun hand outstretched.

The shot echoed louder than she would have expected. She'd always thought a silencer would dampen the sound of the gunshot to a dull rumble. But this was different, louder, deafening.

Paralyzed, she stared at the assassin's back, expecting him to turn around to her now and finish her. But instead, his knees buckled and he collapsed onto the dirty floor. Her gaze flew to the door. Nick stood there, a gun in his hand.

"Are you all right?" he asked, rushing toward her.

She nodded, but couldn't get a single word over her lips.

Nick sidestepped the dead body and reached for her, pulling her out of the stall. "We have to leave. Now. Before anybody sees us."

She nodded numbly and clung to his hand as he dragged her out of the bathroom and around to the other side, away from the entrance.

The van, its engine running, was waiting for them. For a moment she wondered how that was possible, since she still felt the key to it in her pocket. But Stingray probably had a second one on him.

"Hop in, quickly!" Nick demanded, helping her into the van and jumping in behind her, then slamming the door shut.

The van was already in motion, making her stumble before she was able to sit on the bench.

"Get us outta here, Stingray!" Nick sat on the bench beside her and pulled her into his arms.

His erratic breathing and heaving chest mirrored her own.

"I thought I'd be too late."

Michelle buried her head in his chest, still not being able to comprehend how she'd escaped certain death. "You came. You killed him before he could kill me."

"Shame the guy's dead. Would have loved to question him about this Smith character. Guess we blew our chance there," Stingray threw in.

"Yeah, well, I had no choice," Nick answered.

He put his hand under her chin and tipped her face up. His mouth was on hers a moment later, kissing her with a desperation she'd never felt from him before. When he released her moments later, he stroked his hand over her hair.

"You scared the shit out of me, Michelle."

"I didn't know he was gonna send an assassin. And I couldn't know he'd be an hour early." Then she looked around the van for the first time and a twinge of panic raced through her. "Where are Ranger and Lisa? Are they okay?"

Stingray answered in Nick's stead, catching her eye in the rearview mirror. "They're in the Toyota, making sure nobody's following us. They'll meet us at the safe house once the coast is clear."

Relieved, Michelle exhaled. Then she looked at Nick. "What happened at Langley? Did you get the file?"

Nick grinned and patted his jacket pocket. "We got it, baby."

24

After arriving at the safe house, they'd analyzed the files Nick had copied, which turned out to be a veritable treasure trove of information. The files identified over thirty Phoenix agents. Mostly codenames, real names, and pictures were there, but the files didn't contain any mention of relatives or where the agents were from. However, there were other useful tidbits: hobbies, special skills, as well as the professions the agents had previously held. It would help Nick and his two new friends in their search for the others.

Several hours after rescuing Michelle from the assassin and analyzing the files in the safe house, Nick kicked his apartment door shut with the heel of his boot and trained his eyes on Michelle who'd entered ahead of him.

She walked toward the sofa, sashaying her sweet ass for his benefit, making it hard for him to concentrate on what he had to get off his chest. When she turned and let herself sink into the cushions, resting her head against the backrest and blowing out a breath, Nick marched toward her.

His heart was still pounding out of control at the recollection of what had happened this morning. It had been close. Too damn close. And it had made him realize one thing: that he didn't want to lose Michelle. Which was why it was so hard to do what he'd promised her. To help her get away. But a promise was a promise. She'd upheld her part of the bargain, and he had to uphold his.

She smiled at him, clearly oblivious to the turmoil raging inside him. And how should she know? He hadn't told her even once what he'd started feeling.

"Something wrong?" she murmured, reaching for him.

Nick remained standing in front of her, searching for the right words. "I don't think I'm able to uphold my end of the bargain about getting you out of the country."

She shifted on the sofa. "But you promised to give me a new identity."

"I did. But I can't help you disappear." He shook his head. "Not the way you were hoping to anyway. Smith has you in his crosshairs. And knowing what I know now, that one of our own turned bad and worked for our enemies, I have to assume that Talon wasn't the only one. Smith might have other Phoenix on their side."

"But what's that got to do with you giving me a new identity?"

"Everything. Any of those Phoenix who've gone bad can have a premonition about you, where you are, what you're doing. If I send you away to South America on your own, you'll be without protection if one of them comes after you."

"But the chances of that happening—"

"—are real," he cut her off. And that made his blood curdle.

"But if I stay here as myself, he'll get me, too."

"If you stay here, I'll be able to watch out for you.

To protect you."

To be close to you, he wanted to add, but didn't.

He could see how the wheels in Michelle's brain turned feverishly. Hesitantly, he said, "You'll get a new identity, but you'd be staying close... close to me."

Her eyelashes lifted, almost hitting her brows. Blue eyes stared at him with an intensity that almost knocked him off his feet.

Slowly, her lips parted, curving into a tentative smile. "So that's what this is about."

"What what's about?"

"You actually want to go out with me. You want to be my boyfriend."

"It's just so I can keep an eye on you," Nick said quickly.

Shit, he wasn't good at talking about stuff like this. He'd much rather discuss some software code with Michelle than confess what he was feeling. Besides, what if she didn't feel the same? After all, she barely knew him, he'd lied to her for half of the time they'd known each other, and he'd put her in mortal danger. Not exactly a good place to start from when applying for the position as lover and boyfriend. How was he ever going to overcome that kind of handicap?

She rose from the couch. "What exactly do you want to keep an eye on?" She unexpectedly pulled her black T-shirt over her head and tossed it on the sofa, casting him a saucy look. "My boobs?"

Nick's breath caught as he stared at her black bra. Was she going to strip in front of him?

She kicked off her shoes, then opened the button of her jeans and pulled the zipper down. "Or are you more interested in my ass and legs?"

Before she could push her jeans down, he imprisoned her hands, stopping her.

"This isn't about sex, Michelle."

She lifted her chin. "Then what is it about, Nick? What is it that you want? Because unless you tell me, I'm not gonna know what you really want."

"You're gonna make me say it, aren't you?"

She nodded slowly. "Don't I deserve that?"

He swallowed. "Oh, you deserve so much. It's just, I'm not the kind of guy who's used to talking about… well, about what he feels."

"And here, I thought you were such a smooth talker, flirting with me so I'd sleep with you."

"It's different now."

She took a step closer. "Yeah? What's different?"

"After what happened today, after almost losing you…" He shoved a hand through his hair. "…I don't think I could handle if something happened to you…" He sighed. "Damn it, Michelle, maybe you could help me a little here."

"How?"

"By telling me that I mean something to you?"

A soft smile that extended to her eyes formed on her lips. Her hand came up and she stroked his cheek. "Oh, Nick, the shy boy from Indiana. He's still in there, isn't he? And he's afraid to say what he feels because he's worried that he'll be rejected, just like his parents rejected him." She shook her head.

How could she know what was holding him back? "How do you—?"

"You told me so yourself, Nick. You told me that your parents didn't really want to see you after the divorce. I don't need to be a psychologist to guess what that would have done to that boy." She ran her finger along his lower lip. "Now try again. Give me a reason to stay."

Nick took a deep breath. "I'm in love with you. I know it's happening too fast, but if you believe in love at first sight, then believe in this. Believe that I've fallen for you and that I'll do everything in my power to protect you."

Her fingers stroked gently over his cheek. "Now, was that so hard?" She brushed her lips on his. "So does that mean I get to move in with you?"

He pulled his head back, grinning, his confidence at an all time high now. "I think you're forgetting something."

She looked at him quizzically. "What?"

"That you have to give me a reason to let you move in."

She chuckled, and her breath tickled his lips. "What if I told you that despite you lying to me at every turn, you've managed to work yourself into my heart?" She paused for a moment. "And then there's the fact that you saved my life, not once but twice. I think that needs to be rewarded."

"Rewarded, how?" He slid his arm around her waist and pulled her against him.

"You get to choose your reward."

Nick grinned from one ear to the other. "Well, in that case…" He lifted her into his arms and carried her into the bedroom.

"You're very predictable," she said, a soft laugh rolling over her lips.

"Yeah, well, I'm not really concerned about that right now." He placed her on the bed and rid himself of his suit jacket. "Get naked, baby, 'cause I'm ready for my reward."

Moments later, he joined Michelle in bed, both of them now naked.

He rolled over her, bracing himself above her. "As to your question about what I'm gonna keep an eye on most... That would be this part here." He tapped against her temple. "Just to make sure you don't come up with another brilliant idea that puts you in danger."

"I did n—"

He drowned her protest with a kiss. Like a kitten, she yielded to him immediately. He pulled back for a second. "Now about that reward..." He rolled off her then pulled her on top of him. "I don't think you've ridden me yet."

She pushed herself up, her legs sliding to either side of his hips. "Are you sure you really want to relinquish control to me?" Her eyes sparkled and her smile was sinful.

Nick felt himself grow harder beneath her core. "Michelle, when it comes to you I never had any control to begin with. So why start now?" He rocked his hips upward, nudging her with his cock. "Can't you feel what you're doing to me? This shy boy from Indiana is at your mercy."

She shook her head, laughing, and leaned toward the bedside table to snatch one of the condoms there. "Then let's put this shy boy out of his misery." With skilled hands she sheathed him, then got on her knees, adjusting her position above him.

He placed his hands on her hips. "Yes, let's," he agreed and thrust his cock upward, while pulling her down onto him at the same time.

A surprised gasp burst from her.

Nick pressed his head into the pillows, fighting against the intense pleasure that nearly sent him over the edge. Fuck! He'd never been so sensitive.

"I thought you'd given me control," she said.

He flashed her a grin. "But you *are* in control, Michelle, because you're the one guiding my body. You're the one who's making me thrust into you." To underscore his words, he lifted her hips up again, then pulled them down onto him, once more impaling her on his shaft.

Michelle grabbed his wrists and pried them from her hips, then leaned forward and pinned them to the sides of his head. Her breasts brushed his chest, sending a thrill through his body.

"I don't think you grasp the concept of giving control to somebody else. Now be good and let me teach you."

"I can't wait for that lesson to start."

The moment Michelle started to rotate her hips, grinding her sex against him, moving up and down on him, he realized that he would thoroughly enjoy this lesson. She released his wrists, and he didn't lose any time bringing his hands to her breasts. He caressed them and palmed the warm flesh, playing with her rosy nipples, turning them into hard peaks.

Like a goddess, she rode him, her movements smooth, her rhythm even, her tempo increasing with every minute. Her torso started to glisten, pearls of sweat beading on her skin, a rivulet of it soon trickling down between her breasts.

He feasted his eyes on her, drinking in her beauty, and reveling in the sensations she sent through his body.

Her sex was slick and warm, her muscles tight around his erection. Her dark blond hair brushed against her shoulders with every movement, and her breasts bounced up and down, providing him with a tantalizing sight.

Unable to resist, he pulled her down to him, close enough so he could capture one nipple in his mouth and suck on the delicious bud. She moaned out loud then, and he moved to the other breast, inflicting the same treatment there, while he squeezed both breasts, kneading them.

Lower, his hips moved more urgently now, thrusting upward on each of Michelle's downward movements, slamming his cock harder into her in a quest for more friction.

Her muscles tightened around him, sending a shockwave through his body. He expelled a breath of air, and with it, his climax unexpectedly broke over him.

"Fuck!" he cursed, unable to hold back now. He looked at Michelle's face and saw how she'd thrown her head back, eyes closed, and moaned.

Then he felt her muscles spasm around him, and relief flooded him at the knowledge that she was climaxing with him.

He pulled her head down, his lips finding hers in an all-consuming kiss. He couldn't stop devouring her. Couldn't stop exploring her mouth and showing her what she meant to him, knowing that words would never be enough to express how Michelle made him feel.

Whole.

25

Nick hung the towel over the rack in the bathroom and pulled on his shorts, glancing back at Michelle who was stepping out of the shower, water pearling off her perfect skin.

"Damn, you look tempting," he said, letting his gaze roam over her curves.

"Haven't you had enough for today?"

He grinned, already stalking toward her, his cock thickening again. "Apparently, you've given me an endless appetite."

The ringing of the door bell stopped him from pulling Michelle into his arms. He turned his head involuntarily.

"That'll be the Chinese I ordered," Michelle said.

He arched an eyebrow.

"Considering the calories we burned earlier, I figured we needed some food."

He grinned. "You figured right." He pressed a kiss on her cheek. "I'll go down and get it."

Nick snatched a T-shirt from the hook on the bathroom door and slipped it over his head, already walking into the hallway. He reached for his wallet and headed down the stairwell, leaving the door to his apartment ajar. The buzzer in his apartment had been broken for months, so he had no choice but to run down to the first floor.

"Coming!" he called out a few seconds before he reached the entrance door and ripped it open.

The guy standing there wore a baseball cap, kept his head down, and carried a white plastic bag with several food cartons bearing Chinese symbols. It was the food Michelle had ordered, all right, but the guy delivering it wasn't working for the Chinese restaurant around the corner. He was neither Chinese nor the kind of guy who'd take a menial job like delivering food unless it was to gain access somewhere.

The stranger lifted his face, giving Nick a full view of his features now. It was confirmation of what he already knew, what he'd already sensed by the prickling sensation spreading over his skin.

"I'm—"

"—a Phoenix, I know," Nick cut him off, darting quick looks up and down the street to see if they were alone.

"I came alone."

"How did you find me?"

"Sheppard's ID card. When it was activated, all kinds of alarm bells went off. I got an alert. Missed you when you left Langley, but I found you again."

His pulse kicked up. "How? I covered my tracks."

"Don't worry, the only reason I was able to see your picture on Sheppard's ID was because the alert came through the moment you activated it. When I got the second alert after the system administrators disabled access, your picture was gone already." Ace winked. "Lucky for me that I took a screenshot."

Nick sighed a breath of relief.

"I hope you found what you were looking for at Langley."

"Your father was a very clever man."

The other man's eyes widened. "You recognize me?"

Nick opened the door wider, motioning him into the entrance hall. "You're Ace, Sheppard's adopted son." He offered his hand and Ace shook it. "I'm Fox. I recognize you from the picture in your father's files." Which was also the reason why he knew he could trust this man. Sheppard's son was the person who'd loved him most and would have never betrayed him.

"You found his files?" Excitement shone in Ace's eyes.

"I'm not the only one who has a copy of them though. Whoever killed your father knew about the files. He tried to delete them, probably copied them for himself first. But I was able to find a backup copy."

Ace's jaw set into a grim line. "So that's how he's been able to set those assassins on our tail. He knows who we are."

"We?"

"I'm in contact with another Phoenix, Zephyr."

"You trust him?"

"One hundred percent."

"Good. We'll need him. There are two others I know: Ranger and Stingray. They're in D.C. We're working on a plan to bring the Phoenix back together."

"That's better news than I expected," Ace admitted.

"We can do with a bit of good news, because the rest… Something bad is gonna happen." He met Ace's eyes.

"The inferno," his fellow Phoenix said without hesitation.

"Yes. We need to find out where and when it's supposed to happen so we can prevent it," Nick said.

"It won't be easy."

Nick smiled. "We have everything we need now: a list of agents with pictures and names, and five Phoenix working together to find them. And once the Phoenix rise again, we'll find the asshole who took out Sheppard and sent us running for our lives. And we'll finish this."

A slow smile built on Ace's face. "I'm glad I found you."

And for the second time in three years, Nick was glad that somebody had been able to track him down. Because having a man like Sheppard's son on their side, a man who probably knew more about the program than anybody else, was an asset they couldn't do without.

"Come on, we've got a lot to discuss."

~ * ~

ABOUT THE AUTHOR

TINA FOLSOM was born in Germany and has been living in English speaking countries for almost her entire adult life.

Tina has always been a bit of a globe trotter: she lived in Germany, Switzerland, England, worked on a cruise ship in the Mediterranean, studied drama and acting at the American Academy of Dramatic Arts in New York and screenwriting in Los Angeles, before meeting the man of her life and following him to San Francisco.

She now lives in an old Victorian in San Francisco with her husband and spends her days writing and translating her own books.

She's always loved vampires, Gods, and other alpha heroes. She has written over 25 books, many of which are available in German, French, and Spanish.

For more about Tina Folsom:

www.tinawritesromance.com

tina@tinawritesromance.com

Twitter: @Tina_Folsom

www.facebook.com/TinaFolsomFans

www.facebook.com/PhoenixCodeSeries

Don't miss the first heart-stopping romantic
adventure in the "riveting and suspenseful"
PHOENIX CODE SERIES

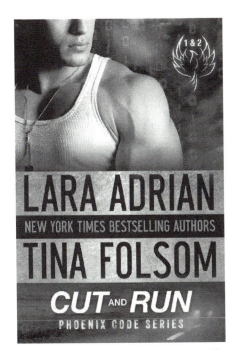

**Available in ebook, trade paperback and
unabridged audiobook editions.**

For more information on the series and
upcoming releases, visit:
www.PhoenixCodeSeries.com

* Fresh Fiction

Never miss a new book from

LARA ADRIAN or TINA FOLSOM!

Sign up for their email newsletters at

www.LaraAdrian.com

www.TinaWritesRomance.com

www.PhoenixCodeSeries.com

Be the first to get notified of new releases and be eligible for special subscribers-only exclusive content and giveaways.

Sign up today!

24030731R00204

Printed in Great Britain
by Amazon